CATHAR MAIDEN

# A WINTER TALE

EDITION OCTOPUS

This novel is a work of fiction. Any resemblance to actual persons, living or dead, events or localities is entirely coincidental. Real-life characters, locations and organisations, when mentioned, are used exclusively in a fictional way.

cathar maiden, 'A Winter Tale'
© 2005 der vorliegenden Ausgabe: Edition Octopus
Die Edition Octopus erscheint im
Verlagshaus Monsenstein und Vannerdat OHG, Münster
www.edition-octopus.de
© 2005 cathar maiden

Alle Rechte vorbehalten
Satz: Claudia Rüthschilling
Coverdesign & -layout: Barbro Hagman

Druck und Bindung: MV-Verlag

ISBN 3-86582-226-6

*To my sister*

Without you, this book would probably never have been written. Thank you for your tireless enthusiasm, encouragement, criticism and unwavering support. In short, thank you for being you.

Charlotte the harlot
Let me see love

Iron Maiden: *Charlotte the Harlot*

September 23rd, 1988

The two boys huddled closer. Outside the sun shone bright, but they had shut the blinds and a soothing twilight enveloped their naked, skinny bodies. The elder of the two, a handsome young man with shoulder-length blonde hair, mumbled soothing words into his friend's neck. Like a mother, comforting her child. The younger lad sobbed and choked on his tears. He was maybe fifteen, a shy kid with big, fearful eyes that seemed to harbour a soul too tender for the hardships of this world.

They hugged each other for a long time. A thundering round of applause rose up from the football ground below. Laughter and cries of happiness rapped against the window, but the boys ignored them. They were lost in their own private universe of sorrow and pain.

'I don't want to live anymore,' whispered the kid.

'Yes, you do. Of course you do. She wouldn't want you to say such things.'

'I don't care.' A sudden flicker of hope crossed his face. 'Can't you take me with you, please? I don't want to stay here.'

'You know I'd love to do that, but I can't. He'd never allow it. But hey, it's only for two more years. What's two years, compared to a whole lifetime. Hm?' He lifted the boy's chin and placed a fond little peck on his cheek.

For a while, they lay together in silence. Outside, the fans broke into another round of cheers.

'They're not bothering you anymore, are they?'

The boy shook his head. 'Don't worry about me. They've got enough younger kids to torture.'

The minutes ticked by in silence. At last, the blonde got up and walked to the door. He rummaged through his coat, muttering under his breath. Then he returned to the bed and handed a music cassette to the lad. 'Listen to it when you're feeling lonely. It'll tell you that, somewhere in time, everything will work out just fine.' He got back under the blanket and snuggled up. 'Did you like what we did?'

'It was the first time I ever liked it.'

'That's good then. That's how it should be. It's supposed to be fun, and not embarrassing and shameful, like what *they* do. You know that, right?'

The boy nodded.

'And remember, you can always call me, no matter what, no matter when. Day and night, twenty-four seven. Alright?'

'Alright. Thank you for coming over.'

The young man tried a cheerful smile. It didn't turn out very comforting. Cheerful smiles and red, swollen eyes don't match too well. 'I love you,' he said earnestly.

'I love you, too.'

# 1

November 24th, 2004

*... It's raining men. Hallelujah, it's raining men! ...*
Charlie tapped her heels against the barstool and took another sip of her Vodka Orange. Outside it wasn't raining men, but rather cats and dogs. Pedestrians were bustling along the sidewalk, trying to dodge oncoming umbrellas and treacherous puddles that had formed at the kerb. A bulky tourist had stopped in the middle of the pavement to consult his inconveniently unfolded map of London. From the left, a young woman in high heels approached. She was gesticulating angrily on her cell-phone and noticed the human roundabout too late. His ham-sized elbow almost knocked her off her feet. She glared angrily at the man and set out to give him a piece of her mind. At that moment, a truck thundered by. Charlie held her breath. Ploughing along the kerb, the truck's tyres splashed up a generous amount of dirty water that rained down on the hapless bystanders. Charlie exhaled and grinned. Miss High Heels was not amused.

Charlie turned back to the counter and sighed. To think that this little incident had been the highlight of the evening. She had been sitting here for three hours straight, waiting for customers, and so far, not a single one had shown up. Damn. In one week the rent was due, the Christmas holidays were fast approaching and on top of it all she had to sit through a couple of very mean tests at school. Jacobs had been threatening his students with these tests for weeks. There was always so much to do, and never nearly enough time to do it. She felt herself heading towards yet another chase-me-through-dark-alleyways nightmare.

She looked around the pub. The *Puss in Boots* definitely wasn't what it used to be. But she still preferred it to walking the streets in this terrible weather. Outside, Miss High Heels and the tourist had moved on, but the downpour was unabated. Charlie made a note in her mental agenda: no matter whom you leave with tonight, make sure that he has enough money to pay for a taxi. Both to his place and back. If you want me wet, baby, you better keep me dry.

'Nice song, huh?'

Charlie needed a few seconds to realize that the ingenious comment had been made for her sake. Long enough for her eloquent neighbour to spark off another proof of his wit: 'Geri Halliwell. *It's raining men.*'

Charlie stared at him in disbelief. He couldn't be serious. From his greasy hair and the yes-I-hate-toothbrushes smile to every single one of his smutty, trembling fingertips, this guy was a study in embarrassment. A very accomplished study, in fact. If this was the best the *Puss in Boots* had on offer tonight, she would have been better off at home, giving the final touches to her paper for Jacobs. Which, come to think of it, was due this Friday. Only tomorrow afternoon and evening to work on it. Not that much time, considering that she was hoping for an A. Rumours had it that Jacobs was not only a very competent, but also a highly dedicated tutor (hard to believe, but apparently true) and thus Charlie had decided (quite unilaterally, so far) that Professor Jonathan Jacobs would be her tutor during her practical training next spring. He might not yet know about his luck, but it was nevertheless an unchangeable fact of life. Still, it would not hurt to convince him of her intellectual merits early on.

Seeing that she was not at all interested in a conversation with him, the Geri Halliwell fan added: 'Do you come here often?'

Ahh. Almost as ingenious as talking about pop music. She'd better put an end to this brainless chitchat and explain to the nitwit that she was definitely out of his league. Miles. He couldn't afford her, even if he were the Sultan of Brunei. Which he wasn't, anyway. She turned around and gave him her most charming forget-about-it smile. Time to launch into her sorry-but-no speech, which she kept ready for occasions such as these.

'You know ...' she began, when a grass-green plastic jacket shoved itself into the gap between their two barstools. At the same time, a pair of slender, manicured hands started brushing up and down her arm.

'Scusey-scuse, I'd need a bit of space. Just for a teensy little sec. Barman! Another red one, thingy, please and a Lemon Ice and a ... can I get you something as well, honey? For the trouble?'

Charlie gaped at the apparition in green that had so miraculously separated her from Mister Unwanted. Unfortunately he looked happily gay and thus did not qualify as potential customer. But never mind that now. He had rescued her, albeit unknowingly, so he deserved at least the honour to buy her a drink. 'I'd like a Vodka Orange, thank you.'

'The Russian and the Big-O it is. Barman: do your duty. Vodka à l'orange for my new friend here. Do you want to come over to our table, honey? Much more comfy-cosy than at the bar.'

Charlie had to laugh. This guy was really something. Quite an original, from ponytail to toe. Why not have a drink with him? Seeing that her regulars seemed to make a point of *not* showing up at the pub anyway. Without a further glance at the Geri Halliwell fan, who tried to regain her attention with a sleazy wink, Charlie accepted the invitation, the drink and Ponytail's hand.

'Ok, you lead the way.' She hopped from the barstool and followed her rescuer through the throng of customers to a table under the large windows. Outside it was still raining, but there were less people on the pavement now. Judging from the crowd in the pub, most of them had taken refuge in the *Puss in Boots*. Ponytail squeezed himself onto the bench next to a young man and motioned for her to take a seat opposite them. Ok. Definitely not a potential customer.

'There's your Lemon Ice, honey, and this is ... do you have a name, honey?'

The first honey gave her a friendly smile, so Charlie thought that she, being the other honey, should introduce herself. 'I'm Charlie.'

'Charlie! What an oh so very nice name! Hi, Charlie. I'm Blake, like William, you know, the bloke with the Tyger, and this is Chris. I'm very much in love with him and he also with me, I think. So, Charlie, anything planned for tonight?'

Rocking back and forth on the edge of his seat, Blake gave Chris' thigh a lusty squeeze and flashed her a wide, expectant grin. He definitely looked eager to get into her pants. But then he also looked very, very gay. So much so in fact, that she started to wonder whether it might just be an act. She knew that a lot of women felt attracted to homosexuals, if only because of the challenge to bring these hard-to-get guys back onto the 'right' path. Not that the proselytisers were ever successful in their endeavours. But her thoughts were wandering. Back to Blake and Chris. The former was still grinning expectantly, so Charlie turned her attention to the latter. Gazing into his bottle of Lemon Ice like a clairvoyant into his crystal ball, Chris might as well have been a deaf-mute. In any case, he still had to utter his first syllable. A deaf-mute. Interesting. A hearing impediment probably was a blessing if you were going out with babbly Blake, who, Charlie noticed, had been constantly talking to her for the last half minute. She focused back on the verbal waterfall cascading down in front of her.

'... not like we were really hoping to meet anyone interesting in an ordinary pub like this. The *Puss* was more meant as a, you know, sort of a diving board into deeper waters. A jet stream taking us down to the darker realms of Poseidon, where shady sharks meet sirens sweet, to stay in the picture. Speaking of sirens, Charlie, what's a girl like you doing in a haunt like the *Puss*? It's not your usual pick-up bar, by the looks of it.'

'What makes you think I want to be picked up?'

Blake gave her an even wider grin. 'Touché! Charming Charlie - twelve points. La charmante Charlotte - douze points ... But, to answer your question: What made me think that? ... I don't know. You're alone, you're sexy. I'm alone ... well, sort of, alone with Chris, but still - we're both pretty alone together. So ... you aren't? Waiting to be picked up, that is? Because if you *are*, we'd propose us.' Ultra-wide grin. End of speech.

Charlie smiled to herself. A candid waterfall and his mute friend. Jay and silent Chris. This promised to become a very interesting night indeed. 'You'd propose yourself for *what*, exactly?'

Damn, she hated that part where she had to bring up the money topic. She never knew how to steer the conversation into that direction without feeling slightly embarrassed. A pity there wasn't a fixed rate, like for other basic goods such as petrol or milk. That would be a useful task for Labour. Maybe she should talk to her local MP about it? ... Oh my, her thoughts kept drifting off, and Blake was tireless. She'd again missed half of what he had been saying.

'... or whatever thought will strike our fancy.' End of speech. Oops, she'd missed the important part. Focus on the task at hand, Charlie: how to push this friendly chat into Sterlingshire.

Chris leaned over and whispered something into Blake's ear. To Charlie's delight, he even nibbled teasingly at his friend's earlobe. Who in turn nuzzled his nose into Chris' neck and murmured an answer. Charlie felt a warm, pulsating throb building up in her pants. She pressed her legs together and alternately moved them back and forth. The hard seam of her jeans created a most delicious friction against her crotch. Mmmmh. Okay, guys, what's the deal? Maybe she should be straightforward. She could look this Blake guy in the eye and say: 'Whatever you want, I'm ready for it, but you know it'll cost you, right?' She wondered how he would react to that. Laugh? Grin? Be offended?

'Chris here was wondering whether you'd do it for the fun of it, or whether you'd like us to ... how shall I put it? ... engage into a pecuniary transaction, thingy.'

Charlie exhaled. The subject was breached. Perfect. She smiled her most charming thanks-for-mentioning-it smile and nodded emphatically. 'That would be so obliging of you. You know, I'm a poor student, and London is quite an expensive city.'

Now it was Blake's turn to nod vigorously. 'Oh, definitely! Exorbitant cost of living. Way up there. A shame, really. Such a beautiful city and no one can afford to live in it. ... Well, sort of, I mean, seven million people obviously *can* afford it somehow, but still. Whore's prices, that's what they're asking. Oops, sorry, no offence, just a manner of speaking, you know.'

He grinned apologetically. He had a face you could fall for. Not her, of course, but a romantic, young girl might. Somehow, he reminded her of that actor who played this private detective in *Sweating Bullets*, back in the early nineties ...

'No offence taken. To come back to the pecuniary matters, well, it would of course depend on what you want exactly. What was it again you said you wanted?'

'Whatever strikes our fancy? From the back and from behind, you know. Me'n Chris are quite open-minded.'

'I have no doubts whatsoever about that. So. You were thinking about the whole night, right? At least a few hours? That would be 150 pounds. That's what I usually ask one guy, and you're two, so it's quite a deal.' Please say yes, next Wednesday's the first of December and I'll have to pay my rent, so pleeeease.

'Fair enough. Sounds good to me. So I'll go call a taxi, ok?'

'Oh, and the cab money back downtown ... I forgot to mention that ... if you don't mind.'

'No prob, honey. We'll get you safely back to home sweet, don't worry. Now, if you 'scuse me for a moment, I'll go grab a cab.'

Blake glided out of the bench, as gracefully as a panther strolling through a mountain scenery. A self-assured, slender predator flexing his muscles for the kill. Or in this case, stepping out of the pub to call a taxi on his cell-phone. Charlie watched in fascination as he strolled purposefully towards the pub door.

Chris smiled reassuringly at her. 'Don't worry if you only get half of what Blake says. He loves wordplays. And he speaks seven languages, which obviously doesn't make things any easier for us common mortals.'

Charlie laughed. 'I actually find his way of speaking quite entertaining. Is he always so talkative?'

'Mhm. Twenty-four seven. 365 days a year. More, if it's a leap year. You eventually learn to shut it out. Like the traffic that drones on and on, but you don't really notice it anymore.'

Charlie was about to answer, when she felt the metallic zip of a plastic jacket in her back and two strong hands pressing down on her shoulders. Massaging her expertly. Mmmmh.

'Cab's coming in a sec. Oh, and it has almost stopped raining. How about we wait outside, honeys? Such a nice smell of freshly washed tarmac in the air. Much better than the stale cig'n booze fog in here.'

He didn't stop talking all the way to Notting Hill. By the time the cab had turned left onto Marylebone Road, Charlie knew that Blake was a professional artist, a sculptor in fact. Right now, he was in his clay phase, as he put it.

'... the urge to create beautiful objects by moulding a soft, moist, pliable texture,' explained Blake, his hands sensuously grabbing the air in front of him. Charlie listened with interest. He sounded so earnest and excited when he talked about his art.

Somewhere on Westway, his constantly roving hands brushed as if by chance against her shirt, and Blake let out a little squeak. 'Is that a breast?' he cried, utterly astonished.

Charlie laughed. 'Is that so strange?' she asked him, amused. 'What were you expecting to find on my chest - hands and feet?'

Blake shook his head, his eyes wide with wonder. 'No, of course not. But still - the female mammalian appendages never fail to fascinate me. Do you mind if I touch? Just a bit?' He prodded her shirt carefully, as if afraid that the soft protrusion might suddenly jump out at him and swallow his hand. Emboldened, he then pressed his palm against her chest, kneading and moulding in expert sculptor's fashion. 'Mmm, so nice,' he murmured under his breath, 'so sweet.' His other hand wandered up her thigh, gliding into the warm slit between her legs. He rubbed his thumb against the hard seam of her jeans and moaned sensuously into her ear.

The driver stared straight ahead, focusing on the road. He didn't pay any attention to the curious scene unfolding in the back of his cab. After all, this was London. The city of loonies and nutters, the town that truly harboured Bedlam. He didn't mind driving any of its inhabitants, as long as they paid the fare and none of them threw up in his car. These three seemed fine on both accounts, so he was more than happy to ignore an occasional squeezed ma'am alien what's-its-name.

Blake unlocked the door to a slightly run-down Victorian house and motioned for Charlie and Chris to climb the steps to the second floor. The apartment was a pleasant surprise. The place had all the ingredients of a classic artist's loft: most of the walls had been removed, and the beams supporting the ceiling stretched up under the roof of the house. During the day, large windows on three sides provided a generous amount of natural light. The flat was sparsely furnished, with an enormous bed in one corner and a worn-out couch, CD player and heavy oak wardrobe in the other. Next to the bed stood a glass display case which obviously served as liquor cabinet. The rest of the room was cluttered with all kinds of artist's utensils: two wooden tables on which several clay objects in various stages of progress awaited further treatment, three chipped blocks (Charlie guessed they were marble), a pot containing a strange sticky fluid, several brushes, wooden spatulas, a few inches of thick wire, chisels, drills, rasps and other curious instruments which she couldn't even put a name to. While Blake took off his jacket, neckerchief and tennis shoes and flung all three items from across the room into the open wardrobe, Charlie had a closer look at the objects on display. Although they came in every size and material, they somehow all reminded her of ...

'What can I offer you, honey?' Blake opened the glass cabinet and pointed at each of the bottles in turn. 'We have green, red, yellow, blue, orange, milky white and creamy brown. I take red, and I know Chris wants blue, don't you, honey?'

Charlie turned around and eyed the bottles curiously. She decided on a Baileys. 'A brown one for me, please.'

'Brown it is. I see you take an interest in my work. Are you an art lover, by any chance?'

'I don't know.' Charlie took a sip from the glass Blake had handed her. 'I like romantic paintings, but I'm afraid I don't know the first thing about modern art. I admire an artist's talent though, the way he manages to recreate life out of a block of stone, or with the stroke of a brush. But I'm not an expert. I couldn't really explain why I prefer one work of art to another. I ...'

'Oh, but that's perfectly fine!' cried Blake. 'You have to go with your feelings. Don't ever let some self-proclaimed art critic tell you what to like and what not. Listen to your gut instinct, honey, and you cannot go wrong.' He picked up one of the clay objects lying on the worktable. 'This, for instance, is a very interesting piece that I produced in a kind of catatonic state yesterday morning. I had been out all night with Chris here, and when we came home I was so tired that I just couldn't fall asleep. Fed up with tossing and turning, I jumped out of bed, started running around the apartment all naked, restless and unhappy. I was in a very blake mood, pun intended. Then, all of a sudden, the first ray of sunshine struck my bed. An epiphany! So pure and beautiful. It boyishly tugged on the sheet and as I pulled the linen away, it flitted across Chris' naked belly and shyly hid in the shimmering moistness of his short and curlies. Elation gave way to inspiration - I set to work, et voilà! here's the result of my early-morning prouesse: I call it *mèche d'amour*.'

Blake carefully handed her the sculpture. Charlie doubtfully turned it around. Its main part consisted of a thick six-by-two inch tablet. A multitude of curves and undulations played over the front, like waves washing across a rough seashore. At the left, the object ended in a softly rounded curve, while the right side bent in a semicircle and joined the backside half-way in the middle. The sculpture was smoothly chiselled and very pleasant to the touch.

She looked up inquiringly. 'Mesh dumb moore?'

'Love lock,' Chris threw in from the couch. 'It's French. So's Blake's art.'

Charlie nodded as if she understood what he meant. 'Nice. Honestly. But as I said, I'm not really an expert in modern art. I'm afraid my tastes rest more in the nineteenth century.'

'Oh, but that's nothing to be sorry for, honey.' Blake took the *mèche d'amour* out of her hand and put it back on the table. 'The nineteenth century has produced the most exquisite works of art. Just think of Rodin's Kiss - such sensuous curves! Mmmh, gets you hard, doesn't it? Or consider the literature: Byronic poems and Wilde plays! Speaking of wild, how about we take off our clothes? A much more natural state to be in, as Monsieur Rousseau would say.'

He stepped behind Charlie and helped her remove her shirt. His hands glided over her hips and stomach, slowly progressing up to the tender skin around her navel. His breath left a warm, moist film behind her ear. He smelled of musk and blackcurrant liqueur. The red one. Blake's fingers moved on, sensuously caressing her belly, moulding her hips, her butt. His right hand found its way into the back of her jeans, his middle finger audaciously venturing deeper. Charlie closed her eyes and leaned back against his chest.

'Blake,' she murmured under her breath.

'Hmm?' His belly pressed against her butt. She could feel the bulge in his pants.

'The money.' She felt a bit bad for interrupting the moment. It did feel good. But it would feel even better, once she had the rent money safely tucked away in her pocket.

'Um. Right. The money. I forgot. Sorry.' Blake took his hand out of her jeans and moved over to the wardrobe. He took three fifty-pound notes out of a drawer and, upon consideration, added a fourth one. 'There you go, honey. Cab fare and tip included.' He wedged the notes into her pocket. 'That settled, can we turn our attention back to the nicer things in life?'

Charlie nodded eagerly, and Blake motioned for Chris to join them. 'Come here, honey. Show Charlie what a really cute butt you have. Not even a hint of cellulite on it, you'll see.'

Charlie laughed. She had seldom felt so relaxed with a new customer. Blake's fingers played through her hair, making the soft skin of her nape tingle. Gently massaging the muscles in her neck and shoulders, he pushed her down onto her knees. Chris positioned himself in front of her, his knuckles caressing her flushed cheeks. Blake unzipped his boyfriend's pants. His chest rubbed eagerly against Charlie's naked back, his left hand searching for the zipper of her jeans. Its harsh metallic sound mingled with his hot breath in her ear, the released tightness of the fabric making room for a new, sweeter tightness deep inside her belly. Charlie rubbed her temple against Blake's warm mouth, her half-parted lips moaning into his neck. She closed her eyes and bent her head forward, deeply drinking in the musky smell of sweat and sex. And to think that she even got paid for this.

# 2

Charlie gasped and panted. Beads of sweat had formed on her brow and she puffed a few loose strands of hair out of her eyes. Her face was flushed and droplets trickled down between her breasts. She knew she was supposed to move in rhythmic, fluent motions, but that was easier said than done. She might look athletic, but she wasn't really used to this. When she had started out ten minutes ago, she had felt cold and stiff, but her muscles had soon warmed up and now she felt uncomfortably hot in her woollen jumper and raincoat. She wondered once again why she was doing this to herself. This wasn't jogging - this was Saturday morning torture. Besides, she wasn't getting any better at it. She'd been coming to Bloomsbury Park every weekend for the last one and a half months, and she still hadn't experienced that exhilarating feeling you were supposed to get during a run. But she was determined to reach the goal she had set for herself. She squinted through the rain and tried to make out the little ivy-covered shed at the far end of the lake. It couldn't be that far anymore. There behind the next bend, where the ducklings played close to the water's edge: that's where it had to be, next to the large willow trees. It had seemed much closer when she had set out at the other side of the pond. Could it be that the distance between her and the shed was growing, instead of diminishing? She felt like that girl in *Labyrinth* and she had the distinct feeling that there was a David Bowieish character hiding behind the bushes, laughing at her vain efforts. She clenched her jaws. You have no power over me, Jareth. No matter how exhausted she felt, she would reach that damn duck-house, or die trying.

'Poo-Poo! Poo-Poo?'

It couldn't take more than another five minutes. She looked back over her shoulder, trying to assess the distance she had run so far. Yes, five minutes max. That was five times sixty ...

'Poo-Poo, no! Stop! Poo ... watch out!'

Charlie's hands grabbed air in a desperate effort to keep her balance. Preparing for a rough fall, she stumbled instead into a guy's arms. The furry thing that had caused her to trip dashed out from between her legs and turned in circles around them, pink tongue hanging out and tail wriggling in eager excitement.

'Poo-Poo, stop it! Are you alright, miss?' The guy looked genuinely concerned. Soft hazel eyes gazing out at her from under an unruly mop of light brown hair.

Charlie noticed that she leaned heavily on his arm, quite unnecessarily in fact. The stumble had been an unexpected, yet more than welcome interruption from her self-inflicted torture. She better pull herself together now though, if she didn't want him to think that she had swooned or something. Straightening up, she pulled back the hood of her raincoat and looked up at the man. 'I'm quite alright, don't worry.' She smiled at the relieved expression on his face. 'Your dog just caught me unawares while I was calculating how many seconds I still had to jog.'

The guy laughed. As she really seemed to be fine, he relaxed and brushed a strand of hair out of his eyes. A futile gesture, because the lock immediately settled back in its previous place. 'Poo-Poo is sometimes a bit too excited. And he never cares about what I yell after him, do you, Poo-Poo?' He crouched down, took the yelping westie in his arms and gave the dog's wet coat a fond ruffling. 'Little rascal, hm?' He straightened up and gave her an apologetic smile. 'I shouldn't have let him from the leash. It's only the second time we're going for a walk and he's not yet used to me.'

'You only bought him recently?' asked Charlie, trying to cuddle the struggling dog.

'Not really. I kinda inherited him from my ex-girlfriend. She broke up with me, and she left me Poo-Poo.'

Charlie was astonished. 'She left you her dog?'

'Mhm. I guess she broke up with him, too.' He gave her an embarrassed little grin and made another futile attempt at brushing his hair out of his face. Then his eyes lit up. 'Listen, do you still want to go jogging? If not, we could have a hot chocolate at the Pond Café. They make it with milk and real chocolate flakes on it.'

Charlie didn't take much convincing. 'With real chocolate flakes, you say? That settles it, Pond Café beats Jogging 10-0.' She held out her hand. 'By the way, my name is Charlie.'

'Hey, Charlie. I'm Damian. Nice to meet you. Come on, Poo-Poo,' he struggled with the leash to put it on the excited little dog's collar, 'we're going to the Pond Café with Charlie.'

'That just sounds so awfully boring.' Damian shook his head in disbelief. 'And you're sure your parents didn't beat you into that school?'

They were sitting at a table in the little sandwich shop at the western end of the park. The entrance door stood permanently ajar, so that it wasn't much warmer inside than out. They had chosen a place next to the only heater in the café, which gave off a feeble current of lukewarm air. The table was also conveniently located out of the draft. A blessing not to be underestimated, Charlie thought. They each had a cup of steaming hot chocolate in front of them and Damian had insisted on buying her a brownie as well, to compensate for her unpleasant encounter with Poo-Poo. She had accepted, admitting that she hadn't had any breakfast yet. That had made him buy her a butter croissant as well.

'So, Charlie,' he said, ignoring her vociferous offer to pay her part of the bill, 'what do you usually do when you're not running through London's parks?'

Charlie told him about her studies. When she mentioned CO-BEL, he was highly impressed. He couldn't imagine that anyone would deliberately choose to study management at the College of Business and Economics. She laughed heartily at his sceptical look. 'Beat me into school? My parents thought I was crazy for wanting to go to university in the first place.' She mimicked her father's stern tone: 'With your A-levels, you will easily get a good job in an office. Work there for a few years, save the money, and then find yourself a man with whom you can found a family. All that talk of studying and living in London - that's not the real life. That's just romance nonsense out of your novels. Real life is a battle, you'll just wait and see.'

Damian joined in her laughing. A moment of silence ensued. They both nursed their hot chocolate and enjoyed the relative warmth of the little coffee shop. Damian looked thoughtfully into his cup, then gazed up sheepishly and heaved a mock-dramatic sigh. 'So you weren't beaten into it. But still - management? Why not art or history or some other *interesting* subject?'

Charlie smiled. 'You know, management is a very interesting subject. In fact, it's not really a subject, it's a way of seeing the world from a broader perspective, of approaching a problem from many different angles. It's not merely about how organizations are structured or how markets work, it's essentially about how people think and interact. For me, management is basically about understanding human behaviour. Of course we have to learn about economics and finance and law as well, but we also have courses in psychology and social sciences.'

She paused to catch her breath. Damian smiled at her. 'Amen. Seriously, hearing you talk about it, it does sound interesting. I'm still not convinced that I would like it, though.' He laughed. 'So, aren't you homesick sometimes?'

'For Swallop? Definitely not. London is such an exciting city.' She lifted her nose in a mock teacher's stance. 'And as Dr Johnson aptly said: Who is tired of London, is tired of life.'

He nodded knowingly and brushed a lock out of his eyes.

Charlie waited for it to tumble back over his eyebrows, then she asked: 'So, what you are you doing, when Poo-Poo is not walking you around the park?'

He laughed. 'That's a very apt way of putting it. ... Hm, what am I doing? Not much, really.'

'Not much?' Charlie pondered this. 'You have to do something. Or is babysitting Poo-Poo a full-time job?'

'Believe me, it is. But, seriously,' said Damian, his gaze lost in the distance, 'I don't really have a job.' He looked at her and smiled apologetically. 'I guess I'm kinda like a bum.' He gave her an embarrassed little laugh.

Charlie felt sorry for asking. He clearly didn't feel comfortable with the subject. Maybe his girlfriend had left him when he had lost his job. If so, he was better off without her. 'I'm sorry.' She took his hand. 'But see, that way you have more time for Poo-Poo. And I'm sure ...'

Damian was almost knocked off his seat. Poo-Poo had become restless and was pulling on his leash which was bound around Damian's chair leg. The chair started to move on the uneven floorboards and Damian had to sit down forcefully to keep it from scratching over the wooden planks.

'Stop it, Poo-Poo. Charlie and I are having a conversation. ... Sit.'

Poo-Poo ignored his command.

Damian repeated forcefully: 'Sit!'

The dog ignored both the command and the exclamation mark and darted under the table, winding the leash around Damian's legs.

'Poo-Poo!'

Charlie laughed. 'It's so funny when you say Poo-Poo, all stern and serious. It's rather a strange name for a dog.'

He nodded, defeated. 'I know it's silly. But that's what Amy used to call him. And I can't really change his name, can I?'

'Why not?' She tried to push the dog back on his tracks, to help Damian get his feet out of the leash. 'Maybe he doesn't like the name, either? Might be a reason why he keeps ignoring your commands. I'm sure I wouldn't listen to such an offending name.'

He looked thoughtfully at her. 'Maybe you're right. I've never thought of that. It sounds plausible.'

Charlie took hold of the dog's collar and pulled him out from under the table. 'Let's make a test. Poo-Poo, look here.' The dog ignored her and tried to dart back under the table. She held tight onto the collar. With the other hand, she seized her half-eaten croissant and thrust it under the struggling pup's nose.

'Bobby.' The dog stopped struggling. He curiously eyed the pastry and wriggled his tail in eager anticipation. Charlie held the croissant up. 'Bobby. Sit,' she ordered solemnly. He stayed put, staring spellbound at the food.

'I think Bobby deserves a reward, don't you?' Ignoring Damian's open-mouthed puzzlement, she offered the dog a generous bite of her pastry. Then she looked up and grinned. 'There we have it. The truth of the matter has been revealed. Your dog's name isn't Poo-Poo. He's called Bobby.'

Damian shook his head in amazement. 'No wonder he has never listened to me. Poor creature. He must have thought me pretty naff, yelling Poo-Poo after him all the time.'

Charlie laughed and patted his hand. 'Don't chastise yourself. The misunderstanding has been resolved and that's what's important, isn't it? The past's already history, and so on.'

Damian stared at her in candid confusion. He had such a sweet and innocent face. Cute, somehow. Maybe she now had a new reason to go jogging in Bloomsbury Park. A reason with six legs and two pairs of hazel eyes.

Shaking herself out of her reverie, Charlie looked at her watch. 'I'd better be off. I still have loads to prepare for a course on Monday. And a paper to finish for the end of the week.' She stooped and ruffled the dog's coat. 'You be nice to your master, Bobby. Don't hold it against him that he called you Poo-Poo. He didn't know any better, you know.' She stood up and put on her raincoat. 'It was really nice meeting you, Damian. Maybe we'll see each other again? I come to Bloomsbury Park every weekend. Saturday morning torture.' She grinned.

Damian grabbed the dog's leash and beamed at her. 'Bobby and I are in the park every day. I'll be on the lookout for you next Saturday. Oh and have fun at your lectures.'

'I will.' Charlie waved a cheerful goodbye at the pair and trotted off towards Gower Street.

# 3

Life was beautiful. This morning she had paid the rent for December, her Process of Management (PoM for short) teacher had shown a real interest in her argumentations and tonight for the first time in ten days it did not rain. Charlie was in an excellent mood. She was on her way to the *Puss in Boots* to have a drink and hopefully bump into one of her regulars on the lookout for a good time. It was only half past eight, but there were hardly any pedestrians or cars around. Swinging her arms to the left and right, Charlie hummed *I was made for loving you, baby*. Just imagine Paul Stanley on holiday in London, having a drink in the *Puss in Boots* ...

A car approached, passing her slowly by. Hmm, a black Mercedes, very classy. Charlie grinned good-humouredly at the driver. The driver smiled back at her. She only got a fleeting glance at his face, but she did notice a very expensive-looking suit. Unfortunately the car turned left on the next corner. The *Puss in Boots* was straight on. Well, of course it would have been more than unlikely for him to have the same destination as her.

But now Charlie was in her smile-at-the-driver mood. She scanned the next car: a red Ford Fiesta with a sticker in the rear window saying 'Shannon on Board'. Shannon was screaming her head off in the baby seat at the back, and the woman behind the steering wheel looked as if she had a mind to change the slogan to 'Shannon overboard'. Charlie smiled to herself. Poor Shannon was teething, and mummy was seething. Mental note: Don't become pregnant for the next ten years.

Next car: a dark blue Vauxhall, year 1980 or older. An old-timer. Definitely. Anything older than herself must be an old-timer. By comparison, the driver looked astonishingly young. Around her age. She got ready to give him a friendly nod, but he was busy banging his head spasmodically over the wheel, mouth wide agape. Aha. Either an epileptic seizure candidate, or a heavy metal fan. For the sake of her peace of mind, Charlie opted for possibility number two and turned her attention to car number four.

Oh. The Mercedes again. Cruising at an even slower pace than before. Wasn't there a minimum speed requirement on this road? Charlie bowed her head and peeped curiously into the sedan's interior. Oops, he was looking back at her. Smiling, in fact. Being a well-behaved girl, she smiled back. The car slowed down some more. So did Charlie. The car stopped. The window on the passenger side went down. This was fast becoming very interesting.

Charlie leaned down on the window. 'Hi.'

'Hey, little girl.' Expensive suit, matching tie, white shirt and just a hint of a very sexy aftershave.

'A nice block to cruise around, isn't it?' Charlie bit her lip. Let's hope Mr Mercedes had a healthy sense of self-humour.

It seemed like he had, because she received a smile in return, coupled with a concerned frown. 'Isn't it a bit late for a little girl like you to walk around on your own?'

Charlie gave him her best now-I'm-offended pout. 'It's not that late. Besides, I'm not a little girl.'

'You sure look like a little girl to me. Shall I give you a ride ... back home?'

Charlie had a hard time suppressing a delighted squeak. Her regulars would have to wait, a new and exciting hunting ground had opened up! 'Sure.' She opened the door and hopped into the passenger seat. 'You have a nice car.'

Mr Mercedes gave her a benevolent smile and motioned to the seat belt. 'You better buckle up, darling.'

The darling obliged. They were cruising through Soho, moving northward.

'Do you have a name, little girl?'

No need to shove it in my face, Charlie thought. I got it the first time around, Mr Upright-citizen-with-a-big-bank-account: you want me to play a teeny girl.

She awarded him with a bashful I'm-so-brainless-it-hurts smile. 'Well, yes. I'm Charlie.'

'Anyone waiting for you at home, Charlie?'

'No, not really. I've finished homework, so Mummy doesn't mind if I stay out late.'

The reaction was instantaneous. He sharply sucked in his breath, and his belly-muscles jerked forward. It's the tiny things that make it. Charlie grinned inwardly.

'She doesn't, hm?' he said. 'You shouldn't be getting into cars with strangers, though.'

'You wouldn't hurt me, would you?' Wide-eyed innocence.

'No, of course not.' Mr Mercedes concentrated on getting onto the dual carriageway. They were heading west now.

'Where are we going?'

'How about going to a hotel? Ever done that with a man, hm, Charlie?'

She was really getting into the game now. 'To a hotel? No. What would we be doing there?'

'You'll see.'

They drove on in silence. Charlie had a surreptitious look at Mr Mercedes. He was rather good-looking, in a businessman sort of way. Early forties, she guessed, hair greying at the temples and a few wrinkles around the eyes. Not fat, but a strong, solid body. And steady hands, calmly guiding the steering wheel. A gold band on his ring finger. Married. Aren't they all.

She should be asking about the money. He didn't look like he couldn't afford her, but you never knew. He might be a miser. Or just a guy who got off on shagging a girl and throwing her out of the car without paying. 'I have a little problem.'

'Hm?' He gave her an earnest, caring look.

'I'm a bit short of pocket-money.' She innocently raised her eyes up to him and secretly congratulated herself. Talk about staying in the game.

Mr Mercedes (he hadn't told her his name yet, had he?) gave a short laugh. 'I think we can remedy to that easily enough. Have a look in the glove compartment, will you?'

Charlie did as she was told. A couple of CDs, some paper tissues and a roll of money.

'I guess that should be enough for an afternoon at the movies, don't you think?' He gave her a conspiratorial smile.

She unrolled the bills. Five twenty-pound notes. Miser. She pulled a disappointed face.

'If you're a good girl, you'll get some more later on.' He steered the car into the driveway of a four-star hotel and pulled up at the barrier to an underground garage. He put a card into the slot and the barrier swung up.

Charlie was impressed. 'You have your own parking slot at the hotel?'

'Not really. But as a preferred customer, you get free parking in the garage.' He pulled the car into a free slot and shut the engine down. Then he turned to her and gave her a friendly grin. 'Wanna go play, little girl?'

They had checked in at the reception and taken the elevator to the sixth floor. Like a gentleman, he unlocked the door to their room and held it open for her to step in first. As expected, the room was top-notch. Generously sized, it featured a thick carpet, a king-size bed, a sparkling bathroom with walk-in shower and a balcony with view over the Thames.

Charlie inspected the bathroom, gleefully clapping her hands when she noticed that the shower was equipped with jet stream power. Her companion (she really should be asking for his name, this was getting silly) stepped up behind her and let his hands glide over her shoulders and arms. 'I'm glad you like the room, sweetie.'

Charlie beamed up at him. 'What's not to like? I don't think I've ever been in such an expensive hotel. Are you very rich?'

He gave a short laugh and pulled her closer, his palms kneading the soft skin under her pullover, searching their way up to her breasts. She rubbed her cheek against his chest and purred like a happy kitten.

'You like that, don't you, little girl?' His breath was smooth and warm in her neck. She nodded and pressed closer. His tongue played along the rim of her ear. 'But you're getting me excited. You know what that means?'

Charlie shook her head and looked up at him in wide-eyed concern. 'Nothing bad, I hope.'

'No, nothing bad. Not for me, at least. It might hurt you a bit, though.' His caress became rougher, more demanding. 'See, that's what happens when little girls get into cars with strangers.' He cupped her face in his hands and pushed his thumb hard into her mouth. 'I told you it was dangerous, didn't I? But you wouldn't listen. Too bad for you.' He pushed her head down, forcing her down on her knees. 'Poor little baby.' His voice was nothing more than a hoarse, excited whisper.

Charlie whimpered. 'No, please don't hurt me. I'll be a good girl, I swear.'

With his right hand he unzipped his trousers, while his left was firmly lodged at the back of Charlie's head. Slowly but determinedly, he pushed her face into his crotch. 'Oh yes, you'll be a good girl. A very good girl. I'll make sure of that.'

He did make sure of it. First he quietly insisted on a long, intense blowjob, guiding her head to take in his slow, hard thrusts. He was a calm, but unrelenting teacher. Whenever Charlie let out a piteous moan or tried to turn her face away with a helpless whimper, his arousal intensified, and more than once he seemed hardly able to control his passion. Yet it became a long lesson. After a while, Charlie's knees started to hurt in spite of the thick carpet. Just on the off chance that he might care, she confessed ruefully that she found her position quite uncomfortable. Babyblue eyes begging him to let her lie on the bed instead.

His thumb softly brushed along her cheekbone. 'Your little body's hurting? Poor baby.' He helped her up and guided her to the bed, making her lie down on the sheet. 'Such a soft body you have. And those cute blossoming titties.' He rubbed his cheek against her breasts, his tongue teasing her nipples. 'So tiny.'

Boy, he was really in the game. She wasn't a full C-cup, but 'tiny' was definitely an understatement. 'Well, I'm still young,' she pouted.

'Yes, so young. You're fourteen, right?'

Boy, was he fucked up. She grinned sheepishly. 'Almost fifteen, though.'

'Well, it's still some time until your birthday.'

Aha. Fifteen was too old. Already half-way to menopause, hm, Mr As-yet-unnamed? She opened her mouth to reply, but he put a finger on her lips. 'Shhh. You'll be a good girl, right?' His voice was a soft, enchanting whisper.

Charlie nodded, eyes wide and frightened.

His hand buried itself into her long hair. 'A very good girl, hm?'

Obediently, Charlie nodded again.

A satisfied smile played around his lips. 'Well then, little girl,' he said, his voice turning into a soft threatening hiss, 'turn around.'

He came hard and deep in her butt. With a satisfied grunt, he rolled down to the side. After having disposed of the used condom, he let his fingers glide absent-mindedly over her bare arms. They lay for a while in silence, relaxed and content.

Finally, he propped himself up on one elbow and gave her a quizzical look. 'You're alright, aren't you, Charlie?'

He sounded genuinely caring. She smiled. 'Are we out of the game now?'

He nodded.

'Yes, I'm fine. My ass is in shreds, but I feel great.' She grinned. 'I'm glad I'm not really a fourteen-year-old little virgin, though.'

He shook his head and laughed. 'So am I. Would have been less fun if you had struggled for real. ... So, am I correct in the assumption that you liked our little game, too?'

Charlie smiled and nodded.

For a moment he was quiet, lost in thoughts. 'I would never have done this to a fourteen-year-old. Care to tell me how old you are?'

'Sure. I just turned seventeen.'

He stared at her, unsure whether she was joking or not.

Charlie laughed and patted his arm. 'No, I'm just kidding. I'm twenty. Born on March 13th, 1984. I can show you my ID if you want.'

He relaxed. He was clearly very relieved. 'No, I believe you. You look young, but not that young. I would have guessed you're around nineteen, twenty.'

He mused about this for a while, and then said: 'You were fast at picking up on the game.'

Charlie mockingly lifted an eyebrow. 'You made it pretty obvious what you wanted.'

'Still. Most girls don't get it. Usually I have to explain what I expect from them, have to remind them to stay in the game. When your knees started hurting, you simply incorporated that into the play. That was fantastic.' He dropped back onto his back. 'You're perfect.'

She nuzzled her face into his shoulder. 'Do you often play these ... games?'

His hand caressed her arm. It was a warm and reassuring gesture. The sort of touch that promises shelter, and always, always keeps its promises. 'Not that often. Once a month, maybe twice.' He made a hesitant pause before adding: 'Whenever the need arises.'

Charlie was quiet. He obviously wanted to talk, to tell his story. She was ready to listen. When the silence stretched on for too long, she prodded softly: 'The need?'

'There's no harm in pretending, is there?' He wasn't looking at her when he explained, his gaze lost in the myriad colours on the tapestry. 'We both know you're not really fourteen. You're a 'consenting adult', as they say. Hell, you even enjoyed it, too. It's fun, it's innocent. Isn't it?'

'Yes, it's fun,' she agreed.

A pregnant pause again. 'It's a relief to play it out,' he finally continued. 'Otherwise, I just keep thinking about it, fantasizing about ... them.'

Charlie nodded. She did not really understand what he was trying to tell her, but she was sure he would get to it eventually, at his own pace. She pulled the sheets over her bare shoulders and snuggled her feet under his warm legs.

He hugged her. 'She's fifteen, you know. Turned fifteen last spring.'

'Nicky?' she asked. When she had begged him to stop, he had moaned the name and thrust his hips forward yet more forcefully. She wasn't even sure he had realized that he had said it.

He froze. His whole body went rigid. Oh. Obviously he *hadn't* realized it.

'You mentioned the name during the game,' she explained.

His muscles relaxed. He leaned over and pulled the sheet higher up, hugging her closer. It wasn't too warm in the room. 'Nicky is the youngest. She's thirteen. She has the cutest blonde locks, comes right after her mother. And she loves to laugh. I love to hear her laugh.'

Charlie waited for him to continue.

'Elsa is fifteen. Turned fifteen last March. She's ... difficult. A difficult age. She wants to be independent, doesn't want to be told what to do. I try to reach her, try to talk to her, but it's ... difficult.' He looked sad, defeated.

Charlie wasn't sure if she should ask, if maybe he wanted her to ask. 'Your daughters?'

He nodded. 'I've never touched them. Not like ... that. I want them to be happy. They're my darlings, my life.' He sighed, a slight quiver in his voice. 'But I just can't help having those fantasies.'

Charlie held him tight. There was so much she could have said: It's just fantasies. Thoughts don't hurt anyone. It's good that you play it out with me, instead of hurting them. Be proud that you resist the temptation, there are so many sickos that don't. Sicko? Hm. Better not use that word ...

He turned around and looked her in the eye. Warm hazel eyes. So serious and sad. 'Can I see you again?'

She smiled. 'Of course you can. I'll give you my cell-phone number if you want. Then you can reach me twenty-four seven. Whenever you need to talk ... or play a game.' She got up and searched through her handbag for one of her cards. It said *Charlie*, in soft, curved letters. And a cell-phone number. Nothing else.

He took the card and smiled. He actually had a very sweet smile. 'Why don't you stay in the hotel till tomorrow morning,' he proposed. 'The room is paid for anyway. And their breakfast buffet is excellent.'

Charlie hopped into the bathroom. 'Maybe I'll do that. I only have to be at school at ten tomorrow morning. Is there a bus or tube station close by?'

He leaned against the shower door while she relished the hard stream of hot water running down her back. 'Kew Bridge Station is just across the street. I'll give you some money for the ride back into town. I'd better go now. It's getting late.' He turned back into the bedroom.

Charlie finished her shower, while he was putting on his clothes and checking his cell-phone for messages. She had the distinct feeling that there was something she had forgotten to ask him. Something important. She stepped out of the shower, grabbed a towel and scanned the row of tiny shampoo-bottles, lotions and other complimentary bathroom utensils lined up on the sink. She mustn't forget to pack those in before she left tomorrow morning.

She heard the creak of the front door being opened. Peeping into the bedroom, she noticed two fifty-pound notes lying on the bedside table. It seemed she had been a good girl, then. And now she also remembered what it was she had wanted to ask him.

'Hey,' she called after him, 'you haven't told me your name yet.'

He turned around and gave her a good-bye smile, before he closed the door behind him. 'Gerald.'

# 4

The Vauxhall's tyres screeched in painful slow motion along the edge of the pavement, finally coming to a halt in front of the *Puss in Boots*.

I'm glad I'm not one of his tyres, Charlie thought. Brushing that silly thought aside, she took a discreet peep at her watch and rejoiced. Yay. Not even eight o'clock, and she was already back at her hunting ground. She turned to the driver and gave his thigh a friendly nudge. 'So, you have fun celebrating tonight, ok?'

The man nodded and picked nervously at a zit on his nose. His nails were bitten to the quick, and Charlie felt the urgent need to grab his hands in order to stop him from further mutilating his frail body. But that wouldn't do. She knew he hated to be touched.

He looked up at her, smiling gratefully. 'Carnations of many different colours, right?'

Charlie patted his sleeve encouragingly. 'Carnations will be perfect, Edmund. Every woman loves them, and they will still be beautiful at the weekend, when your kids come to visit. That'll be a nice touch of colour in your living-room, don't you think?'

Edmund nodded vigorously, his eyes lightening up at the mention of his children. Yes, they would definitely like to see the beautiful bouquet that he was going to offer their mother for their thirtieth wedding anniversary. 'Thank you, Charlie,' he said, chewing off a piece of calloused skin from his thumb, 'I'm so happy I met you tonight. I was looking for you yesterday, but you weren't around.'

Was that an accusing undertone in his voice? 'Yesterday I was busy learning. You know I'm a poor student, slaving away day and night behind my books. You could have called me on my cell-phone, though. That's why I gave you the number, remember?'

Edmund rubbed his fingers along the edge of his palm. 'Yes, I know, Charlie. But I don't like calling people on the phone. I told you that.'

'Right. I forgot. Sorry.' Charlie tapped her wristwatch and reached for her coat. 'Listen, it's getting late. I better be going.' She wanted to bend forward to blow him a kiss on the cheek, but at the last moment, she thought better of it. 'Have a nice evening with Gerda. How about you buy a bottle of champagne to go with the carnations? Might get her into a romantic mood.'

'I don't know. I shouldn't be drinking alcohol, I get rashes from it. But I'll buy her the flowers, I promise.'

Charlie nodded and pulled the door-handle. 'You do that. I'll see you around, ok?'

'Ok. Good night, Charlie.'

'Night, Edmund.' Slipping into her warm coat, she waved after the departing car. She couldn't help feeling sorry for the guy. Each time she met him, he told her about a new allergy or ailment. What a terrible way to spend your life, in constant fear of invisible but deadly viruses, radiation and germs. Such a waste of ... Her train of thought stopped midway between two stations. Hmm? She suddenly had the distinct feeling someone was staring at her. She turned her head left and right, scanning the pavement. A few pedestrians hurried by, but no one paid her any attention. Hmm.

'Hey, Charlie.' She almost jumped at the sound of the voice coming from right behind her back. She whirled around and found herself face to face with the boy from the park.

'Damian! What the hell d'you think you're doing, scaring me like this?' Her eyes searched the area around his legs. 'Where's Bobby?'

'Uhm, I left him at home.' He brushed a lock of hair out of his eyes and gave her a lopsided grin. 'He doesn't like the big city too much. He gets nervous when there are too many people around.'

'Aha. Yeah, I guess it's nicer for a dog to fool around in the park,' she agreed. What a coincidence to meet Damian in Soho, in front of the *Puss in Boots* of all places! ... All of a sudden, the implication of this hit her like a fist in the stomach, and her excitement faded rapidly. Here she was, chatting with a sweet guy, and any moment one of her customers could be showing up, asking her if she was free for the evening. Charlie's thoughts raced. She had to get rid of him, and fast. She gave him a toned-down version of her standard sorry-but-no smile. 'Listen, Damian, it was really nice meeting you, but I have an appointment and I'm already running late ...'

'Oh, you do? I was thinking maybe we could have an ice-cream together, or ...'

Charlie laughed, exasperated. 'An ice-cream in December? No, seriously, I really don't have the time for that now. As I said, I have a date.'

'Was that your father?' Damian gestured in the direction in which the car had taken off. 'The guy in the Vauxhall?'

'Oh. Yes.' As soon as she had said it, Charlie bit her lip. Damn, why was he being so inquisitive? And why did she keep lying to him? After all, there was no harm in what she was doing. Although she didn't *really* want him to know ...

'Uhuh.' Damian buried his hands deeper into the pockets of his coat. 'Well, I don't wanna keep you ...'

Great. Then don't, Charlie thought. She waited. He didn't move.

'Right.' She took a step towards the pub, signalling him subtly to please head off in the other direction.

'So,' he said, taking a step in the same direction. 'Maybe we'll see you on Saturday?'

Charlie sighed. He clearly didn't get 'subtle'. Damn. 'Sure.' She leaned her hand against the pub door, pushing it half open. 'I'll see you and Bobby in the park. We can have a hot chocolate if you want. Actually, I've been looking forward to that all week.'

'Really?' His eyes lit up. 'I've been looking forward to it too, Charlie ... and so has Bobby,' he cried after her.

She nodded cheerfully, waved and let the door fall back into his face.

There weren't many people in the bar. Charlie had ordered a coke at the counter and took her glass to a table at the back. From here, she had a nice view on the entire room and was sure to spot her customers, if one of them showed up. Sipping her coke, she switched her mobile on and checked it for messages. A text from her brother: Mum was having headaches and was asking when she would be coming home for the weekend. Charlie sighed and pushed forward to the next message: Alice, asking whether she wanted to meet her at the library for joint studying. Thanks, but no thanks, she thought. 'Joint studying' was Alice's code for 'coffee and gossip'. She had no time for such nonsense. Between her studies and her customers, she didn't have much spare time, and those few hours were precious to her. She loved to spend them just doing nothing at all. Daydreaming and watching the clouds drift across the sky. She certainly wasn't going to waste a whole afternoon hanging around with Alice. She pushed the forward button again. No more messages. Hm. She popped the cell-phone back into her coat pocket and looked around. The room was still almost deserted. Odd, for a Thursday evening. A few youngsters hanging at the bar, watching a football game on TV. A couple smooching in a corner. Three guys in suit and tie, discussing business matters over a chicken and mushroom pie. Funny, that even rhymed. Two old men stoically nursing their beer. A young man balancing his pint from the bar to the nearest ta... Charlie froze. Then she closed her eyes and sighed. What the devil was wrong with this guy? Why was he so persistent? Hadn't she just told him that she had a date? Charlie started to become angry. It had been so much fun talking to him last weekend, and his little dog was quite simply a cutie. She hadn't lied to him when she'd told him that she had been looking forward to meeting him again in the park. Why did he have to jeopardize their pleasant acquaintance by running after her like this? She decided to ignore him.

He caught her eye and cheerfully raised his glass in her direction. Grmb. She pretended not to notice the gesture, and rummaged in her coat for a Wrigley's. She needed something to chew on.

'Mind if I sit here?'

Charlie looked up, desperately trying not to panic. 'Damian. Why are you following me like that?'

Damian smiled on, undaunted. 'I'm not. I felt like having a drink. This is a pub. A public place, as the name says. ... Didn't you say you had a date?'

'Yes, I am. Having a date, that is. He just hasn't shown up yet.'

'Oh.' He dropped down on the chair opposite her. 'I can keep you company until he comes.' A pleading smile from under a mop of hair.

Charlie took a deep breath. 'Look, Damian. You're a nice guy. I really like you. But I don't want you sitting here right now. We'll see each other in just two days in the park. We can have a long, pleasant chat there, just like we said we would. But right now I need to be alone. Please? There are at least ten free tables in the room. Take one of those.'

Damian looked puzzled and slightly hurt. Don't make me feel sorry for you, Charlie thought. If you do, I'll have to hate you for it.

'What are you doing in Soho anyway?' she asked, suddenly fearing that he might have been following her since last Saturday. Quite an irrational thought. She was getting paranoid.

'I had a appointment with my brother,' he answered, happy that she had decided to talk to him after all. 'We were talking bills and letters and such. Pretty important stuff.' He nodded gravely. 'He has ...'

The pub door had opened again. She craned her neck, trying to see past Damian's head. Wasn't that someone she knew? No, he had his arm around a girl. The couple took a seat under the TV set, and the girl got up to buy the drinks. Charlie relaxed and turned her attention back to Damian. 'So, where is this brother of yours now?' she asked sceptically.

'As I said, he drove home. Actually, he offered to drive me back as well. But I felt like taking a stroll through London by night. I don't come downtown that often.'

'Hm.' She took a sip at her coke. 'You shouldn't leave Bobby alone for too long. He's only just been left by his former master. Amy, right? You don't want him to feel abandoned again, do you?' What am I talking, she thought. For some reason, she felt the need to hurt Damian, to make him feel guilty. She hastily tried to make up for her sarcastic comment. 'You're doing a great job caring for Bobby. One can tell that you like him a lot. And he's such a cutie.'

Damian nodded. 'I'm the only friend he has, poor little bugger.' Abruptly changing the subject, he asked: 'Looks like he forgot about your date.' Intense don't-tell-me-stories stare.

Charlie felt herself blush. Damn. She hated to be caught in a lie. How should she reply to this? She decided to ignore the comment. For a while, none of them said a word. Damian stared into his pint. He slowly turned it in his hands, carefully brushing away the droplets of condensed water.

'How would he have to be?' he finally mumbled into his beer.

'Hm?' Charlie wasn't sure she had understood him correctly. 'How would who have to be?'

'Your date.' He eyed her through a curtain of unruly locks. 'You're not waiting for someone in particular, right? You're just ... waiting.'

It wasn't a question. He was simply stating a fact. Charlie closed her eyes. This was so embarrassing.

He looked at her pleadingly. 'Is it my clothes? My hair? My nose? My height? My ...'

'Stop it,' she interrupted him impatiently. 'Don't be silly. Of course it's none of that. I don't know what you're talking about anyway. You look good. Very good, in fact, and I'm sure you know it.' She made a steeple with her fingers and pressed her mouth against it. 'Listen, Damian: I'd love to go out with you. If I wanted to go out with *anyone*, you'd be the first guy I'd call. Honestly. But I just don't have the time for that. Not now, anyway. It's Thursday evening. I should be working. I shouldn't be sitting here with you, chatting like I had all the time and money in the world. So there. Now you know. Happy?' she ended on a slightly bitter tone. She knew this was probably the end of their short-lived friendship. If only he hadn't come in, hadn't insisted on sitting at her table. She was close to tears.

Throughout her speech, Damian hadn't said a single word. He was simply watching her, with a candid, understanding look on his face. Charlie had the feeling that his soft hazel eyes could see right through her, all the way into her soul. A disconcerting thought.

None of them said a word. An irritating rap-beat emanated from the loudspeakers over the bar. The same line of music, repeated over and over again. Computer-generated sounds replacing real instruments of wood and brass. Charlie felt like being trapped in a time-loop. Maybe she could sit here forever, hearing the same numbing beat again and again, staring into Damian's eyes. Not having to say anything. Not having to answer anything.

When he finally spoke, his voice was so soft that she could hardly make out the words. 'Are you saying that if I paid you for it, you wouldn't mind chatting with me?'

The rap noise abruptly finished with a final beat of the drum-machine. The first notes of a Robbie Williams song came up. Charlie took a deep breath and looked at Damian. 'No,' she replied honestly, 'I don't mind chatting with you, whether you pay me for it or not. But at the end of the month, I have a rent to pay, a stomach to feed and books to buy. You cannot afford to live in London as a full-time student just by working night-shifts at UPS and McDonald's, or by scrubbing the floors of office buildings. Not if you want to sleep in a place that remotely looks like a home and eat anything else than bread and pasta. This doesn't mean that I want money from you. Because I don't. I liked our conversation in the park very much.'

'Yes, me too.' Damian nodded. 'Hm. I understand your dilemma. But it *would* be solved if I paid you for our chat, wouldn't it?'

Charlie stared at him. 'Do you understand what I've just told you? Aren't you shocked at all?'

Damian considered the question for a moment. 'No,' he finally said. 'As a matter as fact,' he gave her a boyish grin, 'how about I get some money from the teller and we continue the conversation at my place?'

First they trudged to the bank at the corner, where Damian pushed buttons at the teller machine, while Charlie was waiting with very mixed emotions. On the one hand, she felt excited about having sex with Damian. He was very attractive. His personality was a charming combination of boyish innocence and male charisma. And he seemed completely oblivious of his effect on women, not noticing that he was turning more than one head, both in the park and at the pub. So going to bed with him *was* a thrilling prospect.

But on the other hand, she had first met Damian as the friendly dog-owner, the nice bloke next door. She didn't know many people in London apart from her customers and the people at school. It had felt good to laugh with him, precisely because he knew nothing about how she earned her money. She had even fantasized about having sex with him one day. Carefree sex, untainted by money issues. Seeing him readily accept the fact that she was a hooker had hurt her more than she cared to admit to herself. When he had followed her into the pub, she had for a second entertained the vain fantasy that he might be having a little crush on her. Turned out, all he wanted was a good fuck. He didn't seem to mind that he had to pay for it, either. Probably told himself that it made things easier, that she wouldn't be clinging to him later on.

She tried to shut these bitter thoughts out. She should consider herself lucky to get paid for what she loved to do anyway. But it was hard to ignore the nagging little voice in her head, telling her that just this once, just with this one guy, she would have preferred to do it for free.

After Damian had finished his transaction, they took a taxi to his flat in Bloomsbury. They spent the journey in awkward silence, with Damian trying to catch her eye once in a while, flashing her a cheerful grin or a reassuring smile. Charlie was relieved when they finally got out of the cab. She was astonished to find herself in a well-to-do residential area, just north of Bloomsbury Park. Damian let them into a beautifully restored three-storied Georgian building. They walked through a marbled hallway. Ignoring the staircase, Damian motioned her into the lift. He put his key into the elevator's security system and pushed in a four-digit code. The cabin glided smoothly to the second floor and opened onto a spacious modern apartment.

The first thing Charlie noticed were the huge potted yuccas and ferns that gave the place an almost Mediterranean flair. She wanted to comment on this, when a white bundle of energy darted out of the adjacent room and almost knocked her off her feet. Yapping and tail-wriggling, Bobby dashed around them. Leaping up first at Charlie, then at Damian, he voiced his pleasure of seeing his master and his newly-found friend in high-pitched, excited yelps. The little dog broke the awkwardness that had reigned between them without the least effort. Charlie dropped down on the couch and set to the task of ruffling his soft, furry coat.

Damian brushed a lock out of his eyes and pointed in the general direction of nothing in particular. 'Make yourself at home, ok? I'll be right back.' Picking up an object from the sideboard behind the couch, he disappeared into the adjacent room.

Charlie turned her attention back to Bobby. 'So little rascal, did you miss me? I sure missed you.' She buried her face in the dog's coat. She needed the cuddling just as bad as Bobby.

Damian reappeared in the doorframe and grinned at her. 'Wanna see what Bobby learnt this week?'

She nodded. He stooped and picked up a little red rubber ball from under the low glass table. Bobby barked excitedly. Grinning like a naughty schoolboy, Damian held the ball up for the dog to see, declared solemnly 'Fetch!' and threw it across the room. It flew over the couch and landed behind an enormous yucca. Bobby darted over the sofa, barely avoided the sharp edge of the tea table and skittered around the potted plant. The tree shook dangerously, bits of moist earth were flung into the air, but seconds later a triumphant member of the canine species emerged, ball firmly lodged in his mouth, stiff little tail wriggling faster than ever. He dropped the ball into Damian's outstretched hand and was rewarded with a fond pat on the head.

Charlie laughed with glee and clapped her hands. 'What a wonderful performance!' she cried. 'See, I told you. Now that we know his proper name, he doesn't mind obeying your orders.'

Damian chuckled. 'Well, I strongly suspect it depends on the order, though. But you taught me a very good lesson in the Pond Café: don't ask more of the little rascal than he can give.'

Charlie got up. 'Exactly, my Little Prince,' she said seductively and put her arms around his neck. 'So, have you made up your mind what you want to ask of me?'

Damian buried his nose in her hair and deeply inhaled the smell of her shampoo. 'Whatever you're ready to give,' he murmured. He held her tight in a strong, tender embrace. Charlie closed her eyes. She felt warm and happy. This could have been so wonderful, if it weren't for the nasty little voice reminding her that she was here on business, that he was paying for her company and that she was expected to deliver a perfect service.

Pressing herself against his chest, she expertly unbuckled his belt, opened the button on his trousers and unzipped his jeans without so much as a single glance down. Her right hand softly stroked the warm, hard bulge in his underpants. It was obviously yearning to be released from its confinement. Her fingers moved on, gently cupping the sensitive skin, teasing it through the fabric. Meanwhile, her left hand found its way under the rubber band of his undergarment, gliding along his skin, tickling, touching, teasing the sensitive nerve-endings, sending prickling flashes of excitement through them, such soft, sweet torture ...

Damian gently stopped her hand. He straightened up and cupped both her hands in his, lifting them to his mouth and bestowing a soft kiss on each. Charlie was puzzled. Why was he interrupting her performance? She couldn't believe that he really wanted her to stop. He had been highly aroused and his dick had been more than eager to be stroked, there was no doubt about that. So why did he give her that crooked smile now, almost as if he wanted to apologize for a faux pas?

'What's the matter?' she asked. She had to clear her throat to even get the words out. Her sober voice broke the spell, the erotic tension evaporated. They were back in reality. A dog, lots of green plants and two human beings in an expensive apartment. The apartment ... A thought that had been nagging at her subconscious since she had entered the building broke to the surface: he had told her in the park that he did not have a job. He had even compared himself to a bum on the streets. This wasn't a poor man's flat, though. Not at all.

Charlie pushed herself away from his chest. 'Didn't you tell me that you're on the dole?' she asked suspiciously.

Damian was taken aback. Embarrassed, he re-zipped his jeans. 'Well no, not really,' he replied. 'I said I don't have a job.'

'That's the same, isn't it? How can you afford this place if you don't even have a job? This apartment must cost a fortune in rent.'

'I don't really know,' he admitted. 'It's not mine, not really, I mean. My brother lets me live here, but he's handling all the money things, so I wouldn't know how much it costs. I guess it isn't too cheap ...' His voice faltered and he seemed at a loss for words.

Charlie shook her head. 'Some people are lucky. Your brother is paying for this? Boy, you two must be close. You have a generous brother, Damian.'

Damian nodded. 'I do appreciate what he's doing for me, believe me. But, um, listen ... can I offer you a drink or something? I'm afraid I'm not a very good host.' He laughed nervously.

Charlie nodded. He disappeared into the kitchen and soon returned with two wine glasses and a bottle. Charlie sipped at her glass. Cheap table wine in an upper-class apartment. Damian was a walking paradox.

'Is there something else you want to know about me?' he asked, settling back on the couch.

Charlie snuggled closer. 'Yes,' she whispered into his ear and squeezed his thigh. 'Whether you like this.'

When she went down on her knees to give him a blowjob, Damian pulled her up and suggested that they move to his bedroom. Charlie agreed and profited from the occasion to remind him of the money issue. With an impassive face, he handed her four fresh fifty-pound notes, asking whether that would be sufficient. She assured him that the sum was indeed very sufficient and made a mental note to give him the shag of his life.

But now Charlie felt like the experience was fast turning into a disaster. She racked her mind, trying to figure out where she had gone wrong. She had started out with a slow, sensuous strip. Smiling bashfully up at Damian, she'd first removed her shirt and the jeans. The bra had followed after. Then she had moved closer to him, slowly rubbing her naked body against his. Teasingly, she had started to undress him as well. Throughout the procedure, he hadn't said a single word. He had just stood there, letting her do her thing. Charlie hated it when men were so passive. You soon run out of ideas, trying to make love to a phlegmatic piece of flesh. But she knew from experience that there was one thing every man adored. So she had dropped to her knees once again, pulled down his pants and grabbed his buttocks. The result had not been as expected, though. Instead of bulging out at her, his penis seemed, if anything, rather to shrivel up. Before she'd had a chance to take it in her mouth, Damian had stepped back and gently pulled her up. Her cheeks were burning with shame when he had given her that thoughtful smile of his. Why did he keep spoiling the moment? Not sure what he expected her to do, she had waited for him to make the next move.

After an awkward silence, he had proposed to lie down on the bed, and there they were now, lying next to each other and staring at the ceiling, both naked and not the least bit aroused. Damian seemed determined not to break the silence first, and Charlie wasn't in the mood for small talk either. She felt sad and disappointed. This wasn't how she had imagined sex with Damian. He obviously wasn't into it. But then why had he asked her to come back with him to his apartment in the first place? Maybe it had something to do with her body. He might not like the fact that her boobs were rather smallish. Well, not small, but not your average silicon balloons, either. Sick of racking her brain over his incomprehensible behaviour, she turned to him and gave him a challenging look.

'Something not the way you like it?' she asked.

With a start, Damian woke out of his reverie. 'Hm? No no,' he gave her a reassuring little smile, 'everything's fine. Seriously. It just went a bit … fast.'

Fast? They hadn't even started out yet. Charlie was puzzled. What did he mean? 'Is there something you'd like me to do?' she asked, ignoring his enigmatic explanation.

'Mhm.' His fingers caressed her face, brushing imaginary strands of hair from her brows. 'How about we just enjoy each other's company?'

'Okay ...' Enjoying each other's company, now that was an elusive way of putting it. What the hell did he mean? She sure wasn't enjoying his company right now, the situation was much too awkward to feel anything but unease. She peeked down. Soft and tiny. Oh my, what an evening. She caught Damian's eye. He had followed her gaze and seemed to guess what she was thinking. Damn. Not good. She opened her mouth to say something, anything to lighten up the situation, to get him aroused, to make him want her. ... She couldn't think of anything.

Damian lay down on his back and stared again at the ceiling, studiously eyeing the plaster. What a fascinating pastime. Charlie felt like crying. The minutes ticked by in silence. Outside, someone's car alarm went off. Charlie counted the beeps. Sixteen beeps, before the owner turned it off. Or was it the car-thief who had managed to disable the alarm? She would have thought it would take an experienced thief less time than that. But maybe he wasn't experienced. Maybe it was the first time he stole a car. Maybe he was now sitting behind the wheel, heart hammering in his chest, wondering whether he would get away with it. Scared at his own courage. Maybe, just maybe, wondering if that guy in the car was really him, a juvenile delinquent who stole other people's property, a breaker of the law, who deserved to be shut away, to be banned from society ...

Damian's fingertip carefully traced the path that the tear had taken down her cheek. When had it trickled down? She had been too lost in her thoughts to even notice.

'It's getting late,' she said, without looking at him.

He didn't reply.

'I have a class tomorrow, early in the morning,' she explained. One more lie.

'Mhm.' That was all he said.

She got up and looked for her clothes. Her shirt lay in a bundle at the foot of the bed. She had thrown it there when she had been stripping. A lifetime ago. ... The jeans. Her socks. The shoes. ... Why didn't he say anything? Why didn't he try to make her stay or at least demanded to get his money back? She wouldn't offer to give it back unless he asked her to. This had been harder than any sex position she could think of. Mental torture. Fucking around with her feelings. As far as she was concerned, she deserved the money.

'I'm off now, ok?' At last she looked at him. He lay there, alone on his bed, looking unspeakably lonely and sad. Her heart went out to him. She wanted to run back to the bed, hug him, caress him, love him. But she didn't do it. He had paid for her services. He didn't want her love. She gave him a final, apologetic look and softly closed the bedroom door behind her.

# 5

The din in the pub was so loud that she almost didn't hear her cell-phone ringing. Robbie Williams moaned some extremely unbelievable love story out of the booming loudspeakers above the counter. A booming moan. Oh my. On top of that, the couple next to her had been arguing heatedly, ever since they had got in half an hour ago. It had been fun listening in on their bickering for, say, the first five minutes, but their whiny complaints soon became annoying, with both parties talking and no one listening. No one except Charlie, of course. She could have given them a hint or two on how to resolve the matter, but they probably wouldn't care to listen. She brushed these thoughts aside and reached for her mobile. She popped one finger in her right ear and pressed the phone against her left. 'Hello?'

'Hey, honey! Remember me?'

'Blake!' Charlie jammed the finger deeper into her ear, trying to shut out a super-screech from Miss Misunderstood. 'How could I forget you? How are you doing?'

'Oh, comme ci, comme ça, as they say in La Douce. Overall quite well, I guess. I've entered a new creative phase.'

'Really?' Ultra-boom from Robbie. Her poor eardrums. 'You have to tell me all about it. But, listen, it's a bit loud in here, I can't hear you too well.'

'Ah yes, a bit squishy-squashy, your pus in boots, huh? Uhm, but in other news: I dumped Chris.'

'Oh, you did?' Charlie was concerned. 'Did you quarrel?'

'Nah, I wouldn't really call it quarrel. It was more like an ongoing malaise, a je-ne-sais-quoi that just didn't click between us. Well, and then he was only really after my money, so ... I dumped him. Bye-bye, bébé. Blake is a free man again.'

Charlie smiled to herself. He was trying hard to sound cheerful and unhurt. Too hard.

'So, Charlie. Wanna go on a binge with a free man? Checking out the lowlife of London? You could help me find a new boyfriend.'

'Blake, that really sounds great, but it's Saturday evening and I should be working.'

'Scuse me? Are you telling me that, this precise minute, you're hanging on someone's dick and I'm preventing you from doing your ... thingy?'

Charlie laughed out loud. 'No, of course not. But I'm hoping to find a customer. And I won't meet anyone if I'm hanging out with you.'

'Are you saying my money isn't good enough? You naughty girl, you! I'll pay you, of course. Come on, honey: a hundred bucks if you help me find a cute butt tonight. How's that for working, huh?'

Charlie considered the offer. Blake had been fun to talk to last week. And he sounded like he needed a friend tonight. 'Deal. I suppose you're coming down to Soho?'

'A supposition beats ten suppositories, that's what I'm always saying. I'll spot you out, don't worry, honey. No way I could miss you, with that super-sweet green sweater you're sporting.'

Charlie's heart skipped a beat. She heaved herself up on the crossbar of her stool and scanned the room. No Blake in sight. 'Are you in the pub, Blake?'

'Of course I am, honey. Have a lookie to the right.'

She turned her head towards the entrance to the men's lavatories. Blake gave her a cheerful wave and came closer. Still speaking into the phone, he said: 'So, did you miss me, honey?' and gave her a big smack on the cheek.

Charlie disconnected the call and gave him a bear hug. 'You silly boy. You almost gave me a heart-attack when you mentioned my pullover. Why didn't you simply come over and say hi?'

'Weeell,' said Blake, using his hands for more emphasis, 'you know, I didn't want to ... intrude. You might have been waiting for someone. Or not waiting for anyone, but hoping to meet someone ... someone other than me, you know. And me being more the shy type, the unobtrusive, quiet guy, I ...'

'Ok, ok, I got it,' she laughed, 'discretion, thy name is Blake.'

He held up his hand. 'Blake the Artist, to be precise. Let us not forget the title. And now,' he looked around for the barman, 'I very dearly need a red thingy.'

Ten minutes later, they had secured themselves a free seat on a couch in a relatively quiet corner and snuggled up together in a 'feel-good position', as Blake called it. Charlie lounged against the arm of the sofa, with Blake's head in her lap and his feet dangling over the other end of the couch. Blake had been complaining about headaches, so Charlie was massaging his temples while he told her about his short-lived love-affair with Chris. They had met in a bar some weeks ago, when Blake had been out celebrating his thirty-ninth birthday with his brother. Not really a reason to celebrate, as far as he was concerned, but his little brother meant well, so he had not wanted to spoil the fun for the kid. They had been to a gay bar in North Kensington, not far from Blake's apartment.

'The *Bellybutton* on Blake Close,' explained Blake. 'A very sweet bar, a pity it got closed down two weeks ago. Have I ever mentioned Blake Close to you? Blake Close - close to Blake. It's close to ...'

'Ehm, yes,' she interrupted him gently, 'you did mention it last time, when we drove up to your place. Five times, in fact. At least.'

'Oh, really? Must be the age, I guess. I keep forgetting things. It's quite scary, actually. Can you imagine: thirty-nine. That's only months away from the naughty forty. Do you think it's a bad omen that forty rhymes with naughty? And haughty. All very ominous words.'

'Forty also rhymes with sporty,' she pointed out, 'you could take that as a good omen.'

'Hm. Yes. Maybe.' He tipped a spot above his left eyebrow. 'Could you rub there, please? ... Thank you, honey, you're so sweet.'

Charlie brushed over his forehead in gentle strokes. 'You don't look your age. I'd have thought you were at least five years younger.'

Blake darted up so fast that he almost knocked his head against her chin.

'You're such a honey!' he cried, hugging her tightly. 'You're really my very best lady friend.' He sank back into her lap. 'Come to think of it, I only have one female friend. Apart from you, of course. She's a very distinguished lady, a contessa. From Italy. Italia, un paese bellissimo. Ever been there?'

Charlie shook her head.

'It's definitely worth the trip. So much to see. So much culture. Just think about the Roman sculptures - very sexy. You can't help getting horny when you walk through a museum full of naked statues. And they're all so good-looking, these Roman gods! The sweetest little butts! And such cute balls! Makes you almost want to take a bite ... speaking of which,' his head darted up again and he grinned mischievously at her, 'wanna come with me to *La Mouche*?'

After running through Soho for half an hour, Blake finally localized the place he had been looking for. From the outside, the *La Mouche* was a rather run-down place, with a crooked neon-sign above the entrance. The light bulbs in two of the letters did not work, so the sign read *Louche*. Not very reassuring, Charlie thought. The bull-dog asking for her ID wasn't very confidence-inspiring, either. In his tight leather pants and tiny white shirt, his stern pockmarked face with the squashed nose unblinking, he looked like a gay version of Frankenstein's monster. Blake paid their entrance fees and pulled her after him into the innards of the *La Mouche*.

Charlie felt instantaneously claustrophobic. The music was deafening. Loud techno beats vibrated through the hot, stale air and stroboscopic lights transformed the dark room into a dizzying scenery of surrealism. The bar's theme seemed to be 'stone-age'. Rough, unhewn steps led down into the main room, where people sat on large blocks, nursing their drinks or watching the show on the wooden platform in the centre of the room. Two sweaty males were performing an eerie dance, contorting their painted limbs in a strange, drunken frenzy. Above the stage hung the huge realistic-looking namesake of the place, hovering ominously over the dancers. This feels like the *Titty Twister*, Charlie thought uneasily. She expected George Clooney and Quentin Tarantino to show up any minute.

Blake nudged her in the ribs. 'What a vibe, huh, honey?'

Charlie gave him a hesitant smile. He couldn't seriously enjoy this. Apart from two girls passionately French kissing, their multi-pierced tongues flicking in and out of each other's mouths, she seemed to be the only female customer in the room. Men sat around in pairs of two or three, kissing and holding hands. Charlie wondered why the bull-dog had even let her in. She belonged as much in here as a feminist at a freemason's meeting. As a paté at a vegetarian's meal.

Blake motioned for her to wait and took off to the bar. Now she felt even more exposed. She had the distinct feeling that she was being assessed by unseen eyes from out of the dark recesses of this vault. Lovecraftian creatures looming in the shadows, watching her through age-old scaly eyes. Charlie began to look around, guarding her back. She was hoping that Blake would soon be back.

'There you go, honey,' he screamed into her ear, making her jump. Now she had tinnitus. Great. She took the glass with the red liquid from Blake and suspiciously smelled at the rim: ultra-sweet blackcurrant flavour. Syrupy. Sigh. Charlie took a sip. Another rib-nudge. Blake motioned to a stone block in the corner. Caveman sign-language. Translation into modern-day English: Wanna sit?

Charlie nodded and they moved over to the side. After a while, her eyes started to adjust to the darkness and the din seemed less deafening. Because I'm probably half deaf by now, Charlie thought uneasily.

Blake leaned on her shoulder and screamed into her ear: 'Ow ...out that one?' He pointed to a guy sitting alone at the edge of the stage, staring at the dancers.

He wanted to out someone? Hardly. Charlie frowned. Then she understood: He had said: 'How about that one?' She assessed the guy doubtfully. This gaping ape as new honey? She shook her head vigorously and gave her verdict: thumb down. She wanted to tell Blake that she didn't think this was the right place to go honey-hunting, but she didn't know how to communicate such a complex thought in sign-language.

Blake pointed to another potential victim. Charlie was about to give her reluctant okay, when a gorilla grabbed the candidate's ass. So much for that. She gave Blake an sympathetic smile and a kiss on the cheek. He shrugged, grinned and motioned for her to keep scanning the room.

For a while, they watched the scene before them in silence. Once, Charlie pointed out a guy that looked sexy enough to her: broad shoulders, muscular torso, shoulder-length wavy hair. Blake shook his head like a dog shaking his fur. As an answer to her quizzical look, he mouthed 'too old'. Charlie rolled her eyes. Yet another one who had the hots for teenies. How very annoying. It reduced their chance of finding a suitable boyfriend in here by at least 80%.

She leaned over to yell the word 'loo' in his ear, when she noticed a man leisurely strolling up to their stone. Eyeing Blake. Definitely giving him the twice-over. The thrice-over. Charlie got all excited. Which reminded her that she had to pee. She grinned at the guy, handed her half-empty glass to Blake and made room for a romantic tête-à-tête.

Finding the toilet had not been easy. It had taken her almost a minute to understand that there was no such thing as a ladies' room at the *La Mouche*. The odd female customer had to make do with the unisex lavatory the place provided. If she dare call the dung heap behind the TOILET-sign a lavatory, that is. Six stinking urinals and a dirty seat behind a dilapidated door. An elderly man in black leather pants and cowboy boots leaned against the sidewall. Eyes half shut, he aimed an unsteady stream of urine in the direction of the nearest bowl. His lavender-coloured T-shirt said KISS ME in shiny pink paillettes. Not, Charlie thought. Her bladder fought a painful battle against her sense of hygiene and dignity. She analysed the rusty hook that, in better times, had probably served as lock to the toilet door. Try as she might, she didn't manage to pull it far enough to fit into the metal ring in the doorframe. After a few tries, she gave up. What if she did succeed in putting it in, only to find that she couldn't push it out again? The last thing she wanted was having to scream for help to be rescued from a stinking men's room. Talk about embarrassing.

'Do you know what they say about the prophet and the mountain?'

Charlie turned around. The guy in lavender had finished adding to the mess on the floor and was in the process of tucking his dripping appendage back into its leather cot. When she didn't answer, he looked up and repeated: 'Do you?'

Charlie was taken aback. What did this guy want from her? She shouldn't have been lingering in here, he probably felt offended that she had seen him pee. Not that she had really been looking at him, but who knows what ...

The man shook his head impatiently and came over. Maybe a quick strategic exit would be in order now? Before she could make up her mind on how to react, he had reached the toilet compartment, pushed her in and followed after.

Charlie's thoughts raced. This was supposed to be a gay bar. The safest place for a girl to be. Who had ever heard of a woman being raped in a gay bar? She opened her mouth to protest, but the man held up his hand, commanding her into silence.

'The mountain,' he declared, lifting the rusty hook as far as it would go, 'won't come to the prophet.' He gripped the ring with his right fist. 'So the prophet,' he continued, pulling hard on the ring so that it partly crunched out of its encasement, 'has to come to the mountain.' He let the hook plop into the ring which now dangled an inch out of the wall, then turned to her and grinned. Charlie stared at him, not knowing what to say.

He pushed the hook back and stepped out of the compartment. 'Have a good poop.'

When she returned to the main room, the music hit her like a sledgehammer in the forehead. She squinted a few times to readjust her eyes to the semi-darkness of the place and tried to make out whether Blake was still chatting with that guy. Yes, there they were, apparently in animated discussion. Charlie wondered how they managed to understand each other in this hellish noise. When she came closer, the answer to the question became evident: they weren't talking at all, they were kissing. The language of lovers. Sweet.

Charlie tapped Blake lightly on the shoulder. She didn't want to disturb, but ...

Blake disentangled himself from his newly-found honey's arms. 'Hey, honey,' he screamed, 'sit.'

Charlie sat down. She was definitely better-trained than Bobby. She looked around, wondering what to do with herself. Was Blake expecting her to join in the smooching? If so, he would have to tell her. She wasn't one to impose herself on a blissfully canoodling couple.

Blake nudged her in the ribs and screamed something at her. She made questioning gestures with her hands, signifying him that she didn't understand.

He shook his head and resorted to sign-language: delicate, manicured index pointing to his crotch. Slender sculptor's hand grabbing his new honey's ass. So far for the subject and the object. Then came the verb: index and thumb formed an O, the middle finger of the other hand was repeatedly pushed in and out of the thus formed enclosure. Me-fuck-him.

Charlie sighed and nodded. Ok, that much was clear. She pointed to herself and made the questioning gesture again. What about me?

Blake grinned. He rummaged through the pockets of his jacket, produced a creased ball of banknotes and handed it to her. Then he gave her a hearty smack on the cheek. 'Mission accomplished,' he yelled into her ear.

Charlie smiled. He was so sweet. 'Have fun,' she screamed back.

He grinned, nodded and wriggled his fingers at her. Ta-ta, honey.

She fondly ruffled his hair and got up. The dancers were still performing their languid body moves. Passing next to the stage, she was struck by their relaxed, blissfully entranced faces. They looked happy, lost in a delightful, enchanted universe of fluid motions and painless dreams. She noticed someone waving at her from the other side of the platform. Her restroom-acquaintance. She waved back and blew him a kiss. He laughed and raised his drinking glass to a good-bye toast. In the flashing light, the paillettes on his shirt twinkled like raindrops in the summer sun.

# 6

'I'd sack the lazy bastards. Outsourcing and off-shoring - that's the ticket.' Pretty boy Marcus gave Jacobs a smug grin. The teacher looked like someone had just gagged him with a slug. Marcus raised an eyebrow. 'It works for my dad, you know,' he added nonchalantly.

What an ass, Charlie thought. So what if his father owned half of Kensington. That cheap Donald Trump imitation wouldn't score him any points with Jacobs. And indeed, the teacher turned away with a disgusted sneer. He accepted nothing less than excellence from his students. Even that, it was rumoured, was sometimes not enough. Divination of his thoughts definitely came in handy if you wanted to pass his courses.

Charlie had been bobbing back and forth on her chair for a while, eager to speak up and shine. Now Jacobs turned around and noticed her. With a resigned wave of the hand, he gave her the go-ahead. At last: this was her chance to show her soon-to-be tutor what mettle she was made of. She leaned forward and assumed a businesslike arguing stance. Thirty pairs of eyes were set on her. She opened her mouth to speak ... and that's when her phone went off. Noo-hoo, Charlie thought desperately. Jacobs hated students who forgot to switch off their cell-phone before classes. It was said that he had once grabbed a girl's ringing phone and had thrown it out of the second floor window. Another version of the story was that he had indeed flung the girl herself through the open window. Charlie didn't pay much heed to such gossip. Still, Jacobs had his irrational moments. But he was also a damn good teacher.

Charlie gave him an apologetic grin and quickly stepped out of the classroom. Closing the door behind her, she heard Marcus say to his neighbour: 'Thank God for cell-phones. Saved us from yet another Hermione Granger speech.' Idiot.

She pressed the phone to her ear and pushed the green button. This better be really important. 'Hello?'

'Hey, little girl.'

Charlie's heart made a jump. Mr Mercedes. 'Hello, Gerald. You rang me out of class.' Naughty school-girl voice. Boy, was she good.

'Really? Ah, but you shouldn't leave your phone on during classes.'

'If I hadn't, you wouldn't have reached me,' she pointed out.

'Smart girl. Feel like earning yourself some pocket-money?'

'Right now? I have to get back to my class.'

'Ah, but it won't take more than a few minutes. Just the time for a quick walk to the toilet. Hm? What do you think?' He sounded tense and out of breath. He wouldn't be jerking off, would he?

'Okay.' Charlie settled down on a bench next to the coffee dispenser. She could do with a mocha to go with the phone sex. Surely he wouldn't notice.

'Are you in the girls' room yet?'

'Mhm.' Charlie tried not to make any betraying noises while she rummaged through her pockets for some change.

'Flush the toilet, will you.'

Damn, he was suspicious. Grumble, grumble, what a difficult customer. She got up and headed for the lavatories. 'Actually, I'm almost there.'

'Hm. You've been lying to me, haven't you? Naughty little girl. Hasn't your mummy taught you that you should never lie?' His voice still sounded tight. Mr Hands was definitely playing with the one-eyed snake.

'I'm sorry. Won't happen again.' She heaved herself against the lavatory door. 'I swear I'll be a good girl.' A quick look around the room - all the stalls were empty. She stepped into one of the compartments and flushed. When the sucking noise of the water ebbed off, Charlie heard his soft chuckle at the other end of the line. She rolled her eyes, settled down on a closed toilet seat and got ready for some baby-talk.

'Are you sitting on the toilet?'

'Yes.'

'With your panties down?'

Charlie hesitated. If she said yes, he'd probably ask her to pee. 'No,' she replied truthfully, 'not yet.'

'Oh, but you should. That's what you do before you sit down on a toilet. You know that, right?'

'Yes.' She held the mobile to her zipper and slowly pulled it down. Then she grabbed her jeans and brushed the fabric against her hips, making the procedure as noisy as possible. That done, she put the phone back to her ear.

'... really good.' Damn, she had missed his speech. Never mind. If it was an instruction, he would just have to repeat it. Surely he would love the opportunity to call her a naughty girl once more. Only silence and static were coming out of the phone. Oops, she was supposed to reply something. 'Gerald?' she ventured.

'Does it feel good?'

Does what feel good? What was he talking about? 'Um, I didn't get your last sentence, I'm afraid.'

A pause. Then: 'I asked you to touch yourself.'

'Oh.' One second to adapt to the new situation. Then, with a teasing pout: 'You want me to stick a finger in my pussy?'

A sharp intake of breath. Of course he did.

'I sometimes do that at night. When I'm lying in my bed, all alone.' She was getting into the game. 'It feels so good when I'm rubbing down there. Makes me all warm in my belly.'

He was positively panting now. 'Yes, you like that, don't you? Rub harder, sweetie, come on, rub that little cherry.'

Charlie rolled her eyes and had a look at the watch. Jacobs would be furious. 'Mmmm,' she moaned, 'oh, this is so good.' She let a few breathless gasps follow for good measure.

'Oh yes, you're a naughty girl indeed. Playing with yourself like that.' He had trouble speaking. Should be shooting any moment now. Countdown to ten.

'Oh, I'm so wet,' she whimpered into the phone. 'My fingers are all sticky and moist. Mmmmmhhhh.'

A fast series of hacking gasps out of the earpiece announced the end of the session. 'Naughty - little - girl!'

Charlie grinned. Countdown over. She waited for his breathing to become more regular, then she said: 'I have to get back to my class. My teacher will be very angry.'

'Yes, you better get back.' A pause. 'Can I see you tonight?'

Yes! 'To give me the pocket-money you promised?' she pouted into the phone.

'That, too. But there's also something I want to show you.'

They agreed to meet at six o'clock in front of the school library's gates. She promised to wait at the kerb, so that he would just have to pull up for a moment. That settled, Charlie switched off the phone and leaned back against the toilet's water container. She smiled to herself. Gerald. He was really something. But she shouldn't be lingering here, she had already missed too much of the lesson. She got up, then hesitated, and finally pulled down her jeans. Might as well do a wee-wee while she was here.

Charlie craned her neck and squinted through the pouring rain. It was hard to distinguish the cars that headed down the avenue in the early-evening traffic. She hopped impatiently from one foot to the other. It was almost ten past six and she had been waiting for the better part of twenty minutes. She felt soaking wet and stiff with cold. Where the hell was Gerald?

'Oh hi, Charlie. There you are. I was looking for you at the library.' Alice. Shit, this must be her unlucky day.

'How about we have a coffee together at the canteen? You look frozen, poor thing.'

Trust Alice to turn a conversation into a monologue if you ignored her. Not like she would ever get the hint that, just maybe, you were not interested in talking to her. Oh no, not Alice.

'I'm waiting for a friend to pick me up,' she replied determinedly. 'I don't have time for a chat, sorry.'

'Oh, that's a pity.' Alice firmly rooted herself next to her. 'What shitty weather to be waiting in. Do you want me to keep you company?'

I have déjà vu, Charlie thought desperately. Why did people always hang at her neck when she least wanted them to?

'Look, it's really raining heavily,' she made one more attempt at getting rid of her. 'We need not both get wet. Anyway, he's bound to show up any minute.'

'Oh really? Well, I hope so for you.'

Why was she always starting her sentences with 'oh', Charlie wondered. Must be a bad habit of hers. One of her many annoying habits.

'Oh you know what?' started Alice again. 'How about you call your friend and tell her to meet us at the canteen? So none of us would have to get wet.' Alice beamed at her, proud of her ingenious idea.

'It's him, not her. And I promised him to wait at the kerb in front of the library.' Charlie squinted at the passing cars. Headlights and rain both made sure that she could distinguish exactly nothing at all.

'Oh really? Is he like your boyfriend or something?'

Take off, pleeeaase, Charlie chanted inwardly, trying to make the girl leave with the sheer force of her willpower. She didn't manage. Alice grinned cheerfully on. Mental note: look for a beginner's course in voodoo. It might come in handy in situations such as these.

A car pulled over from the first lane and came to a stop at the kerb, just a few yards further down the road. A black Mercedes. Charlie jogged over, waving a quick good-bye to Alice, glad that she did not have to answer the girl's last question. She pulled the door open and hopped into the car.

'Hey, little girl.' Gerald eyed her wet clothes and hair. 'Sorry

I let you wait. I received an important phone call, just as I was about to leave the office.'

'Don't worry about it.' Charlie shook herself like a wet dog. 'You're here now.' She gave him her sweetest smile.

He smiled back, then concentrated on the traffic ahead. 'There's a little something for you in the glove department,' he said, without taking his eyes from the road.

'Right, you said you wanted to show me something.' Charlie bent forward eagerly.

'You remember that, hm? Actually, I'll show you at the hotel. I'm curious to see whether you will like it. But there's the pocket-money that I promised you in the glove department. Oh and, Charlie ...'

'Hm?' She was busy thumbing through the roll of banknotes in her hands.

'Buckle up, will you?'

Charlie was standing in 'her' bedroom. She had come to think of this room as hers, having woken up the last time very refreshed after an excellent night's sleep in a bed that was not only huge, but also hugely comfortable. So now she was standing in the same room once more, and enjoyed the view over the Thames. Millions of tiny pinpoints twinkled on both sides of the river. The mysterious beauty of a big city by night. Gerald deposited a plastic bag on the bed and stepped behind her. He gently laid his hands on her shoulders and proceeded to knead the muscles in her neck and arms. Then his fingers glided down her back, over her butt, her hips, her belly. His hands roved up again, cupping her breasts, his thumbs massaging her nipples through the thick cotton fabric of her pullover. She leaned her head against his chest and sighed happily. Gerald knew how to make her feel at ease.

'You like that, hm, little girl?' he whispered into her ear. She nodded.

'How about this? You like that as well?' His hand slid into her jeans and panties. His index and middle finger moved up and down in rapid alternating strokes, untiringly tapping against her crotch, applying and releasing pressure in fast expert movements. Charlie's belly muscles constricted and relaxed in a rhythmic pattern, slowly building up tension, releasing it, building up some more tension, just a little bit more than would be released with the next easing of muscles. Her whole being concentrated on this one tiny part of her body. With each stroke of his fingers, each movement of her hips, it seemed to swell up more, taking on ever larger proportions, filling up her thoughts, her mind, her being. Her heart raced and her pulse beat hard against her veins. This must be what they tell you to do in self-hypnosis: focus on one single part of your body, concentrate your whole energy on it, become conscious of every minute detail of its anatomy, feel it respond to the lightest touch, like sweet electric pinpricks racing through you.

Gerald only slowed down his beat when he felt her muscles constrict firmly. Once. Twice. Three times. He reached further down and stuck one finger deep inside her. Her body gave off a soft, moist, sucking sound.

'And now, sweetie,' he whispered into her ear, 'I'll show you what I have bought for you.'

The dildo looked amazingly lifelike. The flesh-coloured rubber even sported thin veins running down the base of its shaft, while the head strained tightly at its connection. With respectful awe at the sheer size of the toy, Charlie gripped it and let her hands carefully glide up and down its sides. She didn't manage to grasp it all around. She looked up at Gerald, who was smiling at her.

'Have you ever used a vibrator?' he asked.

Charlie knew he expected her to say no, to admit bashfully that she had never in her life used a dildo. But this time, she didn't even have to pretend ignorance. This was indeed the first time she held a vibrator in her hands. She had never felt the need to use one of these things, being more than satisfied with her fingers doing the job. She strongly suspected that very few women actually used a dildo. This was probably one of the many phallic fantasies traded down from generation to generation of male biological researchers who never bother to ask the objects of their studies what they really feel or want. Like the G spot. The myth of the dick-crazy woman. As if every girl was aching to impale herself upon a big, vibrating rubber stick.

'No.' She looked up at him with big, frightened eyes. 'It's huge.'

He nodded, a concerned look on his face. 'Yes, it's huge. It's probably gonna fill you all up.'

Her eyes became even bigger. 'You wouldn't hurt me, would you?' she whispered.

His knuckles caressed her cheek and he playfully nudged the tip of her nose. His thumb pushed roughly through her lips, pressing against her tongue, her gums. 'Poor little baby,' he murmured under his breath. 'I fear I just might have to.'

# 7

The pedestrians' traffic light had just changed to red. That's almost still green, Charlie thought and sprinted across the street. She was well on the other side of the road before the first cars set into motion. One more proof that London's traffic lights were set for slow-moving grannies, making sure the old ladies did not get run over. A very caring and laudable effort of the council. Able-bodied citizens on the other hand had of course better cross the street at a red light rather than waiting for it to turn green. When the lights are red, you know you have to be careful and watch out for cars, so you wouldn't dream of stepping into the street unless the road is clear. When the lights are green however, you foolishly delude yourself into believing that the traffic-governing laws of your country will protect you. And thus fail to notice the big van taking a swift left turn. The said van's driver, being only human, might be dreaming of the delicious chicken soup his mum is preparing for him. He might have forgotten that such a thing as a walking human being even exists. Man meets van = ouch. Therefore mental note: as far as traffic is concerned, you are well-advised to heed common sense more than laws. Might gain you a year or two of your lifespan. Besides, it makes living so much more interesting. Second mental note: apply aforementioned rule to all circumstances in life. As Kant said in his categorical imp...

She stopped in mid thought and stared at a figure at the corner. No, she wasn't mistaken. It was indeed him, loitering in front of the *Puss in Boots*. With Bobby in tow. Charlie was ready to turn around and head back into the direction she had come from, but it was too late. He had already seen her and waved at her. Shit. Bobby recognized her too and cheerfully wriggled his tail, pulling his master towards her.

'Hey, Charlie,' Damian greeted her.

Charlie's thoughts raced. Was this the eeriest of coincidences or had he really been waiting for her in front of the pub? 'What are you doing here?' she stuttered.

'Bobby and I have missed you last Saturday in the park. You must have been awfully early for your run. ... Anyway, we decided to take a walk through Soho, looking for you. You mentioned that the *Puss in Boots* was your usual bar, so we thought that you might show up here, sooner or later.' He gave her a hopeful grin.

Charlie didn't believe her ears. 'How long have you been waiting here?' she finally asked.

'Actually not that long today. We just arrived half an hour ago.'

'Today?' she asked weakly. 'Do you mean to say that you have been waiting here before?'

'Um, well, when you didn't show up on Saturday morning, Bobby and I were a bit worried. So I came here Sunday night, and again Monday evening and yesterday, too. And here I find you, at last.' He looked relieved. 'As I can see, you're ok. That's good. How about a drink? We could go to the *Puss in Boots* if you want, but there are also other nice pubs in the area. If you want to check those out ...'

Charlie crouched down and ruffled Bobby's coat. He licked her hand and gave a pleased little bark. How should she react to this? Why was he running after her like that? He clearly hadn't enjoyed their evening together, couldn't have enjoyed the embarrassing disaster that their attempt at sex had been. So why was he so keen on seeing her again? She had skipped her Saturday morning torture expressly to spare him an awkward encounter at which he might have felt obliged to invite her for a hot chocolate. And to spare her the embarrassment of seeing him as well. She couldn't bear imagining what he must think of her. A hooker. A girl who spread her legs for money.

'*The Soldier and the Swan* is quite nice.' He gestured down the road. 'Only a two-minute walk from here. And the bartender has already made friends with Bobby.'

She nodded, defeated. Why the hell not. 'Ok, let's have a drink there,' she agreed.

The bartender indeed recognized Bobby and, to the dog's greatest delight, produced a bowl of water and a sausage for him. Charlie and Damian both ordered a beer, Damian a pint of lager, she a half-pint of Guinness, and they settled down at a table in the far corner. There weren't many customers in the pub, and the music was turned down to an unobtrusive background sound.

After they had both taken a sip from their beer, Charlie asked: 'Why did you want to see me again?'

Damian nursed his drink, thinking the question over. 'I think we have to talk,' he finally said. 'Look,' he went on, leaning eagerly over the table, 'I think we both agree that last Friday evening didn't go so well. I understand that you were trying to *do your job*, but that wasn't at all what I wanted. I wanted to talk to you, to get to know you better.' He paused for a moment. 'Understand why you're doing what you're doing,' he finally added.

Charlie didn't reply. Why was he so nice to her? She was sure he could find a girlfriend at a snap of his finger, what with his cute face, his endearing character and that awesome apartment he lived in. So why was he wasting his time, waiting in front of a pub for a girl like her? She just didn't get it.

'I just don't get it,' she told him. 'You certainly don't have a problem finding a girlfriend. So why are you interested in me?'

Damian shrugged. 'First of all, I don't know about not having a problem with finding a girlfriend. My last one just left me, remember? And she made it pretty clear that in her opinion, I'm a waste of breathing space.' He paused, then continued: 'But I liked talking to you in the park. I immediately had the feeling that I had known you for years. And you seemed so fond of Bobby, too. You even found out his real name.' He was quiet. For a while, no one said a word.

'But when you found out what I do for a living, you jumped on the opportunity and asked for sex.' Oops. Had there been an accusing tone in her voice?

He looked up. 'No, I didn't. I offered to pay you so that we could go on talking, remember? That's hardly asking for sex. I thought, that way you get paid, and I get a nice evening talking to a smart and funny girl.' He grinned sheepishly and brushed a stray lock to the side. It immediately fell back on his forehead.

Charlie took a sip of her Guinness. 'You just wanted to *talk* to me? No one would pay two hundred quid just for a *talk*.'

Damian nodded emphatically. 'Yes, I would. We would both have got what we wanted. Only trouble was, you didn't *get* what I wanted ... and I was too stupid to open my mouth and tell you,' he added with a disillusioned expression, that looked almost comical.

Charlie had to laugh. 'Poor Damian,' she said and took his hand. 'How about I make up for it and we go home to your place and have a nice long talk? This time for free. What do you say?'

He beamed at her. 'You wanna know what I'm saying? I'm saying, let's go and call a taxi.'

They had asked the cab driver to drop them at an Indian restaurant where they ordered takeout food. Then they had walked the short distance to Damian's apartment, enjoying the clear, crisp air and the promising waft of curry from the bagged cardboard boxes. Now Charlie set the table, while Damian produced two candles, which he lighted for 'a more romantic atmosphere', as he put it.

They tucked heartily into the food and for a while, this task wholly occupied their mouths and minds. When most of the food was gone, Charlie leaned back, sighing happily. 'Yummy. That was the best Indian curry I've ever eaten.'

'Mhm,' agreed Damian, 'I often go there. There's also a great Mexican place nearby. If you want to, we can check that one out next time.'

He was already thinking about a next time. Charlie felt a warm ache in her belly, and it wasn't from the food. Damian was such a sweet boy. 'Do you want to sit on the couch?' she proposed.

He nodded, and after they had brought the dishes into the kitchen, they settled down on the sofa, each with a glass of red wine in their hand.

'I know a funny game,' he said.

'Ok?' Charlie was intrigued. What would he propose now?

'It's called *Truth or Dare*. I ask a question, and you have to answer truthfully. If for some reason you don't want to, you have to do something funny, like standing on one foot for a minute, or balancing an egg on your nose.'

Charlie laughed. 'How will you know whether I tell you the truth or not?' she asked amused.

He gave her an earnest look. 'I believe you,' he simply said. 'There would be no point in cheating. It's just a game, you know.'

She nodded, feeling a bit foolish for having asked. He was so straightforward, so trusting, almost like a kid. She knew she wouldn't lie to him. She would feel too bad about betraying his blind faith in her honesty. 'Ok, so who's starting?' she asked and settled back on the couch, comfortably tucking her feet under her legs.

'Me.' He leaned forward and looked her in the eye. 'Why did you tell me you would go to college?'

Charlie was astonished. 'Because I am?' she offered. 'That wasn't a lie. I am really going to COBEL. Do you want to see my student card?' She got up and rummaged through her coat pockets. Bobby spotted his chance for a late-night stroll and hopped to the door, leash in mouth and tail wriggling in excited anticipation. She picked him up and carried him back to the couch. She handed a little plastic card to Damian. He took it and looked at it for a long time.

'You look good in that picture,' he finally said and handed the ID back to her.

'Thanks.' She smiled. 'It's my turn now, right? My question is: Why did you think I was lying about my studies?'

Damian looked embarrassed. 'Well, you told me that you were having sex with guys for money. On a regular basis, if I understood correctly. That doesn't sound like something a girl would do who wants to get a job at a bank or a lawyer's office later on.' His voice faltered and he looked at her quizzically, as if afraid she might take offence at his reasoning.

Charlie considered this. It was true, soliciting wasn't something that went down too well with prospective employers. 'It's not like I just tell this every geezer I meet,' she explained. 'And I neither accost guys on the street, nor hang around at the usual prostitutes' haunts. The *Puss in Boots* is just an ordinary pub in an ordinary street. It might take a bit longer to find a customer there, but at least I can be pretty sure that I won't get into trouble with the police. Besides, you would be surprised at how many students earn their living like this. Not everyone has a generous brother like you.'

Damian nodded, understanding. 'It must be hard to be all on your own in this city,' he said and took her hand.

'It was, at first,' she agreed. 'I started out working at a sandwich shop for four hours a day, and at the weekend I was scrubbing office floors. That was a hard time. I was barely making any money at all and the owner of the sandwich shop kept harassing me with indecent proposals. When he grabbed my ass in front of a customer, I threw a bowl of salad dressing in his face. He threw me out without paying me for the last three weeks. I ran through the streets, blind with tears of shame and anger. At last

I sat down on a bench in the parking lot of a supermarket. That's where I met Paul.'

'Your first customer?'

Charlie nodded. 'He was so funny. He cheered me up with silly stories about how he used to constantly get the come-on by his former boss. He congratulated me on my reaction with the salad dressing. And then he asked me whether I cared to consider to earn some money in a less disgusting way, namely by having sex with him. The way he said it, it sounded like the most natural thing in the world. He was completely relaxed and laid-back about it.' Charlie shook her head, fondly remembering the scene. 'Paul was really something.'

'What happened to him?'

'He got offered a job transfer to Seattle, Washington. I only saw him once after that, two months ago. He was on vacation in London and called to say hi. We had a nice evening out together.' Charlie took a sip of her wine. 'But other than that, it's just the odd e-mail. He sent me a funny e-card for Halloween. A ghost disguised as pumpkin. Underneath the picture, it said: Don't give up the ghost, pumpkin.'

They both laughed about the joke. Damian smiled at her. 'You like what you're doing, hm?'

Charlie cocked her head. 'Am I mistaken or have you been asking the last few questions? It's my turn now, dear sir.'

Damian nodded. 'Fair enough. Shoot.'

'Hm, let me think ...' Charlie looked at him appraisingly. 'Why did Amy dump you?'

He winced. 'Aw, do we have to talk about her?'

'We also talked about Paul. Or do you prefer a dare?'

He shook his head. 'It's not that I don't want to tell you. It's just not that easy to explain. ... Let's just say, I didn't live up to her expectations.'

Charlie frowned. 'What expectations? Did you hit her, or fart in bed, or ...'

Damian laughed. 'No, of course not. ... I mean, I didn't hit her. I would never hit another person, and certainly not someone weaker than myself. As for farting ... well, maybe I *did* have to break wind once or twice, but that's rather a sign of fondness, isn't it?' He waited for her to grin, then continued: 'No. I think the reason why she dumped me is that I wasn't as rich as she expected me to be.'

He looked sad and hurt. Charlie nodded, understanding. His apartment was straight-out splendid, and if the girl had based her expectations on this and bargained for a rich catch, the realization that the rare pearl was nothing more than a nicely polished stone must have come as a severe disappointment. She felt sorry for Damian. 'Hey, if that's the reason she dumped you, she isn't worth a single tear.' She patted his arm. 'Your turn to ask a question.'

Damian looked at her with his big, soft hazel eyes. Eyes in which you could drown yourself all too easily. A dreamer's eyes that promised not material riches, but crazy walks out in the park, barefoot dances in the snow, a life of light and laughter. Charlie called herself to reason. She couldn't afford to fall in love with a penniless dreamer. She brushed her romantic feelings aside, and waited for his next question.

'What is your favourite colour and why?'

Charlie was taken aback. 'My favourite colour? I don't know. I don't think I have one. Blue, maybe?'

'Mhm ... Why?'

'I don't know why. Because it's a soft colour? The colour of hope?'

'Hm.' Damian considered this. 'Isn't that supposed to be green?'

Charlie laughed, exasperated. 'Ok, so maybe because I simply like it?'

'That's a good answer. ... Light blue or navy blue?'

'Boy, you don't give up, do you? Sky blue. Satisfied?'

Damian nodded slowly. 'For now.' He smiled and brushed a lock out of his eyes. He looked so young ...

'How old are you?'

'Thirty-two. My turn again.'

Charlie frowned. 'Seriously? You're thirty-two years old? I would have thought you were younger.'

Damian gave an embarrassed little laugh. 'Yeah, people keep telling me. Can't be helped, though. I'm thirty-two.'

Charlie shook her head emphatically. 'You're bullshitting me. You're not twelve years older than me. Show me your ID.' She held out her hand demandingly.

Damian looked puzzled. Then his face lit up. 'Hold on, ok?'

He disappeared into his bedroom. Charlie heard him rummage through some drawers. After a while, he reappeared with a wide grin on his face. He handed her a small booklet. A British passport. It was issued on the name of Damian Winter. Date of birth: August 27, 1972. He looked very cute in the picture, and hardly older than herself.

She handed it back to him. 'What did you do before you went on dole?'

He stared hard at her, eyes unblinking. A stubborn, child-like stare. 'Do you like pleasing men for money?'

The question caught her by surprise and hit right home. The bastard. She abruptly got up from the couch. 'I should be going. It's getting late.'

He remained seated. The same guarded look, devoid of emotion. 'Ok.'

'Ok. Yes.' Charlie nervously brushed an imaginary strand of hair out of her eyes. Damn, she was starting to adopt his annoying habit. She pushed the elevator button and took her coat from the hanger. Why the hell were her hands shaking like that?

Damian picked up Bobby and followed her. 'I can call you a taxi,' he offered.

'Don't worry about it. It's not that late, I'll take the bus.'

'Then I'll bring you to the bus stop.' When she tried to protest, he cut her short. 'Bobby needs to go walkies, anyway.'

He accompanied her down the road and waited with her until the bus arrived. They didn't talk much, but just as the bus came around the corner, he asked for her phone number. With a pleading look, like a beaten dog asking for a cuddle. She fished one of her cards out of her coat pocket and handed it to him. Without another word, she hopped up the steps. The bus took off before she had even found the time to drop into a seat. Gazing back, she saw Damian standing at the kerb, one hand waving after her, the other firmly gripping the leash, determined to keep Bobby from chasing after the departing bus. She sank back into the seat, deep in thoughts. Except for her hasty departure, it had been a very pleasant evening. Damian seemed to have enjoyed their time together, too. ... She bit her lip. Then what was it that was bothering her, nagging at her subconscious to break through?

Ten minutes later, she climbed out of the bus, still lost in thoughts. She knew now what had been strange about the evening. Throughout the fun and laughter, Damian had not even once tried to kiss her.

# 8

Charlie stretched, punched the air above her head with her arms and yawned heartily. A look at the watch: almost 8 pm. Done enough for today. She saved her work onto the hard disk and switched the laptop off. Brr, it was still cold in here. She put on her old feel-good sweater and oversized Sylvester-the-Cat slippers and trudged to the fridge to pour herself a glass of milk. Outside it was already dark, but at least it didn't rain. She didn't feel at all like leaving her (at least moderately warm) flat to fight her way through the icy December wind, but she knew she couldn't just stay in on a Friday night. The Christmas holidays were fast approaching and she still hadn't bought any presents for her parents and Ronnie. Her brother was bound to make a nasty little side-remark, either on the fact that she had or had not spent money on gifts, but she told herself that she didn't care. Let fools babble on, while brave men act. Hm, that sounded like a famous quote, a proverb even.

She finished her milk and slouched to the wardrobe. Damn, most of her clothes needed ironing, but she didn't feel like doing that right now. She finally decided on a purple pullover and a pair of stonewashed jeans. She fished a blue bra and matching panties out of the drawer, and searched under the bed for a pair of reasonably clean socks. ... Her cell-phone rang. A customer! A guy rescuing her from a long, cold walk! Hold on a sec, I'm coming!

She hastily scrambled out from under the bed. Ouch! Fuck, that hurt. Never mind, when wood knocks on wood, the thicker trunk wins out, so her skull wasn't in any serious danger. Rubbing the back her head, she tried to figure out what direction the ringing came from. Her coat pocket! She dashed over and pushed the green button. 'Hello?'

'Buenos tardes, my beautiful lady friend.'

'Hey, Blake.' Charlie dropped onto the chair. 'How's your new-found love? Still cuddling and kissing?'

'Nah, not really. It just wasn't meant to be, I guess. He was more like a seven-day wonder. Gone on the eighth. A bee fluttering from flower to flower, never staying for very long. Hasta luego y muchas gracias for calling. Ah well, never mind.'

'Hm. So, why have you called? Wanna go out again?'

'You take the words right out of my mouth, honey. Great minds think alike, as the saying goes.'

Charlie pressed the phone between her ear and shoulder and put on a sock. Not super clean, but Blake wouldn't care anyway. 'Where do you want to meet?' she asked.

'Wherever you wish, honey. I've rented a nice little sports car for the evening, so I can pick you up at your *Gato Con Botas*, if you wish.'

'My what?' Charlie struggled with the second sock. 'Blake, can you speak English please, I don't understand Italian.'

'Madre de Dio, what a lack of culture! That wasn't Italian, honey, that was Spanish. The language of Salsa and Flamenco. But your wish is my command, the Anglo-Saxon tongue it is. So, do we have a rendezvous at the *Puss In Boots*?'

'Would you mind a lot picking me up at my place instead?'

She have him her address and directions on how to find the street. He promised to be there in an hour at the latest.

'Great. I'll wait upstairs then,' she said. 'What kind of car will you be driving?'

'Look out for a ruby red Peugeot 307 CC,' he said and hung up.


'So, what's on the agenda for tonight?' she asked, when Blake pushed down the gas pedal and propelled the car forward, engine howling and tyres screeching mandrake style. He jumped on the brakes just inches before the red traffic light, and Charlie's body was painfully jerked forward.

'Listen, would you mind driving a bit more carefully? Unless you want me to throw up on your lap, that is.'

Blake grinned and accelerated, less brutally this time. Charlie was wondering whether he even had a driving licence. His style of driving was eccentric, to say the least.

'Mmmh, I was thinking we could try to spot out a yummy little piece of ass. I do the driving, you do the butt-spotting.' Blake took a sharp left turn. The car behind him honked. He babbled on, unimpressed. 'You know, something young, something juicy, something that focuses on pleasing *me* and isn't just permanently thinking about its own orgasm.'

Am I mistaken or is he saying 'it' all the time, Charlie wondered. That guy from the nightclub must have hurt him badly. He sounded like he was hell-bent on enjoying himself tonight, no matter what the cost. Speaking of cost ...

'So you just want me to help you find someone? Or would I be involved in the act, too?'

'Uuum ... no,' answered Blake, while burning a red light and almost running a pedestrian over in the process, 'I'd prefer you to be present though, when we do the deed. You never know, he might try to rob me or something.' He laughed nervously.

'Rob you? Was that what the guy from the nightclub did?'

'No, of course not.' Blake made a deprecatory gesture and the car slithered dangerously close to the kerb. 'I just prefer to be careful. *Vorsicht ist die Mutter der Porzellankiste*, as the Germans say.'

'Do they? Good for them,' Charlie remarked laconically and held on to the side-compartment to steady herself. Blake's driving was making her nervous.

'Yes, they do,' he insisted. 'But let's not quote adages in an idle way. We have arrived, girl, watch - and find a toy to play.'

'Hm, that sounds like a quote, too.'

'Oh, but it is. And an alexandrine to boot. A genuine Blake.' He grinned and slowed the car down to a gentle cruise.

Hm. Charlie resisted the urge to act and talk in classic verses as well. Besides, she couldn't think of any. 'Any specific criteria you want me to apply in my search?' she asked.

'Make it a young, sweet blonde. A very young, sweet blonde. An extreme...'

'I got the picture,' Charlie interrupted him. She craned her neck and gave the guys standing on the sidewalk the once-over. Most of them looked neither young nor sweet. A drag-queen in high heels and impossibly long black hair. Permed. Hm. ... A skinny little man in tight leather pants. For a second, Charlie thought she recognized the pee-stall philosopher from the *La Mouche*. It probably wasn't him after all, though. Blake cruised on, giving her time to get a good look at the wares on display. At the next intersection, he turned into a narrow alleyway. Here the boys stood on both sides of the one-way street, smiling seductively at the drivers. They looked much younger, and some of them were real stunners. Not necessarily sweet, but ...

'Isn't that ...' Charlie pressed her nose to the car window and squinted out into the semi-darkness to have a better look. 'Blake! Isn't that Chris?'

'I said young and sweet,' was the only reply she got. Soon they were too far down the street for her to be sure she had not made a mistake. She turned around and tried to read Blake's impassive face.

'Chris is working the streets?' she asked incredulously. 'Blake, did you pick him up on a street? You told me ...'

'What if I did?' he interrupted her. 'I picked you up in a bar. So?' He gave her a defiant glance and concentrated back on the traffic.

But you didn't claim to be in love with me, Charlie thought. You don't fall in love with hustlers. Not if you don't want to get hurt, anyway.

Blake pointed to a figure leaning against a lamp-post. 'What about him?'

Charlie scanned the proposed candidate and shook her head. 'That's A. a junkie, and B. an underage junkie, and ...'

'... and C. an extremely sweet, blonde underage junkie,' Blake finished her sentence. He stopped and rolled down the window. The extremely sweet, blonde underage junkie tried a tentative smile.

Blake stuck his head out of the driver's window. 'Hi, honey,' he chirped.

The e.s.b.u.j. took two steps forward. This close up, he looked even younger. Much younger. He surely wasn't shaving yet.

'Hello,' he mumbled. Charlie's eyes narrowed to little slits. Fifteen at most, she thought grimly. Oh, Blake.

'I was asking myself a question ...' began Blake.

The e.s.b.u.j. cocked his head. 'What's that?' he asked.

'You see, I was wondering whether you like ... rocks! You know, the usual ones: Brighton rock, cracking rocks ...'

Charlie closed her eyes. What was she letting herself into ...

The boy looked forlorn in Blake's big apartment. When they had come in, Blake had motioned for him to sit down while he showed Charlie his latest work of art: a marble penis, with finely chiselled lines running down its side and the tiniest slit on the top. It even sported a single, sensuous tear-shaped drop. Blake argued eloquently that his was a very practical art: this statuette for instance could be used as the base for a lamp-shade, or even ... as dildo, Charlie thought. It somehow reminded her of Gerald's present. Which in turn reminded her that her butt still hurt. Her sugar-daddy hadn't been overly squeamish when he'd used his gift. Panting all the while about how sorry he was that he had to do this to her.

Meanwhile, Blake had taken out an elaborate arsenal of drug-related instruments and spread it on his little bedside table. Two small plastic wrappings holding a nondescript whitish object. A short glass tube open at both ends. Blake equipped one end with a thin wire mesh (a cut-out part of a sieve, by the looks of it) and placed the makeshift pipe on the table. The boy came nearer, hungry eagerness dancing in his eyes.

'I was thinking,' said Blake, carefully unwrapping one of the white cubes, 'that we might have a good ole smokie first, then fool around a bit, and then I'll provide you with some more rock candy for the road.' He gave the boy an enquiring look. 'Sounds good?'

The kid nodded. He wasn't much of a talker. Charlie sat down on the bed and eyed the proceedings. Blake opened a drawer underneath the table platform and took out a lighter. One of these cheap items that you can buy at every gas station. The kind that has a dressed figure in it, and when you turn it around, a liquid runs down and gradually undresses the figure. Harmless fun for simple minds. In this case, the figure was of course a dressman. Chippendale-style.

Blake carefully cut the cube in two and placed one half of it on the mesh. Mesh-end held up, he slowly brought the pipe to his lips. The boy watched eagerly, as Blake flicked the lighter, and a long, blue flame shot out. He brought the tip of the flame closer to the little white cube. A soft, sizzling crack could be heard. The tube slowly filled with smoke. Blake waited until the smoke got denser, then he started to inhale the fumes. In deep, dedicated breaths. Five seconds elapsed, then ten. All the while, Blake kept the flame steadily against the white rock, until it had completely dissolved. He sucked in the last lingering fumes and leaned his head back, his eyes shut. His lips softly closed against one another. Still he kept his breath, savouring the building up of tension, the imminent release of the craved rush. At last his lips parted just a little, and he exhaled deeply. His shoulders flexed, his chest and belly constricted ever so lightly, the facial muscles slacked into an expression of complete acceptance and surrender.

Charlie watched him, fascinated. She had never tried any drugs. Except for the odd cigarette, which she had puffed with her friends in the schoolyard, making it a sport to dodge the watchful eye of the teacher. Cigarettes and alcohol, her drug experience did not reach beyond these legal drugs. Watching Blake inhale the cocaine fumes, she realized how graceful a carefully enacted ritual of intoxication could be. A celebration of the mind's complete and utter surrender to the body.

Blake handed the crack pipe and the second half of the cube to the boy. 'There you go, honey. Have fun.' He looked at Charlie. His eyes pointed to the table. She shook her head. No, thanks. He smiled mischievously and let his hand glide over her cleavage. His lips mouthed a sensuous promise, then Charlie saw the boy make a move.

Blake anticipated the kid's intention. With two fast strides, he was back at the table and firmly gripped his wrist. The boy let go of the second wrapping.

'Uh-uh. Sorry, honey, but that's for later. First we'll unwrap another package.' Stepping behind him, he slapped the boy's butt hard with one hand, while the other reached for the zipper in front. 'Let's see what we've got here,' he murmured.

Charlie had made herself at home on the left end of the bed, while the boy's upper body occupied the right. She watched with growing concern as Blake slammed harder and harder into him, grunting and panting with enraged passion. The boy didn't seem to mind, though. He took the meanest thrusts without a flinch, his shy eyes fixed on a tiny bronze replica of a Henry Moore sculpture. Two weeks ago, when she had noticed the artwork for the first time, Blake had explained to her that the smooth curves and bends of this sculpture never failed to soothe his pain when he felt down, depressed and lonely. Charlie wondered whether it did the same for the boy. She sincerely hoped so.

Her thoughts travelled to Damian. When she had left him two days ago, she hadn't been sure whether he really wanted to see her again. But he had called her that same evening, just as she was letting herself into her apartment. Had asked whether she had safely arrived home. Whether she intended to go jogging this Saturday. ... Why was she thinking of him now, as she watched this boy staring at the statuette? Staring with the defeated look of one who has been crushed too many times, a victim who has accepted his fate, too tired even to struggle. That haunting hunted stare ...

When Blake had finished, he rolled over and came to his feet with feline elegance. He snatched the remaining wrapping and the pipe from the table and handed them to the boy, together with two crumpled twenty-pound notes.

'There you go, honey.' He gave him a fond little peck on the cheek. 'You can take the pipe with you, no need to smoke it up right away.' Blake crawled over the bed and let his head fall into Charlie's lap. He watched the boy, who had begun to put on his clothes. 'Are you often hanging out on that street where I picked you up?' he asked, as the boy slipped into his sneakers.

The kid nodded.

'Maybe we'll meet again, who knows, huh? In thunder, lightning or in rain, as they say.'

'Sure,' said the kid, and moved to the door. Then he added politely: 'Thanks for the money ... and the pipe.'

'Ah, but you're welcome, kiddo.' Blake grinned. 'And when you're downstairs, pull the front door shut behind you, will you,' he shouted after him. The kid made no reply, but half a minute later, the building's front door clanged shut.

'Good boy,' Blake murmured, and buried his face into Charlie's lap. 'Mmmmh, what do we have here?' He playfully tickled her navel. 'A belly-button. How very cute.' He looked up. 'Care for a drink?' He crawled back the same way he had come, and produced a bottle of *Crème de cassis* from the liquor cabinet. 'A red thingy?'

Charlie shook her head. 'No thanks, I don't like that sweet stuff too much. Listen, Blake. Don't you think that kid was a bit too young for what you did to him?'

'Ah, you worry too much, honey. It's not like I raped him or something. He was a consenting ... teenager, that's what he was. Besides,' he poured himself a generous amount of blackcurrant liqueur, 'if it hadn't been for me, he would have gone home with someone else. And who knows what nutter that would have been. There are some sick people out there, honey. People that take advantage of these kids' addictions, that force them to do all kinds of perverted ... thingies.'

'Like anal sex, you mean?'

Her sarcasm was lost on Blake. He nodded vigorously. 'Yes, and worse. I actually did him a favour, taking him home. Kinda like a public service, as I see it. I paid him well, socialized a bit with him, it was like a family thing, what with you and me and the kid all together in one room.' He pointed his glass to Charlie. 'He liked you well enough, I could tell.'

Charlie ignored the remark. 'So, what do you want to do now?' she asked and snuggled up on the pillow.

'Hm.' Blake considered his options. 'How about we have another smoke?'

Charlie shook her head determinedly. 'No, I don't do drugs. I prefer to keep a clear head. Besides, you can never know just what you're puffing into your lungs there. They cut that stuff with the most dangerous substances. Like rat-poison, strychnine ...'

'Rubbish ...'

'That too.' Charlie nodded pensively.

Blake ignored the side-remark and brushed her fears aside with an energetic wave of his hand. 'I don't buy cut stuff. This is the pure thingy.'

'How can you be sure, though?' she asked sceptically.

'I can.' Blake went to the wardrobe and took out another piece of white rock. He rummaged through a drawer full of socks and underwear, and finally produced a finely chiselled clay pipe with two bowls for stuffing. Charlie sighed. The pipe had the unmistakable shape of male genitalia, complete with balls. Talk about art reflecting nature.

Blake carefully placed the rock into one of the bowls. 'I don't buy crack, you know. I buy first-class cocaine always from the same guy, a man you can really trust. He's not a user himself, which is important, as you really cannot trust these crack-heads. When I get home,' he grabbed the lighter and made himself comfortable on the bed, 'I cook the free-base myself. So I'm sure I get 100% pure stuff. Only way to go, honey.' He gave her a re-assuring wink, put the lighter to the left ball and inhaled deeply.

'I want you to note down a date in your agenda.' Blake traced invisible circles on her belly and chest. They looked like the invisible blueprint for a new and very scary roller-coaster. His index came to a short stop at the top of her nipple, then glided down the slope, slowly gaining momentum. He was such a kid.

'And what date would that be?' asked Charlie.

'Next Thursday. December 16th. Five o'clock at the Galeria Mundo here in Notting Hill. Private view of *Amor Amer*, the newest exhibition of Blake the Artist. You're invited, honey.'

'I'm flattered. I've never been to a private view. What was that name ... ?'

'*Amor Amer*.' Blake started moulding her breasts. 'That's a cross between Latin and French. It means: Bitter Love.'

'Aha.' Charlie sceptically eyed Blake's hands. 'Is there a deeper reason why you mistreat my breasts?'

'I'm not mistreating them, honey,' he cried, highly offended. 'I'm moulding them. There's quite a bit of a difference, don't you think?'

'Hm.'

'When you come to my private view, I will introduce you to some of my friends. Who knows, a few of them might even be interested in your services. Oh, and you'll meet the Contessa, of course. She's such a honey, you'll see. Very open-minded, too. Actually, she's the only woman I've ever had sex with. Real sex, I mean.'

He waited for Charlie to comment on this and when she didn't reply, he added: 'And she's a great art lover, too. She adores my sculptures. Says they inspire her.'

To what, Charlie wondered. If she was a friend of Blake's, anything was possible.

'I'm really looking forward to meeting that lady, then,' she said. She looked at her watch. 'Is there something else you want to do, Blake? It's getting late and I wanted to go jogging tomorrow morning.'

Blake jumped up and returned with a new bottle of *Crème de cassis* from the kitchen. 'Just one more red thingy, ok? For the road?'

Charlie sighed. 'You haven't given me my money yet,' she pointed out, as he filled her glass.

'Honey, are you insinuating that I don't want to pay you? Naughty little thing, you!' He gave her a playful slap on the thigh. 'Drink up, allez, allez!'

She obediently nipped at the liqueur. Blake took the glass from her and snuggled up. 'Mmmh, this feels so good.' His fingers played along Charlie's spine. 'How about you stay for the night? I'll pay you some more ...' He buried his face between her breasts and gave her a huge bear hug. 'Pleeeaaase?'

Damn, she had promised Damian to be in Bloomsbury Park by ten o'clock.

Blake's breath was warm and soft on her skin. His arms held her tight, determined not to let go. She stroked his head and rocked him like a baby. Soon his breathing became deep and regular. She waited a few minutes, until she was sure he was fast asleep. Then she got up and set the alarm-clock on her cellphone for 8 am. She would have to get up early if she wanted to have a quick shower, then hop on a bus home, change into her jogging clothes and run to the park.

Moonlight fell on the row of penises on the worktable. Smooth, polished marble, every detail lovingly carved out by a very gifted artist. Charlie imagined Blake's warm, slender hands gliding tenderly over the cold, hard stone. She shuddered. She shouldn't be standing naked in a cold room in the middle of December. She hurried back to the bed and rubbed her icy feet against Blake's warm body.

Snuggled up in a foetal position, his arms tightly hugging the pillow, he slept on like a baby.

# 9

A pebble, thrown hard and flat by an experienced hand, does not immediately sink with a splash, but skips across the water's surface in two or even three merry hops, before taking a headfirst plunge into the wonders that lie beneath. Charlie watched the ripples echo out across the lake, the ephemeral legacy of a hard, proud land-dweller, buried forever in the soft embrace of mud and algae.

'You look sad,' said Damian, thoughtfully weighing the next pebble in his hand.

Charlie sighed. 'I don't know. No, I'm not sad, really. A bit tired, maybe. I didn't get much sleep last night.'

She patted Bobby's head and took the ball out of his mouth. She pointed it towards a group of trees at the far end of the lawn. Bobby's gaze followed her hand. His tail was a stiff white rod, pointing skywards in maximum alert. She threw the ball with all her force. He dashed off. Charlie watched him skitter across the lane, gallop over the lawn and duck under the bushes.

She turned around and smiled at Damian. 'Don't worry about me, I'm fine. I just had to think about the guy I was with yesterday ...'

Damian nodded thoughtfully. 'I guess you meet a lot of strange blokes on your job, huh?' he asked sympathetically.

'There are some unique characters among them.' She laughed. 'Still, most of them are pretty normal. What passes for normal in London, anyway. What makes you think that most of my customers are weirdos?'

'Well, I'm one of them, aren't I?' Damian chuckled.

'You're not a weirdo. *And* you're not a customer.' Charlie took the pebble out of his hand and weighed it thoughtfully. 'Do you think I could do that as well?'

'Just try,' he said encouragingly.

She narrowed her eyes and scanned the lake's surface, willing it to become rock-solid. Then she gave the pebble a conspiratorial squeeze and flicked it through the air.

Splash. It sank like the stone it was. Charlie sighed. 'I'm no good at this.'

'Practice makes perfect. Try this for some fifty weekends, and you'll be perfect before next year's Christmas.' Damian gave her hand a cheerful pat and stroked the soft skin between her thumb and forefinger. While he was at it, he decided to keep his fingers interlaced with hers. 'Care for a hot chocolate?'

Charlie nodded. His touch sent warm shivers down her spine. It felt gentle and reassuring, yet strong and full of sensuous promises. Promises that he had not yet kept ... 'At your place?'

He looked at her. Soft, hazel eyes behind a curtain of unruly locks. Charlie wondered whether one did not need a licence for such eyes. They were certainly lethal enough to warrant one.

Bobby yapped and turned in circles around their park bench. Damian reached for his leash. 'Come on, Bobby. Charlie wants to go home for some hot chocolate.'

'He has a fear of being touched? Damn, that must really suck.' Damian shook his head in sympathy of the guy's psychic torment.

Charlie nodded and held out her other foot. They were lying on the couch, lasciviously engaged in a most satisfying threesome: Damian was massaging her toes and foot soles, while she tickled Bobby's belly, which he presented to her by lying next to (and indeed half on) her chest, paws stretched out in blissful surrender. Having decided to play the passive part in this tableau, he did not actively engage in the prodding and cuddling, but rather let himself be spoiled.

Charlie's right hand reached to the coffee-table and carefully balanced a mug back to her mouth. Too hot. She blew on the sweet, brown liquid to cool it down, but only managed to stir up a few steamy droplets that splashed on her nose.

'Ouch.' She sat up. Bobby's ears went up in alarm. Seemed like cuddling time was over.

'Hm.' Damian's thoughts were still with the last story she had told him. 'It seems rather strange for such a bloke to ask for your company. I mean, touching kinda comes with the deal, doesn't it?'

Charlie nestled her feet under her buttocks and cupped the mug in both hands. 'It kinda does, yes,' she agreed. 'At first, he just wanted to look at me touching myself, while he jerked off. Then he asked me to do a blood test checking for hepatitis, syphilis and HIV. That seemed to reassure him enough to entertain the risky thought of a blowjob - with two rubbers, mind you.'

'Poor guy. I cannot imagine that you can feel the tiniest sensation through two layers of latex.' Damian laughed.

'No, probably not. But he seemed happy enough. Made him come, in any case.' She paused, then asked: 'Wanna hear another story?'

He nodded vigorously.

'Ok.' She nestled back into her former comfort position and offered him her foot for some more massaging. Bobby wriggled his tail and re-assumed his 'dead-chuffed puppy' pose. Charlie's left hand went into auto-pilot tickling mode. 'Next customer. This is the guy I've been thinking about this morning. He's actually very funny, monkeying around and ...'

The phone rang. Bobby's head went up, but immediately collapsed back onto Charlie's chest. No need to stop cuddling, his body language conveyed.

Damian got up and scanned the room for the phone. The ringing continued, its muffled sound coming out of the bedroom. He gave her an apologetic grin and disappeared behind the door.

Charlie nuzzled her face into Bobby's coat. 'Do you know that you have a very sweet master?' she mumbled.

Bobby's tail wriggled in consent. As long as she continued to stroke his coat, he was more than happy to agree.

In the early evening, Damian proposed a stroll to a Mexican restaurant in the neighbourhood. Charlie immediately fell in love with the cosy little place, the fake bull-hide covering the benches, the smoke-stained beams and walls bedecked with South-American memorabilia and the smell of grilled meat mingling with the sound of fiery guitars and banjos.

After a copious meal, she leaned back and suppressed a happy burp. Chicken fajitas, nachos, beans and a large glass of pina colada. Life was beautiful.

Damian motioned to a little Indian girl passing along the tables. She carried a wicker basket full of flowers in her hand. A coin and a rose exchanged owners, and Damian presented the flower to Charlie. 'A little thank you for a wonderful day,' he said.

Charlie was touched. 'You know that this is the first time a guy offers me flowers?' She closed her eyes and deeply inhaled the perfume of the rose. Then she leaned over the table and blew a quick kiss on his nose. 'Thank you, Damian.'

Damn, why was she blushing now? She, who didn't think twice about having sex with complete strangers, who even relished the accompanying tingle of danger and lowlife, became embarrassed like a teenager about a coy display of affection? Don't be silly, Charlie chided herself.

'Would you like another cocktail?' he asked, pretending not to notice her embarrassment. 'Or do you prefer to go home?'

*Go home.* Charlie knew he meant *home to his place.* A home that was neat and tidy and spacious, not spilling over with books and boxes of clothes. A home in which every room was warm and inviting, and where you did not have to put on woollen socks and a jacket to go to the loo. A home that smelled of wood polish and fresh laundry, instead of a permanent waft of cabbage-soup and cold pizza drifting in from the staircase. Charlie wondered for the umpteenth time how a guy on the dole could afford a place like that. Even with the most generous and helpful of brothers. Mental note: If he invites you over for the night and you manage against all odds not to make a mess of it, ask him again about this.

She got up and grabbed her coat. 'Ok. Let's go home.'

The headlights of a passing car circled around the room like flashbeams in a disco, momentarily bathing walls and furniture in a searing bright light. Charlie watched them highlight the soft marine pattern of the wallpaper, glide along the hard edges of the sturdy old oak wardrobe, flicker over the metallic surface of the door's hinges and knob, barely touch the colourful rug at the bedside, while highlighting the lampshade above it, cross the immaculate white of the linen sheet and pillow, and pass over Damian's relaxed, sleeping face. Then the light reached her and ended its circular expedition around the room. Together with the sound of the car engine, it soon disappeared in the distance.

Charlie's thoughts wandered back to the last hours. She *had* managed not to make a mess of it. When they had arrived back here, they had fooled around with Bobby, and Charlie had played disk jockey, rummaging through Damian's collection of CDs. An odd collection it was, she mused. His musical tastes seemed to range from eighteenth-century chamber music to Lloyd Webber musicals, Tom Jones and heavy metal. But then again, maybe not so odd after all. A lot of the CDs appealed to her as well. She had put on a compilation of evergreens, and soon they were singing along to *American Pie* and *Amarillo*. Giggling and fooling around, she had at last summoned up the courage to kiss him. And he had kissed her back. Carefully, barely touching her skin at first, his mouth flitting ever so lightly across her lips and tongue, making sweet showers of ecstasy run down her spine, making her want him badly, so badly, worse than she had ever wanted a man before.

She admitted to herself that she had been apprehensive about this moment. After the first two attempts at sex had ended in disaster, she had wrecked her brain for days to find an explanation for his behaviour. The obvious explanation was of course that he did not fancy her. However, the fact that he had positively been stalking her seemed sufficient proof to discount that idea. The only other reason she could think of was that he had problems in bed. Erection problems, by the look of it. After she had convinced herself that this must be it, she felt very sorry for him. He was such a nice guy and as far as she was concerned, he deserved only the nicest and most understanding of girlfriends. She had sworn to herself to try and help him overcome his shyness or bodily inadequacies.

She need not have worried. A prolonged foreplay, during which he seemed to divine her every want and need, followed by heated and passionate love-making made her realize that he suffered neither from complexes nor from any other bodily or mental ailment. Unfortunately, it also made her realize that she had hopelessly fallen in love with him.

Two fingers wandered along her hip. Her belly muscles constricted in an involuntary jerk. The pillow to her right moved with a deep, throaty chuckle. Then it spoke: 'Are you ticklish, by any chance?'

She nudged him in the side. 'You startled me. I thought you were asleep.'

Damian turned around, his eyes sparkling with boyish mischief. 'You thought right. I was. And now I'm awake.' He grinned. 'A kiss for your thoughts.'

'I thought about what a nice evening this was. And about your CD collection. It's quite a motley assortment of musical styles.'

Damian reached over and gave her a warm smack on the mouth. 'So you don't think *Jesus Christ Superstar* and *Delilah* match?' he asked.

'I think they match just as perfectly as Handel and Iron Maiden.'

'Those two I blame on family ties,' Damian defended himself. 'My sister-in-law Katie is a trained opera-singer. Over the years, she has started several ill-fated attempts to improve my musical tastes. As to *Somewhere in Time*, well ...' Damian made a little pause, then tried again, '... well, my brother was into Maiden way back when. I guess he thought the album would help me over our parents' death ...'

It is amazing how sharp our senses become when the mind struggles to distract itself from the situation at hand. Charlie suddenly felt the distant hum of the fridge throb a steady bass-beat in her ears, the metallic clicking of the heater providing the accompanying rhythm. Her eyes were mesmerized by the tiny knots at the end of the bedspread. Hundreds upon hundreds of colourful little threads, intricately interwoven with one another to form the most beautiful pattern. Seen from a distance, it looked like quite an ordinary bedspread, a Japanese garden scene printed upon fine, smooth linen. Who ever cares to notice the myriad threads that make up such a fabric? They stay in the background, unnoticed, yet fundamentally important. The stuff the world is made of.

'Your parents died?' she asked softly.

She felt Damian nod. 'When I was sixteen. In a car accident. My mother loved to drive her sports car. She was a real daredevil behind the wheel, never caring about speeding tickets. I remember how my father used to scold her for that.' He gave a little laugh. 'You know what's funny? The day it happened, they had taken my father's company car. He was driving, ever so cautious and law-abiding. The truck hit them full force in the left side and pushed them into the railing. Squished the car like a lemon. They were both dead on the spot.'

'Oh, Damian, I'm so sorry.' It sounded hollow and utterly useless, just like their deaths.

'You know, I just can't help thinking ... if my mum had been behind the wheel that day, they would already have been a hundred miles away before that damn truck hit that damn railing.'

For a while, no one said a word. Charlie felt helpless and inadequate. Some people say the most traumatizing experience in a child's life is the realization that people around you cannot feel what you feel. They may sympathize with you, but when all is said and done, you are still alone with your pain. Charlie often thought that the psychologists had got it all wrong. It's terrible to be alone with your grief, but seeing someone you love get hurt, and realizing that there is nothing you can do to take away the pain or at least share it with them, is a much worse experience.

'I sometimes dream about her. About the way she used to laugh and hug me,' Damian mused. 'Strange that I should remember that, don't you think? I don't really remember much of my childhood. But I remember very clearly how she hugged me ...'

His voice trailed off. His hand snuggled under the low of her back and pulled her closer. She rubbed her nose against his shoulder. He smelled of fresh air and sweat, mingled with a faint scent of dog and fruit shampoo. As incongruous a mixture as his CD collection. And as much an integral part of the man she loved.

He nibbled teasingly at the rim of her ear. His fingertips stroked up and down her lower back, barely touching her skin. 'Ask me something,' he demanded suddenly. 'Anything you want to know. I swear I'll answer you.'

'How come you can afford this place?' The words were out before she'd had time to think. She bit her lip. Damn. Very sensitive, Charlie, she chided herself.

His fingers did not stop their caress. He stared at the ceiling, as if hoping to find the answer to her question engraved in the plaster. 'My father owned a consulting company. Winter Towers. Over the years, he turned it into a pretty prosperous business. When he died, the shares were divided equally between me and my brothers. But I'm not really good at financial matters, so I let my brother handle the business part and I get an allowance every month. Enough to live on, even if I don't have a job. Which doesn't mean I'm not trying to find a job. It's just not that easy. I guess I'm not really good at anything.'

She hugged him. 'I'm sure you'll find a job. The trick is, you mustn't give up looking. Everyone is good at something. You just haven't found the right thing for you, yet. Was there any subject you particularly liked at school?'

'Not really. I hated school. I was at Lambert's Oak, and they expected you to reach top grades in your tests. I guess I was the dead weight in their statistics.' He gave an embarrased little laugh.

Charlie stared at him with wide eyes. 'You were at Lambert's Oak?' she repeated incredulously. 'That's about the best public school you can get. Apart from Eton, maybe.'

'Hm. I s'pose so. I could have done without.'

She was silent. She had never met anyone from Lambert's Oak. That school was a diving board into Oxford and Cambridge and she had a hard time believing that an unemployed thirty-something who had bumped into her while walking his dog in the park had been educated there.

'Did you drop out?' she finally asked.

He shook his head. 'Oh no. My brother insisted that I finish college. I somehow got my A-levels in English and economics and then he enrolled me in the first business school that would have me. I had to fail the first year twice before he finally gave up. He's sometimes a bit slow on the uptake, is Gerry.'

'Hm. But still, you have your A-levels, in languages and economics. There must be some kind of job you're suited for, something that you're good at. You ...'

He kissed her softly on the mouth. 'Linguistics,' he mumbled. 'I'm pretty good at linguistics. Everything to do with the tongue.' His mouth moved down her chest, bestowing little kisses on her breasts and belly. It finally settled comfortably in the warm triangle between her legs. 'Or maybe the back-office? Can be interesting, too.' His tongue wandered on. 'Or maybe ...'

Charlie closed her eyes and pressed her hips against his face. No matter how shitty he might be on any other job, his blow-jobs were pretty damn fantastic.

A nosy little ray of sunlight tickled her face. Charlie blinked, then closed her eyes again. Snuggling deeper into the comfy-cosy warmth of the bedspread, she gave a satisfied little grunt. Damian was busying himself in the kitchen, taking the crockery out of the dishwasher. A promising waft of freshly-brewed coffee reached her nose and mingled with the sweet scent of air freshener. She heard Bobby trot from the living room into the kitchen. Soon after, there was a clunk, followed by an excited bark and four furry paws skittering over the parquet. Charlie grinned. Early morning tyranny. Sweet. She treated herself to a healthy yawn and stretched her body in a delicious play of muscles.

Ouch. Something had stung her foot. She opened her eyes and blinked several times. Hastily rubbing the sleep out of her eyes, she scrambled upright, careful where she put her hands and legs.

Holy ... Charlie was speechless. Mouth wide-open, she stared incredulously at the sea of roses on the bed.

# 10

The meeting had been dragging on since nine o'clock this morning, and there was no end in sight. Gerald's thoughts drifted away from the flip charts and statistics. Yesterday evening, he had come home earlier than usual from his club. When he had turned into his driveway, he had noticed a movement in the back of the company car stationed to the left of the garage. His headlights had caught the interior, and there they were: Louis, shirt hanging out of his unzipped pants, and his darling baby. His Elsa. Just as scantily dressed. Both looking guilty and embarrassed. He hadn't known what to say. Ironically, it had been his idea that one of the company's drivers should bring Elsa and Nicky to school and drive them through town to their piano and riding lessons. He had thought that a private chauffeur would be safer than the public transport system. Quite obviously, he had been wrong. He had sat there behind the wheel, staring into his little girl's defiant eyes, and his world had fallen to pieces. His baby was growing up, and there was nothing he could do to stop it. First she had taken a fancy to applying make-up on her sweet face, then her little titties were perking up under her shirts. And now this. His baby wasn't a baby anymore. Quite the contrary. From now on, he would be fearing day and night that she might become pregnant with a baby of her own. The ultimate rape of a little girl's body. Her one-way ticket out of childhood.

Gerald grabbed his cell-phone and abruptly stood up. He murmured an excuse to the board of directors and left the room. He needed some relief. Now.

Newton's law of gravitation tells us that every object in the universe attracts every other object with a force directed along the line of centres for the two objects that is proportional to the product of their masses and inversely proportional to the square of the separation between the two objects. Or, in less scientific terms, if you jump out of a plane without a parachute, don't expect to float in the air.

Another law holding just as universally true was formulated by Mister Murphy. It tells us that if there is even a small chance that something might go wrong, it most definitely will. And you may rest assured that it will choose the worst possible moment to do so. Transposed on our story, this means that Charlie should not have been at all surprised when her phone went off. Nevertheless, she was. Surprised, that is. Ah well, there is nothing like a little shock to wake you up in the morning.

Jacobs' head jerked around like a velociraptor hearing the snap of a branch. 'If anyone dares to answer that phone, I shall scream,' he declared in a dangerously soft voice.

Charlie's hand deflected from its route and scratched her shoulder instead.

The seminary room was eerily silent. The only sound to be heard was the desperate buzz of a lonely fly on the windowpane. Two seconds ticked by. Charlie's coat continued to ring. Jacobs' haggard figure stood stock still in front of his students. Only his eyes moved to and fro, scanning their faces. Fourteen it's-not-mine-I-swear expressions on wintry-pale faces. And one it's-not-mine-I-swear expression on a strawberry-coloured little mug. Hm.

He slowly turned around and fixed his gaze upon the hapless arthropod. His eyes narrowed to little slits. His fingers flexed menacingly. One more second ticked by.

'Why is it,' he asked with the same soft voice, 'that flies never seem to find their way out, yet at the same time unerringly find their way in?' He made a pregnant little pause, as if hoping for an answer to this puzzle. Neither his students nor the fly replied. Another second ticked by. Jacobs opened his mouth anew: 'Do us all a favour and answer that call, will you, Miss Morgan? Judging by his persistence, it must be of the utmost importance.'

Charlie scrambled out of her chair and fled to the door. Her cheeks were blazing a deep crimson. How utterly embarrassing.

'Hello?'

'Hey little girl.'

'Why the heck do you keep calling me during classes? I already told you last week: I have a seminary on Monday mornings. With a very nervous teacher. One about whose opinion I care quite a bit. I don't know if I made myself clear, but in case I haven't: don't ever again call me on Monday mornings!' Charlie made a pause to catch her breath. The line remained dead. Mental note: If he has dared hang up now, smash the phone against the nearest pillar and scream. 'Are you still there?' she finally asked.

'Yes.'

Hm. So he had not hung up. Good. She couldn't really afford a new phone. 'Then why don't you say anything?'

'Can I see you tonight?'

If he was trying to make her lose her temper, he was on the right track. Charlie took three deep breaths and counted to ten. Her blood pressure returned to almost normal. 'Sure,' she said. Happy baby voice. 'Same time, same place?'

'Ok.'

'Ok. See you then. Now if you'll excuse me, I have an appointment with Wrath.' Charlie clicked the phone shut and braced herself. Acid comments, here I come.


'Oh I'm so happy.' A pause. Was she waiting for a reply? Maybe something along the lines: 'Oh, how great!' Charlie couldn't bring herself to say that.

'You know what?' Another pause.

'No, what?' Charlie sighed. She was pretty sure the monologue would have continued without her interjection, but why not keep up a semblance of a conversation. It made Alice happy and it didn't cost her much effort.

Alice beamed triumphantly. 'This morning? In Jacob's course? Marcus looked at me twice.'

'He did?' She almost added: 'While you were watching him for ninety minutes,' but she just caught herself in time. No need to be cynic. The girl didn't know any better. And being in love with a dick like Marcus was punishment enough for all the sins she could ever commit.

'Oh yes. I think he even winked at me once.'

'Wow.' Was that a coffee stain on her pants? Hm. Maybe she *should* throw in a day at the launderette.

'... at least!'

Oops, the conversation had gone on without her. Charlie hoped an appraising hum fit the context: 'Mmmh.'

'Oh, I almost forgot to ask you: that guy who called you on the phone this morning, you know, when Jacobs threw his fit ...' Thanks for reminding me, Charlie thought. '... is he like a boyfriend of yours?'

Sensation-hungry smile. Sorry, babe, no Sun-worthy news here.

'My dad. Wanted to discuss a Christmas present for my mum.'

'Oh.' Dire disappointment.

Charlie checked her messages on the phone. 'Listen,' she said with an apologetic smile, 'I think I better call him back and tell him the vacuum-cleaner wasn't such a great idea after all.'

Charlie left the girl sitting in the library's patio café and stepped out. She had promised Damian to have dinner with him tonight. She better tell him that she would be late. She had put the call off until now, but it was unfair not to tell him in advance. She just hoped he would not be too angry or, worse, hurt.

'Hello?'

'Hi, Damian. It's me.'

'Hey, Princess. How's your day? Are you busy studying?'

Charlie smiled. He was such a cutie. 'Yes, very busy. I've been looking up articles in the library and I have gone through my lecture notes again.'

'Good girl. At what time do you think you can be here tonight? Bobby and I miss you.'

Sooo sweet. Ok, time to hit him with the bad news. 'Listen, I got a call this morning. From a customer. He wants to see me in an hour.'

'Oh.' Pause. Then he added: 'I see.'

'Are you angry?'

'No, of course not,' he hastily reassured her. 'Why would I be angry?' Pause. Then, in a hesitant voice: 'Is he a nice guy?'

'He's ok. Please don't be jealous, Damian, he's just a customer.'

'I'm not jealous,' he defended himself. 'But ... it's not the double-rubber guy, is it? I just don't want you to do something you don't like,' he added sheepishly.

Nestled against a stone pillar in the windswept library courtyard, Charlie felt warm and loved. 'He's nice, don't worry. And I'll try to be as fast as possible,' she promised. 'Do you still want to see me later on?'

'Of course, Princess,' he replied cheerfully. 'Bobby and I will be waiting for you.'

'Gerald?'

'Hm?'

'Can I ask you something personal?' Charlie played absent-mindedly with his chest hair. If you pressed your fingertip against the skin and swirled your finger carefully enough, you could wrap the tiny curls around your pinkie ...

'No.'

... or not. She was just as shitty at this as at making pebbles skip across the pond. She tried again.

Gerald watched her efforts with an amused smile. 'Are you having fun?'

'Mhm.' She wasn't one for giving up that easily. 'Why not?'

He frowned. 'Why not what?'

'Why can't I ask you?'

Gerald shook his head and laughed. 'Aren't you a nosy little girl.' He caught her fingers in his hand and gave them a tight squeeze. 'And stop that, will you?'

Disappointed pout. 'Spoil-sport.'

'So, what is it you want to know?'

She grinned. 'Who's the nosy one now, huh?'

'Don't be childish.' Gerald turned around and reached for his cell-phone. Charlie stared open-mouthed at him while he checked his text messages. *Don't be childish*? As in: Please play the blue-eyed kiddo while I'm panting on you, but make sure you morph into a stern no-nonsense adult right after the deed? Asshole. Which reminded her of the question she had wanted to ask him.

'Gerald?'

'Hm?' He clicked his mobile shut and held up his arm for her to snuggle closer. Which she did.

'Why don't you want to have normal sex?'

He blew a kiss on her forehead. 'Without the role-play, you mean?'

'No. I meant ...' Charlie struggled to find the right words, '... normal sex. As you do. The missionary position,' she added lamely.

Gerald gave her an amused little smile. 'You mean, why don't I fuck your pussy?'

'Right. That's what I meant.' She nodded vigorously.

'Hm. I thought that was obvious.' He looked into her eyes, a long, intense stare. 'Because I don't want to make you a baby, of course.'

*Why do you keep running around the apartment? She will show up eventually, you know. When she does, we will both be happy, and while she's not yet here, we might as well be happy, too. We could play catch-the-cookie, or go-get-the-ball. Or we could just lie on the couch together and cuddle. You cuddle me, and I lick you. But no ... you prefer to run around, checking your watch every two minutes. What a dog's life.*

'You miss her too, hm?' Damian patted Bobby's head and sighed. 'You look real unhappy, poor bugger. I just hope she's fine. She said she would be as fast as possible. She even promised it. But how fast is as-fast-as-possible, I wonder. She didn't say anything about that. Might not be very fast at all. What do you reckon, hm?'

*Waiting is such a waste of time. I can understand the need to wait if one is all alone. But you're not. You have me. We could pass the time with something more productive. Like catch-the-cookie, for instance. Not interested, no?*

Damian had another look at his watch. Almost eight. 'If only she'd call.'


'Make me a *baby*?' Charlie stared at him in disbelief. 'We use rubbers, remember? Besides, I'm on the pill. I don't think there's a big chance you could knock me pregnant.'

'You never know. And then it would feel strange ... taking you like that.'

'Oh, right. Having sex in the missionary position - what a perverted and outrageous thought. Better stick to the good ole anal fuck, huh?'

'No need to be sarcastic.' Gerald was unimpressed by her outbreak. He gave her a quick slap on the butt and gripped her around the waist. His mouth moved close to hers, his gaze sinking like lead into her eyes. Their lips almost touched. 'Besides, I don't like you using such ugly words. We should be able to communicate like civilized people ... hm, little girl?'

Charlie felt his growing erection press against her leg. Opening gong for round number two ...

'Look, I know you need to go walkies, but we'll just wait for some minutes until Charlie's here, ok? She shouldn't take much longer.'

The phone rang. Damian was on it like lightning. 'Hello? ... Oh, it's you.'

*Whoever the caller is, I hope he has a healthy and robust self-esteem. Otherwise he's likely to fill up the ranks of the bodies floating in the Thames, the way you make him feel unwanted.*

'Sure, I haven't forgotten. Thursday afternoon. ... Look, I'm expecting an important phone call. ... Yep, her. She's coming over for dinner tonight. ... Look, we'll talk about this on Thursday, ok? ... No, I haven't asked her yet. Actually, I'll do that tonight. ... Ok. ... Right. So, I'll see you in a few days. ... Yep, love you, too.'

Damian hung up and stared pensively at the empty display. He just hoped she had not tried to call while he had been on the phone.


'This hurts, hm? No wonder: you're so fucking tight. I imagine - this must - hurt - like - hell.'

Jaws clenched, he accentuated every word with a hard, merciless thrust of his hips. His sweaty stomach pressed against her naked back in rhythmic, sucking sounds. Boy, was he heavy. Sweat dropped down upon Charlie's neck and shoulders. Her fingers dug deeper into the pillow and she desperately tried to relax her muscles.

'You're begging for mercy, aren't you?' she heard a highly aroused voice panting above her.

Damn, she'd forgotten to beg. 'Please, I can't take it anymore,' she whimpered, very convincingly.

'Oh yes, you can,' he took up her cue. 'I've had little girls even tighter than you, and screaming louder. Claiming they couldn't take it. But they all could, in the end. Not like they had much choice.' His voice was still hoarse, but his hip movements had somewhat calmed down. Not good. She had been hoping that he was gearing up for the final thrusts.

He bent his head down and nudged her cheek with his nose. 'You know what?' he murmured in her ear.

'What?' she asked in a fearful whisper. She didn't need much acting skills to appear frightened in this situation.

Propped up on his right elbow, he let his left hand glide along the curve of her breast, cupping the soft, round flesh. Inch by inch, he pushed himself deeper inside her, in sweetest, pain-filled slow-motion. When he was all in, he gently rocked up and down, teasing the soft line between her thighs ...

Charlie let out a weak moan.

'Hmmm?' His lips breezed lightly over her ear, her cheek, her chin. 'You like that, hm, little girl?'

Her lips parted, eagerly anticipating his kiss. His breath touched her mouth, the tip of his tongue barely more than a whisper on her skin. It flicked ever so lightly over her lips. Tingling like an electric pulse on every nerve-end that it reached. The whole world seemed reduced to this warm, padded sensation. Waves billowing down her spine built up a warm throb in her belly.

'And now,' he breathed softly into her mouth, 'you better get ready for a rough ride.' Heaving himself up on the bed, he worked up a steady, hard rhythm.

The waves continued to ripple down her spine. They pooled into her lower abdomen, where they swelled to the forceful onrush of a tsunami, rolling faster and ever faster, until a hard, hot and helplessly unstoppable mount of pleasure washed over her. Her back arched upward, her belly muscles constricted. Sweetest pain ...

But immediately after the tide of ecstasy had ebbed off, her body became acutely aware of the mistreatment it was still suffering. She cried out in protest.

'You didn't - expect this - when you got - into - the car - did you? Hm? Well - here's the bill - for being - a naughty - little - girl.'

Every thrust sent a flame of searing pain up her spine. She struggled to get her hands on his hips. 'Ow, no, Gerald ...' Charlie felt her head spinning and tasted bile in her throat. She couldn't find the right words to make him understand.

The thrusting stopped abruptly. The pressure and pain ceased at the same moment, and Charlie realized with relief that he had rolled down. He took her face in both his hands and gave her a concerned look. 'Are you alright, Charlie?'

She managed to shake her head, fighting the tears that threatened to well up. She bit her lips to stop them from quivering. When she looked up, she noticed his soft, caring hazel eyes. Eyes, to fall in love with. She couldn't get a single word out. Instead, the same thought kept spinning round and round in her head: he didn't say 'little girl', thank God he didn't say 'little girl'.

'Feeling better?'

'Mhm, thank you.' Charlie took another sip and handed the cup back to him. She let out an apologetic little laugh. 'Pewh. Talk about coitus interruptus, huh?'

'You really had me worried. Your face was as white as the blanket.' He gave her a searching look. 'Are you sure you're ok?'

'Yes, I'm fine.' She sat up and pulled her knees to her chin. 'Do you want me to give you a blowjob?'

'Don't be silly.' Gerald brushed a lock of hair out of her eyes and gave her a peck on the cheek. 'I've wreaked enough havoc on your body for one evening. I'm gonna take a shower.'

Charlie heard him step into the shower and turn on the water. She looked at her watch. Almost nine. Damn. She should call Damian and tell him not to wait any longer. And to think that she had been looking forward to seeing him all day long. Damn. Damn. Damn. She sighed, and punched in his number.

'Hello?'

'Hi, Damian, it's me. I'm sorry, it got much later than I expected.'

'Oh.' There was a pause. He seemed to be wrestling with something.

'Damian?'

'Uh, yeah, I'm still here. Bobby and I are going walkies. He's wound the leash around a bush, hold on, will you?'

More wrestling. Charlie waited patiently. He didn't seem to be too mad at her.

'Charlie? Sorry about that. Listen, do you still want to come over? I could fetch takeout from our Indian restaurant and we'll warm it up when you get here.'

'By the time I get there it will be after ten ...'

'No problem. You can sleep over. It's not that far from my place to your school. If you want to, that is ...' His voice trailed off.

'I would love to,' she began, when Gerald stepped out of the bathroom, a study in dripping, self-assured masculinity. 'Hold on a second.' She put the call on hold and looked up. 'Would you mind dropping me off near Bloomsbury Park?' she asked.

'No problem,' he replied.

Charlie pushed the hold button once more. 'Listen, are you still there? ... I'll be at your place in half an hour, ok? Love you.' She disconnected, and hopped into the bathroom to take a shower.

# 11

'Ready?'

'Mhm.' Charlie beamed up at him. Damian and Bobby had waited in the taxi while she had run up to put on some warm clothes. She had wound a long woollen scarf around her neck and pulled a cap deep into her forehead. Her hands were safely tucked away in a pair of warm mittens. Pullover, jeans, walking shoes and overcoat - and she was ready to explore London the tourist way.

The night before, Gerald had deposited her at the closed entrance gates to Bloomsbury Park. She had insisted that she could walk the rest of the way to her friend's place. Not that she didn't trust Gerald, but she preferred to keep her private life private. She didn't think he was the mad stalker type - but her motto was 'better safe than sorry' and so she had waved him good-bye and jogged the few minutes down the road to Damian's apartment.

They had spent a wonderful evening with candle-light dinner, dog-cuddling and smooching on the couch. Fooling around with Damian was so much fun - Charlie felt like she had known him for her whole life. They had talked about their school years ...

'In eighth grade, I totally fell in love with that guy who used to bring his pet-mice to school. He smuggled them into class in his pants. They were the cutest little things you can imagine. I'm not sure whether I was more in love with him or with his mice.'

Damian laughed. 'Wow, that's really something, smuggling mice into school. I never had any pets as a kid. I would have loved to have a rabbit, though. But my father was against animals in the house. And I couldn't have taken them to Lambert's Oak anyway.'

'I always wanted a dog,' she admitted dreamily. 'But my parents were also against it.'

'All parents are pet-haters,' he declared. 'But now you have Bobby. A childhood dream come true.'

'Right.' Charlie stroked Bobby's coat, which the dog acknowledged with a grateful wriggle of his tail. *Go on*, the wriggle said, *it makes you happy, it makes me happy, there's no need to stop the cuddling. Not in this life, anyway.*

'Is there anything else you always wanted to have or wanted to do and never had the chance to?' Damian asked.

'Loads.' Charlie nodded vigorously. 'For instance, when I was a kid, I was fascinated by the stories about the Tower - how they imprisoned people in there and tortured and executed them. I always imagined the Tower sort of like a dark, looming fortress with deep, damp dungeons from which tortured souls are screaming out for revenge. I always wanted to see that place ...'

'So, was it as exciting as you expected?' he asked.

'I don't know. I still haven't been in there,' she laughed.

'What? You've been living in London for, what? - over a year now, and you still haven't visited the Tower?'

'So, have you seen it?' she asked.

'Hm. Yeah, I went there with my school once, when I was a kid. Must have been eight or nine. I don't recall much of it, to be honest. I do remember however,' he defended himself, 'how me and some mates had a match of footie on the lawn outside, after the tour. I have a very vivid recollection of that game, uhuh.'

'I see.' Charlie grinned.

'But seriously, would you like to see it? The Tower, I mean?'

'Yeah, I would love to. But somehow I never seem to find the time. Before I left for London, I had made a list of things I wanted to visit, like Big Ben, Westminster Abbey ...'

'What, you're saying you haven't seen all that yet?' he cried. 'Ok, when's the first day you don't have any classes?'

'Tomorrow, why?'

'How about we go on a bus tour tomorrow, in a real red London double-decker bus, huh?'

And that's what they were setting out to do now ...

They clambered up the narrow stairs to the top of the red double-decker. An icy wind was blowing, and the grey clouds in the sky threatened rain for the afternoon. Not the best day to tour the city in an open bus. At least most tourists seemed to be of that opinion, as only six people were up there: right at the front sat a cheerful couple, laden with maps, guide-books, a photo camera and quite an impressive-looking video camera. Their kid, a boy of about eight, was unimpressed by the sights that the capital of the former British Empire had to offer and clicked away on his Game Boy. Two seats behind the family sat a young man in a red jacket and yet two seats behind him (was this a pattern? were they also supposed to leave a security-seat between themselves and the next passengers?) ... in any case, two seats further up a young couple, both heavily freckled redheads, held hands and watched the houses move by with the sort of enraptured look that you only see on the faces of the mentally impaired and, of course, on lovers on holiday.

Charlie squeezed herself into a seat, followed by Damian, who motioned to Bobby to lie down. He mouthed 'Down!' with all the severity and conviction of a dog-owner who knows how to handle his pet. Bobby looked up at him, wriggled his tail and lay down. He obviously felt sorry for his master.

'... and a very warm welcome on this chilly morning to our latest guests on the bus. My name is Simon and I am your tour guide. What country are you from, if I may ask? Your four-legged friend is, if I am not mistaken, from the West Highlands ...'

Charlie noticed that the man in the red jacket, Simon, had a microphone in his hand. She had taken him for just another tourist when she had first seen him.

'I'm from Swallop,' she answered.

'Swallop - the Pearl of Derbyshire, a very fine town indeed. Welcome to London. Is your friend a Swallopian as well?'

'Actually I'm from London,' admitted Damian.

'Oh, so you have no right to be on the bus. No, just kidding, welcome to you, too. As you can see, we are currently driving east on Eaton, that nice patch of green coming up are the Buckingham Palace Gardens and the building behind, you guessed it, is Buckingham Palace. Have a look to the left and you might just spot her Majesty poking her nose in the royal bathroom.'

The woman at the front grabbed her Game Boy-playing offspring and assumed a proud pose. Her husband filmed, as she beamed into the camera, Buckingham Palace drifting by behind her back. 'Gotcha on tape, honey,' he declared triumphantly, every pore oozing American tourist pride.

The redhead squeezed her boyfriend's arm and giggled.

Charlie squeezed Damian's arm and refrained from giggling. 'I'm so excited, I feel like a real tourist.'

'Yeah, me too. Everything looks so different from up here, with the guide talking. It's really cool.'

Westminster Abbey was coming up in front of them. Charlie let out a little squeak. 'That's Westminster!'

'Its abbey, to be precise, yes,' the guide took up her cue. 'Since Christmas 1066, when William the Conqueror was made king of England on this site, all English monarchs have been crowned in Westminster Abbey. The throne on which British sovereigns are seated at the moment of their coronation is called St Edward's chair. Many famous people are buried within the Abbey, our kings and queens from centuries past, of course, but also many writers, like Geoffrey Chaucer of Canterbury Tales fame, Dr Johnson, Charles Dickens ... they all lie cosily together in what we call the Poets' Corner.'

Charlie sighed happily. 'I'd love to stroll around in there.'

'You wanna get off the bus here?' proposed Damian.

'No, I can do that on some other day. We only just got on.' Charlie looked eagerly around. There was so much to see: they had left Westminster Abbey behind and were driving north now. To the right, she spotted the long facade of the Houses of Parliament, with Big Ben looming behind, and already Simon was pointing out the next highlight: a street cordoned off to the public, with guards at the front: Downing Street.

'Wow, you really don't get in there, huh?' said Damian, impressed.

'... Our Prime Minister, Tony Blair, is in fact not living at number 10, but at number 11 Downing Street, as this apartment is larger and therefore better suited for his family,' explained Simon.

'Imagine living in a street that is permanently guarded,' said Charlie.

'Must be terrible. I prefer my apartment,' replied Damian.

The American tourists were quarrelling. Apparently wife and son had not been quick enough to be filmed both in front of Big Ben and Downing Street. The husband was gesticulating furiously.

The young couple smiled on.

'Coming up - Trafalgar Square,' declared Simon. 'To the north lie Chinatown and Soho, of infamous nightlife fame. It's pretty tame nowadays, but it still offers many interesting places to go to in the evening. There are lots of bars, restaurants and, of course, theatres. ... Here we are now, driving by Trafalgar Square, with Nelson's column. It commemorates the British naval victory over the French in 1805. Also note the big Christmas tree, an annual gift from our Norwegian friends. Trafalgar Square is a popular meeting place, both for Londoners and tourists. There's a saying that you cannot hang around Trafalgar Square for more than fifteen minutes on any given day without bumping into someone you know.'

Charlie nodded vigorously. 'Even I have been to Trafalgar Square, so it must be really popular.' She pointed to the right: 'I once had a pizza in that restaurant over there.'

'Was it any good?'

'Mhm. I remember the place offered all-you-can-eat, too. I never went back there to try it, though,' she added thoughtfully.

'How about we do that next weekend?'

'I think the all-you-can-eat was only on weekdays at noon.'

'Oh.'

The bus turned around Trafalgar Square and headed back down south. The American camera-lover was delighted when he realized that he got a second chance to film his family in front of a Big Ben background. They crossed the Thames just south of the Houses of Parliament and then headed north again, past the London Eye, whose cabins slowly moved up into the low-hanging clouds.

'Can we put that one on the to-do list as well? asked Charlie.

'Sure.'

She huddled closer to Damian. It was really getting cold up here. Now that they had left the inner-city traffic behind, the bus was making good speed on its way north, over Waterloo Bridge.

'Waterloo Bridge,' intoned Simon, 'commemorates yet another British victory over our beloved neighbours. In 1815, Wellington gave the little Corsican, you all know who I mean, Napoleon of course, the coup de grace. It was to be the French Emperor's last battle before his final exile on the island of Saint Helena. And if you ever wondered whether it is by chance that the Eurostar connection from Paris to London ends at Waterloo Station - it is not. Neither is the fact that the French high-speed connection slows down to snail-rail velocity once the train has crossed the Tunnel. The true British way to welcome French visitors into our land.'

Funny, Charlie thought.

'This long and winding road we are currently speeding along is Fleet Street,' he resumed. 'Anyone knows what Fleet Street is famous for?'

'Newspapers,' peeped Charlie.

'Correct, Miss Swallop, newspapers ...'

Damian was delighted. 'Great, you knew that,' he beamed.

The next sight Simon pointed out was St Paul's Cathedral. Then they crossed the Thames once more and were rewarded with a splendid view over Tower Bridge. Charlie was delighted. What a pity she had not brought a camera. She should have thought of that. Come to think of it, she probably hadn't thought of it, because she didn't possess one. Maybe she should buy herself one for Christmas.

The bus passed along the Thames and Simon turned their attention to the HMS Belfast, which was berthed next to Tower Bridge. After its prowess in World War II, the cruiser now served as a museum. Then they crossed Tower Bridge and Charlie stared open-mouthed through the huge blue supporting beams at the impressive masonry.

'Hey.' Damian nudged her in the side.

'Hm?' Charlie bent her neck backwards to watch the construction's huge bows as they sped through the second tower.

Another gentle nudge.

'What? I have to see this ...'

'Ok, you go on looking up at bridges,' replied Damian, and grabbed Bobby's leash. 'Meanwhile, Bobby and I will explore some dungeons.'

The bus came to a halt in front of the Tower. Charlie gave a little squeak and hurriedly followed them down the steps.

'Hm, what shall I take?' Charlie tipped a forefinger on her nose and studied the list of dishes on the menu.

Their visit to the Tower had left them tired, thirsty, hungry and full of new impressions. The experience had definitely been worth their aching feet. They had listened to the beefeater's explanations about the Tower's long history as royal palace and prison, they had admired the crown jewels and the royal armouries, and they had been introduced to the royal ravens, the last permanent residents of the Tower. Charlie had taken quite a fancy to Thor, while Damian claimed that Cedric sported a much nicer plumage. Charlie had loved the gory stories about the political intrigues and subsequent executions. She had listened eagerly as their guide told them the legend of Anne Boleyn who, after being beheaded on Tower Green in 1536, had supposedly been seen walking around the fortress with her head under her arm, bemoaning her dire lot.

'I think I'll go for the chicken and mushroom pie,' she declared, and closed the card.

Damian was still staring at the menu. Charlie glanced over and noticed that he was looking at the list of beverages. 'Do you know what you want to eat?' she asked. 'I can go order at the bar, if you want.'

'I'm not sure,' he said hesitantly. 'Chicken and mushroom pie, you say? I guess that sounds good ...'

'Are you ok?' Charlie gave him a sceptical look. 'You look confused.'

'No, I'm fine. I'll take the same as you, and a large coke. I'm dying of thirst.'

While she waited for their drinks to be prepared, Charlie thought about the discussion they had had this morning. While she had been to the bathroom, Damian had called a taxi to take them to Victoria station. She had protested that cabs were way too expensive, if you could just as well take a bus or the tube. He had replied that he didn't like taking the tube as he found the system confusing. 'A maze', he had called it. Charlie had thought that pretty strange for someone who had been living in London for his entire life. When they had bought their tickets for the sightseeing bus, the lady had handed Damian a map with information about the highlights of the tour. He had not even once glanced at it, although he listened with interest to the guide's explanations. And now the thing with the menu ...

The barkeeper put two pints of coke in front of her. 'I'll bring the food to your table,' he said.

'Thanks.' Charlie balanced the glasses back to their table. She took a large gulp and sighed. 'Now I feel better.' She pointed to the jukebox in the corner. 'Would you mind having a look whether they have a song by Nightwish?'

'By who?' Damian stared at her. 'Never heard of them.'

'They're great. A metal band from Finland. Can you please have a look? They're called Nightwish - night like day, and wish like want.'

Damian looked like he was about to protest, but she gave him her sweetest smile and then turned her attention to Bobby who lay under the table, pooped from an exciting day at the Tower.

Damian took off to the jukebox. He stared for a while at the screen, doing nothing at all. Then he looked around, as if searching for some guideline. But none of the other customers paid him any attention. He met Charlie's eyes from across the room. He blushed. Charlie stood up and walked over to him. He had tears in his eyes.

'I was fifteen when they finally figured out what was wrong with me. Dyslexia. I guess they couldn't have come up with a more difficult word for it. Still, I suppose it has a nicer ring to it than lazy, stubborn, or plain-ass stupid.' Damian sounded bitter. He stared into his coke and ignored both Charlie's concerned look and the plate that the waiter had put in front of him.

'I'm so sorry, Damian.' Charlie reached out and took his hand. 'I don't know much about dyslexia, but I do know it has nothing to do with you being lazy or stupid. It's not your fault.'

'Do you know how embarrassing it is when you're not even sure you've spelled your own name correctly? Something every six-year-old can do.'

She was quiet. She had never met anyone who was dyslexic. She knew that dyslexic people had trouble with reading and writing, but she had always thought of it as a slight impediment, a nuisance which made you stumble over a long word or commit frequent spelling errors. It had never occurred to her that ordinary things like reading a menu or using the tube might represent too big a challenge.

'So you cannot read?' she asked hesitantly. She didn't want to embarrass him, but if they wanted to build up a friendship, he had to understand that there was nothing he could not tell her.

'No, I can read,' he said. 'It just takes awfully long. And when I have lots of words in front of me, like on a menu card, where there are pages and pages of written text, I get stressed. I know I'll never be able to even figure out what's where before you have made your choice. So I spare myself the horror and don't even try.' He looked defeated.

'I don't understand,' she said, confused. 'Didn't you tell me you went to university?'

He cringed behind his glass like a beaten puppy. 'I went to a public school. I guess Dad paid them a lot of money so that they would take me. The teachers left me pretty much alone, save one or two who turned it into a sport to humiliate me in front of their class. I sat three A-levels and they gave me that piece of paper saying that I'd passed them. I was just glad that it was over, that I would never again have to go through such a humiliating experience. But Gerry wanted me to go to university. He didn't even ask what I wanted. Simply enrolled me into the first school that would take me. I guess he paid them a nice roll of money, too.'

Damian's voice was so choked that Charlie had trouble understanding what he was saying. But she knew better than to interrupt him. He needed to get this out, needed to tell his story. 'I even went to a few lectures. It wasn't particularly interesting, but at least I didn't have to say anything. I just sat there and listened to the teacher rambling on about some obscure theory or other. But I couldn't bring myself to go to these seminaries, where you had to read books and prepare papers. And after a while, I didn't go there at all anymore.'

'I'm so sorry, Damian. I never even thought about how hard that must be. I mean, I seem to be reading constantly ... street-signs, advertisements, even the labels on the ketchup bottle.'

Damian gave her a weak smile. 'Yeah, I know. The world's full of words. You cannot avoid them.'

'But did they never try to give you tutoring lessons at your school? Special lessons, teaching you strategies to ...'

Damian shook his head. 'You don't get it, do you? You cannot understand it because you're smart. You think, if you just sit long enough over something, you'll eventually get it. But that's not how reading works for me. The longer I stare at the letters, the more they scramble up in front of my eyes.'

'Yes, but ...'

'No. You cannot understand. Just like Gerry, he didn't understand, either. Until they finally chucked me out of school when I had failed every single course the second time. Then he got it, at last.'

'Got what?' she asked desperately.

'That I'm a hopeless case,' said Damian.

There was a long silence after Damian had told her that he was a hopeless case. Charlie didn't know what to say. She just knew that she didn't want him to think that way. At last, she pushed her plate away, and gave him an encouraging look.

'There's something I'd like to show you,' she said. 'At my place.'

Charlie had insisted that they take the bus instead of a cab. Which meant that they had to walk another five minutes from the bus-stop to her block. That was why they were now trudging through the icy December rain towards her little apartment.

Bobby seemed to enjoy this unexpected excursion into the land of puddles and slush.

'Didn't you tell me this morning that you don't want me to come up to your place?' asked Damian, after they had walked for a while in silence.

'Yes,' she admitted, 'but I changed my mind.' Her heart hammered against her chest, while she wondered what he would think of her. Her cheeks burnt with anticipated shame. All of a sudden, she wasn't so sure anymore that it had been a good idea. But they had already arrived at her apartment building. Too late to turn back now.

Charlie put the key in the lock and opened the creaking entrance door. They stepped into a dark little hallway cluttered with a broken pram, old bikes and various rusty containers of indefinable content. The walls were smeared with graffiti. The smell of garlic and onion soup, stale cigarette smoke and beer mingled with the odour of mould and decay. Charlie stepped determinedly up the creaky old staircase, not looking back at Damian and Bobby, who had come in behind her. On the first landing, they heard screaming from behind one of the doors. It sounded foreign. Charlie didn't understand what they said, but she was pretty sure that most of it conveyed the meaning of the standard English four-letter words. Without stopping, she attacked the next flight of stairs. The light-bulb on the second landing was broken and she had to feel her way up. Open bags of garbage deposited on the landing could be especially treacherous. She had learnt that the hard way, while running down the stairs when she was late for class one day. She had very nearly fallen down the stairs on the rotting leftovers of chicken curry and mashies.

Finally she reached the third landing. Mind-numbing techno beats thundered behind the door on the left. Charlie ignored this and fumbled with the key in the lock. She heard Bobby growl at her neighbour's door. He didn't seem to like techno either.

'Come here, Bobby.' Damian pulled the dog into her flat.

Charlie stood aside and let them enter. She tried to see her home through Damian's eyes: a tiny room, cluttered with books, papers and clothes. An unmade bed, a small table with a laptop, a chair. Behind a curtain, a toilet with a wobbly seat and a tiny shower. In the corner behind the door, a little cupboard, sink, stove and fridge provided a make-shift kitchen. She tried to keep the place tidy, but there was just no room to put everything. And there was not much she could do against the moulding wallpaper and the dark stains on the ceiling. She wasn't going to invest into a flat that she would, hopefully, be able to leave within the next two years.

She tried to read Damian's look. He didn't look shocked. Not even astonished. If anything, he looked sad.

'It's tiny, but it's mine,' she finally managed.

He just looked at her.

'Do you want to sit down? There's not much place to sit, I'm afraid. Maybe on the chair ...' Her voice trailed off. It had been a bad idea. She should not have brought him here.

'You said there was something you wanted me to see,' he said, without moving.

Bobby curiously poked his nose into the laundry-basket.

'Well, yes.' She motioned around the room. 'This.'

'It looks nice enough ...' he began, but she interrupted him.

'No, it doesn't look nice. It's crammed up and uncomfortable and old. It isn't even particularly healthy. Way too hot and smelly in the summer, and in the winter I never get the damp cold out, no matter how high I turn the heater. My neighbour is a brain-dead acid-popper who listens to techno noise day and night, and my closest friends are silverfish who particularly like it in the shit hole that the owner has the gall to call 'bathroom'. It's embarrassing. It's shameful. And on top of all that, it's ridiculously expensive.' Her voice had been quivering with the last sentence.

Damian took her in his arms and held her tight. He didn't say a word, but his hug felt good. So reassuring. She knew that he

understood her, understood that she had wanted to show him that she, too, had things in her life that she would rather forget about. Things that were ugly and shameful and that you did not want anyone to know about. No one, except the person that you trusted most in your life. The one person you could depend on, no matter what. The person that you truly ...

'I love you,' he said softly.

Charlie closed her eyes and buried her face in his shoulder. 'I love you, too.'

'There's pride, and then there's false pride. That's what you call stubbornness. Your reasons sound a lot like stubbornness to me. ... No, Bobby, we're not going to the park. We're going home now.' Damian pulled on the leash. Bobby gave him a reproachful look. *Just because you're bigger and stronger than me, you think you can bully me, huh?* it said.

'Look, it's really getting late,' Damian reasoned with him. 'We'll go to the park first thing in the morning. Deal?'

But Bobby was a westie and not a businessman. Deals weren't his forte. He pulled harder.

'You're just as stubborn as Charlie,' sighed Damian.

'I'm not stubborn. But you have to see things my way,' explained Charlie. 'Let's just assume I accept your offer and move in with you. I would of course give up my flat. And I would tell all my customers that they need not call me again. Then what? I would be totally dependent on you. I'd live in *your* apartment, and spend *your* money. You know what they call that? Entertaining a woman.'

Damian shook his head. 'No, Charlie, you got it all wrong. You know what *I* call that? I call it love. Helping each other. Trusting each other. Depending on each other. And who are *they* anyway? I don't give a fuck about what *they* think. I just care about what *you* think.'

They had arrived at Damian's flat and he unlocked the door. Charlie relished the sweet scent of freshly scrubbed parquet and polished marble that wafted out. His offer was tempting. But it was too risky. Her life may not be easy, but it allowed her to live in London and study for her degree. In less than two years, she would have a university diploma in her hands and everything would become much easier. Then, maybe ...

'I think that I don't want to take the risk.'

'What risk?' he asked, exasperated.

'The risk that things will not work out between us. What if you chuck me out of your apartment in two or three months? I will have no place to live then, and no safe customer base I can fall back on. Do you know how hard it was in the beginning, how awful to get into a car with a guy you don't know? He could be a rapist, a killer, a lunatic on the loose. Sometimes, I was scared shitless.'

The elevator doors opened and they stepped into his flat. Bobby padded to his bowl and looked up expectantly.

'You would never be as helpless as you were when you first arrived in London,' said Damian, and stepped into the kitchen, with a tail-wriggling Bobby in tow. 'You cannot compare the two situations. You have something invaluable, that no one can take away from you: experience. You have done it once, you could do it again. Besides, I don't think that you will really lose your customer base, as you call it. Not in a few months. If you called them, they'd be more than happy to see you again. I would.'

He emptied a tin of dog meat into the bowl and put it on the floor. Bobby threw himself on it like the proverbial starving dog.

'Besides,' he continued, as he filled water into the coffee machine, 'if you don't give things a try, you can never know if they work out or not. Hearing you talk of risks and problems, you sound like your dad, telling you to get a job in Swallop, instead of coming to London.'

'That's unfair.'

'What is?'

'Telling me I sound like my dad.'

'No, it's not unfair. It's just the truth. If you don't want to sound like him, then don't. Come on, Charlie, give yourself a push.'

Charlie bit her lip. Damn, why did he have to be so manipulative? Weren't dyslexics supposed to have problems with words and meanings? Trust her to fall in love with an eloquent one. Damn. Damn. Damn.

'But I want to pay for my expenses.'

'Like food and clothes? Okay.'

'I'd have to get a job, then.'

'I'm not telling you what to do,' he said, with a candid smile. 'If you can accept that I pay for our expenses, at least as long as you are still in school, then that's perfectly fine with me. If you can't, I guess you'll have to find yourself a job. A few hours a week, maybe. Whatever you decide, I will be happy to go along with it. But refusing to move in with me would be downright silly, if you ask me. ... Unless you don't want me around,' he added, less sure of himself. He brushed a lock of hair out of his eyes.

'Of course I want you around, stupid,' she said.

He looked reassured. 'Good then. So, when will you move in?'

'What if I wanted to do the odd trick, say, once a week, to get myself some money?' she asked. She knew she was provoking him, but the words were out before she could stop herself. She immediately felt sorry, when she saw the hurt and confused look on his face. 'No, I didn't mean that,' she said.

'I'm not telling you what to do,' he repeated. He handed her two cups and a milk jug. 'Can you put this on the coffee-table, please?'

'A ride on the London Eye,' he said.

'Watching the telly on a Friday night,' she said.

*Cuddling me every day*, Bobby thought.

'Spending more time in the library to study.'

'Thanks. What a great advantage. If that's all I get out of it, I prefer my old flat.' She giggled.

They were playing 'Name all the things Charlie can do if she doesn't have to work the streets anymore'. They had come up with about fifty things so far.

'Liar. Your turn.' He tickled her toes.

'Stop that! Having a quiet room to study in.'

'You mean this living room? Not that quiet, I can assure you. It is known to be haunted by a canine presence and its mad owner.' Damian rolled his eyes like a madman. 'Hooooaaaaahhhhhh!'

Charlie giggled and have him a playful slap. 'Your turn, you presence, you.'

'Having the comfort of a clean toilet,' he intoned, 'unless I've managed to get to the loo, first.'

They both laughed. All of sudden, Damian slapped his forehead. 'Damn, I forgot something!'

'What? The wife that you have hidden in the attic?'

'Huh? No. I wanted to invite you. To a happening. On Thursday.'

'A happening? That sounds interesting ... oh, but on Thursday I already have an appointment.'

'Oh.' He looked disappointed. 'With a customer of yours?'

'No, of course not. With a friend.'

'Oh, ok. Well, I guess that can't be helped then.'

'Are you very disappointed?' she asked anxiously.

'No, don't worry about it. I'm sure that B...'

Bobby let out a bark. Then a growl. They both looked at him, perplexed.

'What's the matter with him?' asked Charlie.

'No idea.' Damian patted the dog's head and looked around the room. 'What's wrong, hm, Bobby?'

Laughter was drifting up from the street. Charlie stepped to the window and looked out. A gang of children was running after a bearded man in a furry red coat. Santa Claus was coming to town. One of the kids threw a jumping jack on the sidewalk. It exploded with a loud bang. Bobby growled, and hid behind the couch.

'He's afraid of crackers,' said Damian, with a concerned frown. 'Poor bugger, and soon it's New Year's Eve.'

# 12

Charlie reached for the gift bag on the other chair. She had to have another look at that cute mug she'd just purchased. A black mug with an endearing little westie on it. The dog carried a leash with the Harrods sign in its mouth, and gazed up at her with big, trusting eyes. When she had spotted the mug sitting there on the shelf in Harrods World, she'd immediately known that this was the perfect Christmas present for Damian: a mug with Bobby on it. The ideal, personalized gift. She just hoped that Damian would like it, too.

After a fond look at it, she put it back to the other green bags that cluttered the chair next to hers. Her Christmas shopping had taken all of two hours. Not bad, considering that she had not had the least idea what to buy when she had entered Harrods. The huge warehouse had so much on offer, you were really spoilt for choice. She had relished strolling through its vast halls. Those enormous halls! You could get lost among the huge counters and endless shelves. And everything was so lavishly decorated with stucco, marble and glass. The ultimate consumer's paradise. She had selected a bottle of 1849 Harrods lager and a gift set of matching pint glasses for her beer-loving father and brother (Ronnie would complain about his present, no matter what she bought, so she might as well not make it too expensive), and a green Harrods shopping bag filled with a selection of candies and jam jars for her mother, and, of course, a packet of extra fine cookies for Bobby and the westie mug for Damian. Now her purse was much lighter, and she felt tired, thirsty and satisfied with a job well done. A glance at her watch told her that she had almost two hours before Blake's art exhibition opened in Notting Hill. More than enough time to treat herself to something good. On her stroll through the department store she had spotted a cosy wood-panelled café and its name ('Harrods Café and Crêperie') had convinced her that this was just the right place to celebrate her successful shopping spree.

The friendly waitress arrived with her order: a delicate thin crêpe, folded twice, with a scoop of vanilla ice-cream on top. The dish came with a complimentary wrapped lemon. How very posh. Cool. The waitress placed a big mug of hot chocolate next to the plate. Hot chocolate with marshmallows on it. Yummy. This looked so delicious. She seized knife and fork and tucked in. Mmmmh. It tasted delicious, too. So what if this cost over ten pounds? What was the use of living in London if you couldn't even afford a crêpe at Harrods?

'... and you would think that he'd at least *say* something. But no: he just sat there, looking at me with that sad, drooping face. It was, like, sooo embarrassing.'

Two girls of about sixteen passed her table and dropped into the chairs behind her. Heavy make-up and ultra-hip clothes. Charlie smiled to herself. She remembered the time when she had thought dark mascara, eyeliner, eye shadow and shiny lip-gloss made you look sexy and grown-up. The result was to be admired in the Morgan family album in Swallop: a pouting teenager with an impossible hairdo and full facial war-paint. She really didn't miss her teenage years. It was so much more fun to be a twen. You earned your own money and could spend it on whatever you pleased. Which meant, for instance, that nothing stopped you from treating yourself to a ridiculously expensive crêpe on an ordinary workday. Yummy.

'... he's, like, so not cool,' the girl behind her ended her story.

The other one gave her a sympathetic sigh. 'My father would have killed me, for sure.'

'Killed me? He's too much of a chicken for that. What would the neighbours say? And his business partners! Oh my Goodness, what a scandal.' She laughed affectedly. 'He's like one of those monkeys. Shut your eyes, close your ears, if you don't see it, it's not there.'

Charlie took a sip of her hot chocolate and listened on.

'But did you really *do* it with him?'

'Of course, I did. What do you think? I'm not a cock-tease.' A self-confident laugh. 'If a man doesn't interest me, I don't even bother looking at him. But if he gives me the hots,' her voice lowered to a conspiratorial whisper, 'I just let it happen. Easy as that.'

'I couldn't imagine doing it with such an old guy.'

The nymphomaniac laughed. 'Louis isn't old, silly. He's not much older than my dad.'

'That's *old*.'

'Yeah well, I suppose it depends on the person. My father is way old. I'm pretty sure that my parents don't fuck anymore. My room is right next to theirs, and I *never* hear any sounds. And I'm, like, hey! How did they ever manage to make two daughters? But you know what they say, it takes a man to father a ...'

'Ssht, there's your mum.'

A petite woman of about forty passed Charlie's table. She looked way better than her daughter, Charlie thought. Her hair was trimmed into a fashionable messy bob and her cream-coloured clothes looked both elegant and comfortable. Behind her slouched yet another bored-looking teenager. Blonde, maybe three years younger than the other two, and dedicatedly masticating a piece of chewing gum. The woman unloaded her bags and smiled at her daughter. She had the sort of radiant smile that played with the wrinkles on her face. Not pretty, and maybe not beautiful either, but definitely charming. 'So, you two. Haven't you ordered any drinks, yet? We're dying of thirst.'

'No, the waitress keeps ignoring us,' pouted the nymphomaniac.

Maybe that's because you're supposed to wait to be seated, Charlie thought, and took a sip of her hot chocolate. She managed to gobble up four marshmallows with a single sip. Mmmmh.

'Well, then we shall call her. Excuse me, waitress!' She had a very pleasant voice. Melodious and full. A singer's voice, or maybe a thespian's. Charlie smiled. As interesting as this little family get-together was, she should be going now. She wanted to have another stroll through the Food Hall before she left. It would be too bad not to try out the teasers that they offered there for free ...

Half an hour later, she emerged from the gourmet temple with a full tummy and a cloud of perfume hanging around her. The Food Hall was right next to the Perfumery and she had not been able to resist those teasers, either. Another look at her watch: she should be heading towards the bus stop now, if she didn't want to be late for Blake's private view. It wouldn't do to show up at the art gallery with a load of bags, so she had to drop them off at home first. And it was already almost four ...

She meandered among the counters in the hope of finding some exit. This place was a real maze. She entered yet another hall, this one sporting huge escalators. Charlie's mouth dropped open. Wow. This must be the Egyptian Escalators. Charlie felt like inside a pyramid. Huge lamps, dim light, a crammed vault, and hieroglyphs, hieroglyphs everywhere. This was ... she stopped in her tracks. That man standing near the escalators, wasn't that ...? She lingered, unsure whether she should greet him or not. He seemed to be on his own, but maybe he didn't want to be seen talking to her in public. As if he could feel her gaze on his back, the man turned around and looked straight at her. His face broke into a surprised smile. Charlie's mind was made up: he smiled, so that meant it was okay to talk to him. She took a step in his direction and saw his smile vanish. He gave her a hard look and turned his back on her. Ok. Maybe it was *not* okay to talk to him after all.

He looked up the escalators and waved. 'There you are. You're late.'

Charlie followed his gaze. Oh, this was interesting.

'No, we're not.' The woman from the Crêperie gave him a good-humoured laugh. 'We said four o'clock at the Egyptian Escalators. In fact we're five minutes early. Here, take these bags, will you, Gerald.'

Gerald took the bags from her and turned to his nymphomaniac daughter. 'Did you have a nice day, Elsa?'

The girl shrugged her shoulders. 'Sure. I spent three hours in a room with a sadistic moron, and then I got blisters on my feet from running through a huge warehouse. Perfect day.'

'Oh right,' he said, ignoring her theatrical eye-rolling, 'you had a test today. What did Mr Higgins ask you?'

'Questions,' she mumbled, and nudged her friend in the side. 'Are you coming with us? Clive copied me *Nine Lives*. You know, since I told him I admire Paris Hilton, he's hell-bent on copying all her movies for me.'

Her friend nodded. 'I'd love to! But I have to call my parents first ...'

Gerald threw a glance in Charlie's direction. Oops. She hadn't noticed that she was still staring at them. His eyes commanded her to take off. Charlie directed her attention towards the Egyptian symbols on the wall. A woman spreading her arms in a welcoming embrace. What was that thing she had on her head? A cup? Some round thingy, as Blake would say. A sun maybe? Did the Pharaohs worship a Sun Goddess? Wasn't Ra the Sun God? Hm ...

'Where is Nicky?' she heard Gerald ask. He sounded a bit stressed. Naughty Nicky, kept her daddy waiting. Naughty little girl. Charlie analysed the second hieroglyph. A so-called cartouche. She took a step closer to the escalators to have a better look. She heard the woman say: 'She had to use the lavatories.'

'I don't have all day,' said Gerald irritably. 'What a silly idea to meet at the escalators, right in the middle of Harrods. Next time, I will pick her up at home.'

'You said you had an appointment and couldn't wait for us to get home,' his wife pointed out.

'Then she can take the bus. Other people take the bus, too.'

'Louis wanted to drive her,' slurred Elsa. 'But you said ...'

Charlie risked a quick look out of the corner of her eye. The girl's cheeks had flushed crimson, as Gerald stared wordlessly at her. Charlie gazed back at the hieroglyphs. A bird, a knife and a mouth. What could that mean? She sighed. She would never be a Champollion.

'I would appreciate if you pulled your pants higher up,' said Gerald tensely. 'People can see your navel.'

'That's low cut,' mumbled Elsa. 'Everyone wears their pants like this.'

'No one I can see here,' retorted her father.

Charlie looked around. He had a point ...

Gerald had turned to his wife. 'Katie, I told you that I have to be in ...'

'Yes, I know you told me,' she interrupted him. 'She'll be here in a minute. Why are you so nervous? Just drop her off at the horse stable and you're on your way to the gathering. It's not even a real detour, for goodness' sake.'

'There she is,' said Elsa.

Charlie scanned the escalators. Indeed, Miss Chewing Gum was gliding down the stairs.

Gerald reached out for her. 'Hello, darling. Let's go.'

Nicky shrugged his embrace off. 'Do I have to go riding today?' she whined.

Her mother gave her a stern look. 'You wanted Silvermoon, so you will take care of her. I have already told you a thousand times, a horse isn't a toy.'

Nicky sighed heavily and pouted. The family took off through the Perfumery. A delicate young man tried to interest Gerald in a fashionable eau de toilette, but one threatening look was enough to shut him up. Gerald could be mean. Charlie felt sorry for the vendor. After all, he was only doing his job. Maybe she should allow him to spray some perfume on her. She threw a last look at the hieroglyphs. That goddess was sitting on a strange sort of chair ... She shook herself out of her reverie. If she didn't want to be late for Blake's private view, she'd better get going now, too.

She was way too late. The bus to Notting Hill had got stuck in the worst traffic jam, and on top of that, it was pouring. Charlie pulled the hood of her raincoat over her head and ran through the rain. Damn, none of these houses seemed to have numbers. Was she even running in the right direction? Panting, she stopped to catch her breath. Then she noticed a crooked signpost with the words *Galeria Mundo* written on it. It pointed to some steps, leading down into a basement. The windows were hung with brightly coloured drapes and the door stood open. A poster attached to the glass-pane announced: *Blake - Amor Amer* in elegantly curved letters on a sand-coloured background. Upon closer inspection, Charlie noticed the fine outline of several erectile male protuberances (as Blake would put it), blended into the sand.

She took a few steps down. Animated conversation drifted out at her. The official part of the private view did not seem to have started yet. Good. She would try to blend in with the crowd and make herself invisible.

The room was full of people. Some were holding champagne glasses in their hands. Most of the visitors stood around in groups of twos or threes, making small talk. Only a few lonely figures were actually looking at the artwork on display. Charlie strongly suspected them to wait for someone to engage them in a conversation. In the meantime, there's no better way to camouflage your anxiety than to have a look at some clay penises.

'It is, in fact.' That voice. Its calm, deep timbre effortlessly rose above the general din. Charlie froze. 'We will discuss the question at the next board meeting,' the voice continued, oblivious of the effect it had on her. It came from behind a red and green curtain. Anxious not to make herself noticed, she peeped behind the curtain. Animatedly discussing business matters with a wiry old man, Gerald's hand was absent-mindedly stroking a polished brass ring fastened onto a softly curved marble object. A pierced nipple serving as door-knocker. Amor amer. She quickly withdrew her head.

Ok, Charlie, you have five seconds to think. Her thoughts raced. What was *he* doing here? Could it be that his company sponsored this exhibition? Of all possible art exhibitions in London. Talk about bad luck. What kind of a company was he working for, anyway? Maybe stockbrokers, dealing in art? Maybe an auction house? She had never asked him. It didn't matter now, anyway. It all came down to the simple fact that Gerald knew Blake. Damn. She didn't want her customers to know each other. And she was sure Gerald wouldn't want Blake to know that they were frequenting the same hooker.

Five seconds over. She made for the door. Too late. Emerging out of a door to the right, Blake had already spotted her.

'Hey, honey!' he cried.

She dashed up the steps. He took chase and grabbed her coat, just as she turned around the corner.

'Hey, what's the matter? You look like you've seen a ghost,' panted Blake.

Charlie noticed that he had sand on his hands. 'I ...' she began, but he had already caught his breath.

'You've arrived just in time for the happening, honey. It's going to be so cool, what with the sand dunes and the snakes. Snakes and dunes ... those are nice symbols, don't you think? So suggestive.' Blake pulled her back towards the art gallery. 'I'll introduce you to some of my friends before the show starts.'

Charlie struggled to break free of his groping hands. He seemed to have at least three pairs of them. 'No, Blake, listen! I cannot stay, I'm sorry.'

'What?' He finally let go of her coat. 'Why?'

'There's someone in there whom I don't want to see.'

'Seriously?' His eyes lit up. He gave her a mischievous wink: 'A customer of yours?'

'Yes.' She looked nervously towards the door. If he looked out the window, he was bound to see her.

'Who is it? Huh?' Blake grinned eagerly.

'Blake, that's confidential. I cannot just tell you who my customers are. He would probably not want me to tell you.'

'Uhm, I can imagine that he wouldn't. So, you won't tell me? ... Maybe his initials?'

She gave him a reprimanding look. 'Blake!'

'Ok, ok, I got it.' He lifted his hands. 'No names, no initials. Boy, you keep dirty secrets better than the priest at confession. I'm impressed.'

'So you understand that I cannot stay?'

'Uhm, not really, no. But ... I accept it. Of course. Grudgingly.' Another Charlie-look.

'Don't give me that look, will you? It makes me feel, you know, kinda thingy-like.'

'I make you feel like blackcurrant?' Charlie had to laugh.

Blake pouted. 'Are you taking the piss, honey? Can you not at least come in for two seconds? I told the Contessa about you, and she's so eager to meet you.'

'Maybe another time, ok?'

'Well, she's leaving for her castle in Italy, tomorrow. Castle Otranto. I don't think she will be back before the next year.'

'Blake, can I please go now?'

He pulled a face. 'If you can bear to make me totally unhappy ...'

'How about you give me a private tour through your exhibition tomorrow?' she proposed desperately.

His eyes lit up. 'Of course, honey, you'll get the best tour ever. But I'm afraid they won't leave the snakes till tomorrow ...'

'I hope not,' she laughed, and blew him a kiss on the cheek.
'I'll see you tomorrow then,' he cried after her.

She only felt safe once she had put three blocks between herself and the gallery. A pity she had to miss her first-ever private view. Snakes and sand dunes - that sounded like an interesting spectacle. Gothic, somehow. Very Blakeish indeed.

Charlie walked along Portobello Road, feeling the rain slowly soaking through her jeans. It was cold and she didn't know what to do with the rest of the evening. If she went home now, she would feel obliged to work for school. So better not go home, then. Hm. She remembered that Damian had invited her to a party this evening. Maybe she could still join? She pulled her cellphone out of her pocket and dialled his number. After five beeps, his voicemail clicked in. She disconnected and tried his mobile. Again the voicemail. Damn. A sign from heaven: go home and study. With a sigh, she trotted off to the next bus stop.

# 13

Charlie pointed to a larger-than-life marble penis. 'So this represents the fountain of life?' she asked sceptically. 'Isn't that what you usually call the womb?'

'Well, I do think that depends on whom you ask. No sperm - no baby, right? But I agree, a combination of womb and cock would make the imagery even more perfect. Maybe, if I add a round object, out of which it could stick out ...'

Blake's hands cupped an imaginary vessel. Charlie refrained from digging deeper into the matter and moved on to the next artwork.

'Stop!' commanded Blake.

She stopped in mid-stride.

'You have not seen the fountain yet.'

'Yes, I have,' she objected. 'I've had a very good look at it. It's huge, it's made of green marble and it has your name at the base. A genuine Blake. See, I've looked at it. It'll haunt me in my dreams tonight, I swear. Happy?'

'Yes, but you haven't seen it in action,' he chided her gently.

For a second, Charlie feared that he would get it in his head to rape her with it, but to her relief he stepped behind it and pushed a little switch. Water spurted out of its top. A miniature fountain.

'Nice,' said Charlie. 'That's water coming out of it, right?'

'Of course, honey,' he cried, highly offended. 'Did you think it was ...? Oh, you naughty girl, you.' He nudged her good-humouredly in the ribs. 'Nah, sorry to disappoint you, but it's only tap water.' He turned the flow off and gestured into the general direction of another object. As far as she could tell, it was made of fired clay. 'This,' he intoned, 'is a very useful chef-d'oeuvre.'

'Is it?' Charlie eyed the object doubtfully.

'It is. Can you guess, why?'

Charlie sighed and had a closer look at the thing. It consisted of a small tray on which two round objects were placed. Between the two bowls rested an elongated cone-shaped object which reminded her of a salt-sprinkler.

'It looks like a salt-sprinkler,' she stated.

'Correct! To be precise, it's a condiment tray for salt and pepper and spices. To give your life some flavour, ya know. Highly useful, you must admit.'

Charlie readily admitted this. Her glance fell on the brass doorknocker that Gerald had fondled the day before. It was labelled 'sold'.

'Did you sell a lot, yesterday?'

'Oh yes, quite a few objects. You always sell most on the first day, that's why it's so important to organize a successful private view. That piece of art you're looking at went to the Lord Mayor. If you hadn't run away, I would have introduced you to him.'

'The Lord Mayor of London?' asked Charlie, incredulously.

'In persona. I'm sure you two would have got along so well.' He shook his head, disappointed. 'Such a shame you couldn't stay.'

For one second, Charlie wondered whether Gerald was the Lord Mayor. But that was silly, because she had seen the mayor on telly, and Gerald didn't at all look like him.

Blake's head jerked up. 'It's not him, is it? The customer you were afraid to meet?'

'Of course not.' Changing the subject, she asked casually: 'Were there also a lot of business people invited?'

'Oh yes, of course. Bankers, company directors, people from the ministry, you name it, we got it. The movers and shakers of our country. You have to invite them, really, if you want to raise money for a good cause. And they're always happy to socialize among themselves. You know how it is.'

Charlie didn't. 'A good cause?' she asked.

'Oh yes, all proceeds go to a new school that helps children with reading difficulties.'

'Dyslexics?' Strange, Charlie thought, how a word suddenly keeps popping up, once you have heard it for the first time. It was a bit like the concept of déjà vu ...

'Right. I think that's a very laudable initiative. In fact it was my idea. Of course it's also important to help children in Third World countries. But neither should we forget the unfortunate ones in our midst.'

Though his solemn tone made her smile, she realized that Blake was genuinely concerned. She patted his hand. 'You're a darling.'

'Oh, so are you, honey. Want to see the rest of the exhibition?'

'Sure. Lead the way.'

'I feel so alone,' moaned Blake.

Charlie had a hard time understanding what he said, as his head was buried in her crotch. She looked down. 'You don't have to do this, you know,' she pointed out.

His tongue continued its journey into Pussyland. 'But I want to,' he complained. 'I want to feel useful.'

'You shouldn't speak with your mouth full,' she gently reprimanded him. 'Besides, I prefer to look at the people I talk to.'

His head came up from under the blanket. 'Does that mean you want me to stop?'

'It means,' she said dreamily, 'that I want you to offer me something to drink. Nothing sweet, and nothing alcoholic,' she added hastily.

Blake hopped out of bed. 'How about an orange juice? It's not something that I would usually offer to my guests, but it's neither sweet nor inebriating. Besides, the bottle has been open for a while, so it would be a good idea to finish it.'

'Make it expired orange juice then,' she sighed. 'As long as I don't expire when I drink it ...'

He returned with a glass of juice for her and a *Crème de cas-*

*sis* for himself. He slumped down next to her onto the bed. 'I'm so happy,' he sighed.

'I thought you were alone?' she asked.

'Yes, that too, of course. But I can be alone and happy at the same time. My little brother has confided in me yesterday, that he has found the love of his life. Le grand amour. *Elle court, elle court, la maladie d'amour* ... do you know that song? No? It's French. Like the sex, you know?'

Charlie was confused. 'Ok. So your brother is happily in love,' she summed up his speech.

'Right. And of course I'm happy for him. More than happy. If there's a person on this planet who deserves happiness, it's him. But somehow,' his hands grabbed eloquently through the air, 'this knowledge of his dwelling in blissfully united joie de vivre, and with a girl to boot, leaves me, by comparison, even more painfully acutely aware of the very lonely unpurposefulness of my existence.'

Charlie stared hard at him and tried to peel out the gist of this sentence. 'Unpurposefulness?' she finally managed. 'Does that word exist?'

'It does now.'

She had to bow to the logic of that thinking. 'I think you are looking in the wrong places to find your honeys,' she said.

'How so?'

'Well, picking up guys on the street or in bars is a pretty good recipe for heartache. I'm sure your brother did not find his girlfriend that way.'

'Um, no, apparently they met in the park. Maybe I should get myself a dog,' he mumbled thoughtfully.

'You know what?' Charlie jumped out of bed and beamed at him. 'I have a brilliant idea. You don't have a computer, right?'

When he shook his head, she announced triumphantly: 'Get dressed. We'll go to an internet café and find you a boyfriend.'

'A Nick? Why not a Paul or a Dick or a John?'

Charlie shook her head. 'Nick is short for nickname, silly. You should never give out your real name on the internet. You never know what sickos are roaming these forums.'

Blake looked worried. 'Sickos, huh? Ok, so, what nick should I use? How about W. Blake? Or is that too much of a giveaway?'

'Well, it probably isn't,' she laughed. 'I wouldn't use Blake, even if people will think that you mean the poet. I don't think sexual innuendos are a good idea, either. Only attracts the aforementioned sickos. How about something creative, something that hints at you being a sculptor?'

'Artista?' he proposed.

'Well, you're not a girl ...'

'Albion, what are you coming to,' he cried, horrified. 'No class'cal education to be found in here, just mammon lust and filthy lucre everywhere ... Artista is the Latin denomination for an artist. A *male* artist, to be precise. Like poeta, scriba, agricola ...'

'Was that a famous quote?' she asked, impressed.

'Yes, a genuine Blake. Do you like the nick?'

'The nick?' Charlie was confused.

'Artista.'

'Oh, right, Artista. Yes, why not. It's kind of original.'

Charlie filled in the form:

NICKNAME: Artista

HAIR: (a quick look to her right) blonde

EYES: (another quick look) green

PROFESSION: see nickname

INTERESTS: ...

'What are your interests?' she asked Blake.

'Asses and dicks,' was his prompt reply.

'You want me to write that down?' she asked sceptically.

'Better not, huh? We could lie. How about this: art, literature and travelling, especially to France.'

She completed the form and then logged in on the board. A page appeared, featuring several attractive young men and topics of general interest to the British gay community. Another page popped up: two blank forms, separated by a menu list.

'Ok, so what do I do now?' asked Blake eagerly, his fingers resting lightly on the keyboard, like a piano player's hands on the keys.

'There's a list of the people who are online on the first page. We can look through their accounts, and if there's someone you like, we will try to make contact.'

'Making contact, that's good. That's very good. Where do I click?'

Charlie laughed. 'Don't be so nervous, Blake. See that list here on the right-hand side? Pick a nick that appeals to you.'

Blake read through the names. 'Buttfuck - nah, too obvious what *he* wants. Chris71 - oh no, no more Chris. Nomen est omen. Bad omen, in this case. Dandyboy - hm. That sounds kinda cute.'

'Ok, then click on the name.'

Blake moved the cursor over the screen. Suddenly, a message popped up: *Hi cutie pie - Black Beauty here.*

Blake looked at Charlie: 'Help! A horse is trying to make contact. What do I do now?'

Charlie laughed. 'Well, the polite thing to do would be to answer, don't you think?'

'Right.' Blake thought for a while. 'How about I write: Hi, my cute stallion?'

'Sounds witty.'

Blake typed very conscientiously: *Hi, my cute stallion.*

The answer followed on the spot: *I am. A cute stallion, that is. I can be yours.*

Blake frowned. 'Is he implying that he wants to mount me? I'm not a mare, you know.'

Charlie shrugged. 'Don't tell me. Tell him.'

Blake typed: *Want me to ride you, beautiful horse?*

The swift reply: *oooooohhhh - naughty.*

Blake grinned and typed: *Is that a yes?*

A red mouth appeared on the screen. Blake stared at it, confused. 'He's sending me a kiss. What do I do now?'

'What do you want to do? Send him a kiss back?'

'Right. Virtual kissing. Good idea. How do I do that?'

Charlie took the mouse and clicked on the list of emoticons. She scrolled down and clicked on the kiss-mouth.

The answer popped up right away: *Oh yes, you wanna give me head. Are your lips very full?*

Blake looked concerned. 'To be honest, I don't like his answers too much. Can't we find someone less, you know, stallionish?'

'As you wish. Then tell him you're not interested anymore.'

Blake typed: *I'm not interested anymore.*

'Very sensitive, Blake.'

'I'm being honest! What's wrong with that? There's no point in getting his hopes up, is there? I have a very low pain-threshold, ok? I don't want my boyfriends to talk about mounting and thrusting their cock in my mouth on the very first night.'

'Ok, ok, Miss Artista, no need to get all emotional. See there, the next contender.'

On the screen, a certain Vaginas_suck chirped: *wanna have fun.*

'Is that a question or a statement, what do you reckon?' asked Blake.

'Does it matter?'

'Well, a question would mean: Do *you* want to have fun? A statement on the other hand means: *I* want to have fun. There's a huge difference between the two, so, yes, I *do* think that it matters.'

'Then ask him.'

Blake typed: *Does that mean: I want to have fun! or does it mean: do you want to have fun?*

The answer was: *both*, followed by a tongue sticking out and the question *you're not a cunt, are you?*

Blake was highly offended. *Of course not!* he typed, then added: *However, I do not approve of name calling, especially where the weaker sex is concerned*

Charlie nodded approvingly. 'Thanks for defending my honour, Blake.'

'You're welcome, honey.' He beamed at her.

The vagina hater typed: *huh?* The English language did not seem to be his forte. He demanded: *turn on the cam and let me see it*

'Huh?' asked Blake, 'what does he mean?'

'He wants to see your dick on a camera. Tell him, you don't have one.'

Blake typed: *I don't have one.*

Vaginas_suck did not seem to believe this: *come on, don't be shy.*

'What?' Blake gestured at the screen, then typed, very determinedly: *I'm telling you I don't have one. I would prefer to end this conversation now*, and added a pig-smiley for emphasis.

The misogynist replied: *I would prefer to see your dick.*

'Help! He's stalking me!' Blake jumped on Charlie's neck in mock horror. 'You *are* sure he cannot come crawling through that screen, right?'

Charlie laughed. 'Of course he can't. Don't worry. Just tell him again that you're not interested.'

He typed: *Fuck off!* and grinned self-satisfied at the screen. 'Take that, you perv.'

The perv threw an angry smiley at him and disappeared.

'Good riddance.' Blake turned to Charlie. 'I'm not sure this will work. These guys are all so ... extreme.'

Before she could reply, the next message appeared: *Doggie speaking. Woof.*

Blake was delighted. 'A pup, how sweet. I'll be nice to him.'

He typed: *Good doggie. want a cookie?*

The answer was: *me want cookie yes*, followed by a hug.

Blake was ecstatic. 'He sent me a hug!'

The next line appeared: *you an artist?*

Blake answered: *In fact, I'm a sculptor.*

Doggie seemed to be fond of sculptors: *great, then you're good with your hands.*

Blake replied: *oh yes, very good. I can give you a massage, if you want.*

The answer was: *I'm more into rougher stuff. can you give me that as well.*

'At last someone who is not only into his own pleasure,' screamed Blake. He rubbed his behind against the chair and let out a horny growl. 'This one's hot, I can feel that.'

Vaginas_suck remarked acidly: *I can see you're still online.*

Blake stared at the screen in horror. 'What does he mean, he can see me? How can he see me?' He peered around the screen, as if fearing that someone was lurking behind it.

'Calm down, Blake. He can see your name on the board. You are still online.'

'Oh, is that it, yes? Huh.' Blake threw another suspicious glance at the screen. 'Ok, back to my doggie ...' Ignoring Vaginas_suck's remark, he typed: *oh yes, honey, whatever you want.* Then he selected a flower from the emoticon list and typed behind it: *a rose with thorns.*

Charlie clapped her hands in delight. 'How sweet of you, Blake.'

The doggie answered: *a whip with thorns and oil.*

Blake answered: *A whip with thorns and vinegar. And a kiss to make it good.*

Charlie nodded approvingly. 'I see you're getting along well.'

'Thank you so much for introducing me to this internet thingy.' Blake hugged her enthusiastically. 'This is so much fun, honey.' He typed determinedly: *I want to fuck you.*

Doggie jumped on the offer: *can we meet? I'm into kinky. could you do something like this to me?*

A little icon appeared. Blake looked confused. Charlie took the mouse and clicked on the accept button. The computer downloaded the file, then another link appeared: open. Charlie clicked on it and a screen-sized colour picture popped up: a naked man's lower body. His legs were spread wide apart and his balls were squeezed through a wooden apparel which stretched them almost beyond recognition. They popped out at the other side as grotesquely blown-up purple sacks. The tip of the penis disappeared into its foreskin, which was stretched tight, along with the testicles. Blake stared at it in horror.

'I'm getting sick,' he moaned. 'Please remove that horror from my field of vision, will you, honey.'

Charlie obeyed and closed the pop-up window. Blake remained sitting in stunned horror, so she typed for him: *Sorry, but this is too kinky for me. Good luck with finding someone else.*

Glancing back at the screen, she noticed that Vaginas_suck had made another attempt: *Still got no camera?*

That guy was fast becoming annoying. She ignored him and turned to Blake. 'How about we have a look at the accounts again?'

'Ok.' Blake looked pale. The picture seemed to have been too much for his sensitive artist's soul.

They scrolled through the nicknames: DesmondChild58. Blake clicked on the picture. Child my ass, he was at least sixty. Dirty-Dog. Blake wasn't too keen on the canine species anymore. After all, he declared, he wasn't a sodomist or some such thingy.

Meanwhile, a certain Randy_Studd was trying to make contact: *Hey, I'm gay. Oooh, are you too?*

Blake could not be bothered with rhymes just now: *No, I'm a seventy year old granny.*

Randy took it with humour: *oh sorry, lady :) bye.*

Blake clicked on another nick: eleusis. That sounded interesting. The account gave the following information:

HAIR: black
EYES: green
PROFESSION: PR
INTERESTS: anything intriguing

The picture showed a good-looking man in his late twenties. Smart, self-assured and sexy.

'I want him,' cried Blake. He thought for a moment, then typed: *Hello, my beautiful Greek god.*

They waited anxiously. For a while, the screen remained empty. Then a message popped up: *hello artist, how are you? wanna paint me? LOL*

Blake stared open-mouthed at the screen. 'How does he know that I'm an artist?'

Charlie laughed. 'Your nick is Artista.'

'Oh. Right.' He replied: *I'm a sculptor, not a painter. I can make a model of you, if you want.* After some thinking, he added: *you have such a wonderful body.*

eleusis answered: *thank you*, followed by a blush-smiley, and *I have never met a sculptor.*

Blake typed: *Eleusinian mysteries - what an enchanting prospect.*

The answer was: *to be honest, I don't know much about it. but I'm willing to learn*, followed by a smiley.

Blake frowned. 'Why is he calling himself eleusis, if he doesn't even know what it means? That's very suspect.'

Charlie shrugged. 'Maybe he heard the word somewhere. Why don't you ask him?'

'Nah, better not piss him off. How about this?' He typed: *And I'm willing to teach. You will like it.*

eleusis replied: *where are you from?*

Blake answered: *London - Notting Hill, and you?*

'Blake, don't tell him too much of yourself,' warned Charlie.

'Why not?' He stared enthusiastically at the screen, where eleusis' answer had just popped up: *I'm from Manchester - pretty boring, I knwo - know*

He frowned. 'knwo know?'

'He made a typo and corrected it,' explained Charlie, patiently.

'Oh, ok.' He typed: *You could come on holiday to Londno - London.*

'Are you making fun of him? He might not like that, you know,' warned Charlie.

'I'm not making fun of him,' cried Blake. 'I'm just trying out typos, that's all.'

'Hm. Well, your new honey has already written back.' She pointed to the screen.

*can I see a picture of you?*

Blake frowned. 'Why do they all want to see me?' he wondered. 'What do I do now? I don't have a picture of me. At least not here.'

Next to Charlie and Blake sat a young boy of about sixteen. He was wearing a black T-shirt with a sinewy monster holding a bloody axe in his hand. With an evil grin, the monster looked down on his victim, who clutched desperately at his murderer's shirt. The boy had been engaged in a lively conversation on a baby-blue bulletin board. Now he turned around and pointed to a little camera, that was installed on top of Blake's screen. 'You can turn that on, you know.'

'Seriously?' Blake peered into the lens. 'How do I do that?'

The boy reached over and pushed a button. A red light shone up. On the screen, a message appeared: camera on.

'In this window, you can see what he will see,' the kid explained. 'If you click on this icon, he will see you. If you want to switch the camera off, you click on it again.'

'Oh, that's easy.' Blake beamed at the boy. 'Thanks, mate. Uhm, nice T-shirt you have there.'

'Thanks. You're a Maiden fan?'

'Uhm. I used to be, I guess. In my wild youth.'

The kid gave him the thumbs up and turned back to his conversation.

Blake stared at the camera. 'Ok, honey. Let's see if I can make him want me.'

# 14

Charlie's legs kicked over the mattress. Her breath came in rugged gasps and her head rocked forward in little spasmodic thrusts. Her teeth were clenched, her face glowing hot and feverish. A desperate little sob escaped her throat.

Damian rubbed his eyes and looked drunkenly to his left. 'Charlie? Are you ok?'

He only got a panting gasp for reply. He was wide awake now. He propped himself up on one elbow and looked concerned at his girlfriend. She seemed to be having a nightmare.

He shook her gently. 'Charlie. Wake up, Princess.'

Charlie's hand slapped his face and her legs thrashed the sheets even harder than before. Damian was really worried now. She looked like she had an epileptic seizure ...

'Charlie! Baby, you're scaring me!' He shook her shoulder, hard.

She awoke with a jerk. 'Huh? What?'

Damian's face loomed over her.

'What are you doing?' she asked with a start. 'Do you want me to have a heart-attack?'

'You had a nightmare.' His gentle face looked concerned. 'You were thrashing around like you had to fight for your life. What happened?'

'Oh.' Charlie rubbed the sleep out of her face. 'It was nothing. I've been running again.'

'You've been running? In your dream?'

'Mhm. There was a huge warehouse full of books. Old, mouldy books. They smelled like ... old books, you know. Someone was coming behind me. I had to get away, but there was no door. Just piles and piles of books. I started climbing up the stacks of volumes. They reached all the way up to the ceiling, and there was a skylight in the roof. I knew if I could only reach that window, I would get out. I would be safe. But they chased after me and the piles were shaking dangerously. But I had to climb on, couldn't look down.'

Charlie had tears in her eyes. Damian caressed her bare arm. 'Poor baby. Do you have that dream often?'

'Not always the same one. But similar ones, yes. I haven't had it for a while, though.' She paused, then continued: 'When I reached the skylight, I managed to climb out on the roof. I must have got down somehow, but I can't remember that part. I just know that, all of sudden, I was running along the street, and they were still behind me. Shooting at me. I ran faster, but the street seemed to be rolling underneath my feet and I progressed very slowly. And they kept screaming and shooting at me. It was so terrible.' She again buried her face in her hands.

Damian took her in his arms and tried to soothe her. 'I'm here, baby, you're safe now. It was only a dream. A nightmare.'

She pressed herself against him. 'It was so terrible,' she repeated.

'Did they get any closer to you?'

'No, not really. But I could feel their shots in my back. It hurt. And I didn't dare to turn around and look behind me. Because ...' her voice let out a desperate sob, '... because I knew that if I looked behind, I would see myself lying there, dead.'

Shuddering, she buried her face into his shoulder. He stroked her gently and mumbled soothing sounds. For a while, they were sitting like that, then Charlie looked up. 'I'm so silly. I know it's just a dream. But I was so hoping it wouldn't come back.'

'When did you have that dream for the last time?'

'Months ago. Last July, I think, during my ...' She caught herself and finished: 'just before the summer holidays.'

Damian gave her long look. 'During your exams, you mean?'

'I don't think it had anything ...'

'Oh yes, I do think it has something to do with your exams. I've watched you when you were studying this afternoon. You were so tense. As if you were determined to cram that knowledge into your head, no matter what.'

Charlie gave a little laugh. 'That's silly, I wasn't tense. I just tried to get as much done as possible. Because *you* wanted to have dinner later on, so I was under stress to finish. Besides, if I had known that you would be spying on me while I read, I wouldn't have accepted your offer to learn at your place.'

'I'm not spying on you. And I didn't force you to have dinner with me. I just thought that five hours of studying is more than enough. You have to make a break in between to let your mind assimilate what you have read.'

'Listen to you, Einstein. Is that how you managed to fail your first year twice?' She bit on her lip. Damn, why was she insulting him? He was only trying to be nice. But he really couldn't understand the pressure she was under. 'I'm sorry,' she said, 'I didn't mean it. I know you only want to help. But I need to get an A in this test tomorrow. Otherwise Jacobs will never even consider being my tutor ...'

'Jacobs? Didn't you tell me he was an asshole?'

'Well, sometimes he is,' she conceded, 'but a brilliant asshole.'

'Oh. Okay, then, if he's a brilliant asshole. Then you have to lick him, of course ...'

'Don't be cynic. You can't understand. You have a nice apartment, a brother who pays all your bills, and you don't have to do anything for that. But I can't fall back on my family. If I ever want to get a decent life, I have to get top-grades during the next two years. That's the only way to get a good job, an interesting job. So I *need* to win Jacobs over. And for that, I *need* to write an excellent test tomorrow. Because I *need* ...' Her voice was becoming ever more high-pitched.

Damian covered his ears with his hands. 'Ok, ok, I got you, my little siren. Because you don't *need* to scream like that.'

Charlie was quiet. She felt misunderstood. What did he know about pressure and career planning? Nothing. Nothing at all.

She lay back down and hugged her pillow. 'I have to catch some sleep. It's almost four, and I need to get up at seven.' Damn. Why had she used the word 'need' again? She was making it too easy for him to poke fun at her.

Damian stroked her back. 'I'll wake you up at seven. With a hot coffee and the full English breakfast. You just have a good night's sleep now. And I'll chase away every nightmare demon that tries to get into your head while you sleep.'

He hugged her around the waist and pressed his body against hers. Feeling very loved, Charlie fell into a deep, dreamless sleep.

He knew he was about to win his own private bet. Soon she would get up and hand in her test paper. She would be the first to hand it in. And that would mean: bingo! He had been right! Of course, when you really considered it, it was quite pathetic to make such silly little bets with yourself. Only goes to show what a lonely teacher's life can bring a man to. Still, he sometimes wished all his students were as intelligent and eager as her. It was pupils such as Ms Morgan that reminded him why he had wanted to become a teacher in the first place. Of course, there were other advantages to being a professor as well. The extensive holiday periods, for example. Not to forget the look of horror on some students' face when he made it clear that they, for sure, would never pass a single test in this faculty. Jacobs smiled to himself and hummed an annoying little tune. Soon it was time to snatch the papers away and put an end to their torture. Such pitiful little victories in this vale of misery ...

Charlie had another look at her watch. Ten minutes left, and she had already finished. Excellent. She carefully read through her answers and corrected some minor spelling errors. She added an explanatory note to one of her answers, then looked at the watch again. In three minutes, Jacobs would ask them to hand in their papers. Perfect timing. She stood up and walked to the front of the class. The teacher had been lost in narcissistic adoration for the last five minutes, admiring his neatly clipped nails.

Now he looked up and gave her an ironic little grin. 'Ah, Ms Morgan. I hope my questions didn't insult your genius too much.'

Charlie's self-satisfied smile died on her face. Why was he being so nasty to her? While she was still debating with herself about how to react to this, he gave her a reassuring nod. 'Never mind. I see my humour is lost on you, dear child. Just a good hint from a failed stand-up comedian: if you ever want to rule this country, darling, you better start loosening up.' He snatched the paper from her and made a condescending wave. 'You may dispatch.'

Charlie's cheeks burnt crimson red. He was an asshole, indeed. Why did she even bother trying to impress him? Head held high, she went back to her desk and collected her books and pens. She threw her handbag over her shoulder and left the room without so much as a second glance at him.

Outside the seminary room, she leaned against a stone pillar and closed her eyes. She felt drained. Yesterday evening, she had had a headache after reading for too long. Of course she hadn't told Damian this, as it would only reinforce his belief that she was trying too hard to be good. Then there had been that horrible nightmare again. She shuddered, when she recalled the feelings of pure dread and terror she had experienced in her dream. It had all felt so real. And now the test. She had indeed thought that the questions had been easy. Way easier than what they had discussed during the last few weeks in the seminary. She was pretty confident that she had answered them all correctly and exhaustively. But Jacobs' remark had left her shattered. Did she come across as a know-it-all? Did he think she was aiming to be a teacher's pet? She hoped not. She had never had this impression before, but maybe he didn't like her too much? If so, he would probably never agree to be her tutor, no matter how good her grades were.

She clenched her jaws. Fuck. Now she needed a coffee.

She trudged off in the direction of the coffee-dispenser. While waiting for her turn, she rummaged through her pockets and produced the necessary coins. After the machine had spat out the liquid which it shamelessly promoted as 'freshly ground coffee', she sat down on a bench and proceeded to satisfy her caffeine habit.

With the first sip, she burnt her lips and tongue. Ouch. She put the cup down on the bench and took out her cell-phone. Time to check her messages.

The first text message was from her brother: MUM ASKS WHEN U R HOME 4 XMAS RON

Probably not at all, Charlie thought. Next message: YOU HAVE THREE NEW MESSAGES. PLEASE CALL YOUR VOICEMAIL.

Charlie pushed in the number and listened to the recordings. The first was from Damian: 'Hey, Princess. I just wanted to wish you good luck for your test. So: good luck. Love you.' Sweet.

The second message clicked on. Only a static background noise was to be heard. Hm. Just as she was about to hit the delete button, a voice said indistinctly: '... bark, Bobby. It's Charlie. Woof.' Charlie shook her head. He sounded like Doggie. Hopefully he ... A loud bark hit her eardrum and cut her thoughts in two. Ouch. 'Hey Charlie, this is me again. Bobby wanted to wish you good luck, too. So: good luck from both of us. Call us when you've finished, ok? Love you.'

The third message came on: 'Hey, little girl. I see you have switched your phone off, this time. Good girl.' Arrogant bastard. Fondling pierced marble nipples and ringing people out of their classes. Ok, so what did he want? 'I would like to see you this evening. I can be at your library at, say, seven pm? ... I'll call you again at around three. See you then.'

No more messages. She switched the phone off and took a sip of her coffee. It had cooled down somewhat, and left a pleasant warm feeling in her throat. For some time, she just sat there, staring at the graffiti on the wall. Then she sighed and switched the phone on again. No use delaying it. She had to call Damian and tell him that she would not be able to see him tonight.

Gerald let Charlie step into the elevator first. An accomplished gentleman, he was. As long as he didn't catch you alone and naked.

'So, little girl,' he said, as the doors closed behind them, 'how does it feel, going to a hotel with a strange man?'

They enacted the same scenario as always: Gerald picked up a cute little girl (her), who was totally inexperienced, and brain-dead enough to get into the car with an elderly pervert (him). Once he had her in his hotel room, the perv showed his real face and raped the poor, innocent girl. Who, of course, was unable to defend herself against his strong, male body. It felt a bit like in a time loop. But Gerald never failed to introduce some new element in their game, so it didn't become too repetitive. And she had to admit that these role-plays were very, very arousing.

The elevator glided upwards. Charlie gave him a wide-eyed sugar-candy look. 'You told me you would show me how to kiss. I tried that once with a boy from my school. But I would love to practice with a real man.'

The real man's pants bulged out at this. He gave her a tense little smile that was probably meant to reassure her. The elevator doors opened, and he motioned for her to step out first. Once inside their room, Gerald carefully locked the door behind them. Meanwhile, Charlie was leaning against the wall, waiting for him to casually stroll over.

She beamed expectantly at him. 'Will you kiss me now?'

He bent down, until his eyes were only an inch from her face. 'Is that what you want, hm, little girl?'

Before she could even nod in reply, he had pressed his mouth against hers. His hands roughly cupped her face, while he pushed his tongue between her lips. She let out an astonished little gasp. This slight parting of the lips was just what he had been waiting for. His fingers brutally rubbed her cheeks, while his tongue forced its way into the warm interior of her mouth. She tried to turn her face away from him, but it was too late. He had pinned her writhing figure against the hotel room wall, his left hand gliding down her side and under her pullover, while his right played wantonly through her hair. She struggled harder. He gave a mocking little laugh and pulled her towards the bed, making her fall down on the bedspread.

His body loomed over her, broad and heavy. 'It's a bit more than what you bargained for, hm, little girl? Are you afraid yet?'

'What are you going to do to me?' she whispered.

'You'll see. Lots of things. Things that will make me very horny. Very aroused. Which, in turn, will incite me to do even more things to you.'

His hand pushed into the cup of her bra and he began to knead the nipple between his index and thumb.

'Ow, no!' She tried to push his hand off her breast.

He grabbed both her wrists with his other hand and slowly shook his head. Ts, ts, ts. Meanwhile, his fingers continued their massage. She could feel her nipple turn hard and sensitive under his touch.

'I don't like it when little girls try to push my hands away,' he said very softly, his voice a smooth, velvety menace.

'You are hurting me,' Charlie complained.

She only got a scornful laugh in reply. 'Don't be silly. You have no idea what hurt is. But you will find out soon, very soon. Within the next hour, you will know what real pain feels like.'

To give his words more emphasis, he squeezed her nipple hard and pulled it around. Charlie gasped and her body jerked up in pain. Before she could object, he had pulled her sweater over her head. He sat down on her thighs, his legs pinning her to the bed. He contemplated her body with an almost tender look on his face. Her right breast lay full and heavy on her chest, the nipple red and swollen. He bent down and took it in his mouth. He sucked hard on it.

Charlie felt tears welling up in her eyes. Damn, this really hurt. She was about to say something, when she heard the metallic click of his zipper. Gerald straightened up and allowed her a good look at his organ. It stood hard and straight and proud against his stomach. He pulled her up and lovingly brushed his thumb over her cheek. 'And now, little girl,' he said, 'I will show you where a man really wants to be kissed.'

Charlie cuddled closer to Gerald's naked body. He had made her suck him long and deep, but then he had decided that her mouth deserved a little pause. So they had snuggled up under the blanket, and had struck up a little conversation.

'... so his penis was much smaller than mine?' asked Gerald.

'Oh, yes,' she replied, ' thinner, too. It was much easier to take it into my mouth.'

'Hm. It looks much sexier if a girl has her mouth nicely filled up, though.'

'But I had trouble breathing, when you made me take it all in,' she said, with large, pleading eyes.

'That just goes to show that you have to practice some more. You'll learn how to breathe without having to gag.'

'Really? Will you teach me?'

'Oh yes, little girl,' he said, pushing her head down, 'I will.'

He made her turn around, so that he had a close-up view of her butt. For a moment, Charlie thought that he wanted to engage in 69, but she soon found out differently. While she still flexed her jaws to get ready for the job at hand, his hand fell hard upon her butt. She gasped.

'Lesson number one: don't make a man wait.'

She hurried to please him. Damn, that really hurt. He had caught her completely unawares.

*Slap*! His hand had come down again. 'Lesson number two: there is a reason why it's called sucking. So use those muscles, that's why God gave them to you.'

Charlie sucked harder. Please, don't slap me again, she prayed silently. He stroked the round curves of her buttocks and probed a finger into her anus. He seemed to be satisfied with her performance. Good.

*Wham*! Another slap. And another. She moaned with her mouth full.

'Ah yes, I love that, baby, I love that. Come on, moan some more for me.'

His hand fell down again and again. It felt like a million needles pricking in her butt. Her head went up and down, faster and faster, matching the rhythm of his slaps. His left hand pushed beneath her belly, teasing her, exciting her, while his right kept hitting her butt. Just when she thought she couldn't keep up his wild pace anymore, his hips jerked forward and he spilled his cum into her. Two, three hard thrusts, and then he sank down with a satisfied grunt.

She lifted her head and gave him a reproachful look. Licking a few white drops from the corner of her mouth, she declared loudly: 'Ouch.'

'This is probably the last time we see each other this year,' said Gerald, when they lay together side by side. 'Next Sunday, I'm taking my family on a skiing holiday to Saas-Fee.'

'Nice. I've never gone skiing.' Charlie nuzzled into his shoulder. 'Those were your girls, right? At Harrods?'

'Yes. Elsa and Nicky, and Elsa's friend Laura.'

'And the woman who was with them is your wife?'

'Yes, that's Katherine.'

'She looks nice.'

He didn't reply. For a while, no one spoke. Charlie felt his heart-beat against her ear. His breathing lifted and lowered her head in a slow, steady rhythm. She closed her eyes. She felt sleepy.

'We used to do role-plays together,' he suddenly said. Her eyes opened. Oh. Conversation time again. She acknowledged his words with an encouraging grunt.

'It took me a while to work up the courage to show her what I wanted. We never actually spoke about it. During the daytime and after I had come, it was like none of it had ever happened. I sometimes felt like a split personality. Most of the time, I was the gentle father and caring husband, but for an hour or so every couple of days, I would turn into a sex-monster who raped and tortured little girls. It was eerie, not being able to talk about it. Sometimes, I thought I was only imagining it all, that I was in fact going insane, and no one except me was even noticing it.'

'Why did you never talk about it?'

'I just couldn't. Katie is ... very serious. Very down-to-earth. I don't think she ever approved of these sex-games. She just went along, because I wanted it. I suppose she thought it was part of her marital duties.'

'She didn't strike me as someone who could be forced into something,' Charlie pointed out. 'Maybe she liked it, too.'

'No.' Gerald pulled the blanket higher and gently stroked the naked shoulder. 'No, she didn't. She went along with the game-play for some months, but then she became pregnant again. After Nicky's birth, we didn't have much sex. She was a difficult baby, cried a lot. I understood that Katie was tired and often had headaches. So I didn't want to bother her with my needs. But a year passed, then two, and somehow we didn't get back to our normal sex life.'

'You mean, you haven't slept with your wife for over a decade?' asked Charlie, incredulously.

'In the beginning, I made some advances, of course. And she never refused me, mind you. But I could tell she wasn't into it. She just went through the motions to please me. So I asked less and less often. In the end, I stopped asking altogether. And that's how it has been for seven, eight years now.'

'Maybe she has a lover,' ventured Charlie.

Gerald gave her an astonished look. 'No, she hasn't.'

'How can you ...'

'No,' he interrupted her, 'I told you, she's not interested in sex anymore.'

There was no point in arguing. She was well aware that this was probably their last time together. She had debated with herself whether she should tell him that she would stop her work. In the end, she had been too much of a chicken to tell him face to face. Besides, she preferred not to discuss her private life with him. He might get it into his head and try to make her change her mind. She would tell him on the phone, when he called next time.

Charlie heaved herself onto his chest and straddled him. She rocked playfully back and forth. He growled happily and grabbed her around the waist.

'I was thinking,' she said, while her butt rubbed teasingly against his dick, 'how about we take a shower together?'

# 15

Charlie took a deep breath. The cold winter air filled her lungs. Christmas holidays! These two words meant that for almost two weeks, she didn't have to get up early in the morning. Unless Bobby woke her up to go walkies, of course. But then, she could always hand that task over to Damian.

She felt great. She was out on Trafalgar Square, ready to relish a huge all-you-can-eat buffet. On her own. Damian was having lunch with his brother. To discuss some bills, as he had put it. She was supposed to go over to his place after lunch. She had a strange feeling about meeting this larger-than-life brother. He seemed to be quite a character. Hearing Damian talk about him, he sounded so perfect, without any fail or fault. She knew Damian held his opinion in high esteem. What if he didn't like her? He might try to convince Damian that she was only after his money ...

Her phone rang.

'Hello?'

'Buenos tardes, my charming little friend. I have good news.'

'Hi, Blake. I was just about to have lunch.'

'Wonderful. You have lunch. And then you come over to my studio.'

'Listen, Blake, I don't really have time this af...'

'Oh, but you have to make time. Ned's here.'

'Ned?' Charlie was puzzled. Who on earth was Ned?

'Ned. eleusis. My new internet love. Remember I gave him my phone number?'

Charlie remembered only too well. She had strongly advised Blake against it, but as expected, he had not listened to her.

'We talked for over an hour on the phone last Saturday. And again on Sunday evening. And now he has come down to visit.'

'So he's at your place right now?' Charlie heaved a generous helping of fried rice on her plate. Mmmh, and they had watermelons, too. In December. Cool.

'Umm, actually, he's at a meeting. He arrived yesterday evening and we had the most fantastic night. It just - clicked. Wham, bam, bang and slam. If you get my meaning. My dick just fit his ass like a glove, as the saying goes.'

'Is that how it goes.'

'If I'm not very mistaken. Anyway, this morning he had to go to this designer conference. Because that's what he does, you know. Organizing thingies for designers and stuff. All very interesting.'

'Great.' Charlie helped herself to some hot wings. Hm. Come to think of it, the spare ribs looked yummy, too.

'He will be back around six, he said. So, are you coming over? He's got such a cute ass. You'll love it.'

'Blake, I already have a date this evening.'

'What?' he cried, 'without me?'

Charlie laughed, and balanced her plate back to her table. A bit of sauce dripped to the floor. Damn, she should have gone back for the watermelons later.

'What do you mean 'without me'?' she asked. 'We're not a couple, as far as I know. You love Ned and I ...'

'I know we're not a couple, honey,' said Blake, offended. 'But I thought we were friends.'

Charlie took a deep breath. Time to hit him with the bad news. 'I'm not working anymore, Blake.'

'What?' he screamed, even louder this time. 'I hope you don't have any disease ... thingy.'

'No, of course not,' she reassured him. 'I have a boyfriend.'

'Oh. I see.' He sounded hurt.

Charlie tried not to make too much noise while she munched her fried rice. 'Look, Blake, I'm really sorry, but ...'

'So just because you have a boyfriend you don't want to hang out with me anymore? Drop me like a hot potato?'

'Well, I ...'

'We don't have to have sex, you know. If you want it all bourgeois, stuck-up, don't-touch-me-I-won't-touch-you style, that's fine with me ...'

Charlie sighed and bit into a slice of watermelon. The sweet juice ran through her fingers and down her wrist. Damn. She tried to slurp the drops from her hand without dropping the phone.

'... because *I* don't drop my friends that easily. In fact, I ...'

'Blake! Will you listen to me, please?'

'Huh? Oh. Ok. My comment's not wanted? No problem. I can do the sois-belle-et-tais-toi. Pas de problème. Go on, tell me. I'm all mum and listening. Zip.'

She sighed. He could be such a drama queen. She waited for a few moments. When she was sure he would be quiet, she said, 'If you swear that you won't expect sex, we can still see each other from time to time. And of course I would love to meet Ned. After all, it kinda was me who brought you two together. Tell you what: how about we meet this evening for a nice chat? Sounds good?'

'Hm. Sounds suspiciously bourgeois. But, alright, nice chat it is. A six heures?'

'A scissor?' Charlie was confused. 'What do you mean?'

'Will you drop by at six?'

'Ok, six o'clock it is. And now, if you don't mind, I will turn my attention to this delicious little honey rib.'

'Honey rib sounds great,' said Blake, and they both hung up.

He had already left when she arrived. Perfect. No brother meet and greet this time. Bobby acknowledged her with a stoic nod from his cosy spot on the rug under the dining table.

Damian jumped up and hugged her. 'Hi, Princess. I've made a New Year's resolution.'

He had such a proud sparkle in his eyes that she immediately suspected the worst. He had made a resolution. Help. Wedding bells were ringing in her ears. Stay calm, Charlie, she told herself, it might not be all that bad.

'Really?' She reached up and gave him a kiss on the mouth. 'Wanna share?'

Again the disquieting beam. 'I told my brother that I want to handle the mail myself.'

'Oh.' She relaxed. False alarm. 'That sounds like a very sensible decision to take.'

'Right. I thought so, too. He was a bit sceptical at first. But then he agreed that we could try it, at least.'

Charlie frowned. She didn't like the patronizing way of this high'n mighty brother of his. Damian was a grown-up, after all. Why on earth would he not be able to take care of his own mail? He might be dyslexic, but he wasn't dumb.

'If you need my help, don't hesitate to ask.' She gave him a big bear hug. 'I love you, Damian.'

'I love you too, Princess.'

From under the table, a canine tail bobbed approvingly up and down. Letters were so much more fun to chew on than wedding rings.

Nothing beats sex in the afternoon. Apart from, maybe, sex in the morning. Or in the middle of the night. But the afternoon was definitely among her top-ten favourite hours of the day for sex. Charlie bit playfully into Damian's nipple and rolled over. She grinned at the ceiling and whistled softly to herself. That is, she blew air in a vaguely rhythmic pattern. A gentle observer might have let it pass for whistling.

'Do you know that cum tastes differently depending on what the man has drunk or eaten before?' she asked.

'Mhm.'

She turned around and gave him an astonished look. 'You do?'

'Why, yeah. Stands to reason.'

'Oh, it does?' She gave him a suspicious squint. 'Hm?'

'Mhm. It does.' Earnest nod.

They both burst out, laughing. Charlie rolled on his belly and hammered with her little fists against his ribs. 'Are you making fun of me, Mister Winter?'

'I wouldn't dream of it, Miss Morgan.' He grinned.

'Sure?' She jackhammered a finger into his ribs.

'I swear. Ouch! Help! Mercy!'

He struggled helplessly, with both arms and legs flailing through the air to no avail.

Charlie laughed in delight. Sex with Damian was so much fun.

Two hours later, Charlie trudged along the windswept street, her hands buried deep in her pockets. Only her eyes poked out under a woollen shawl into the cold December air. Damn, it was freezing, and the tube station wasn't too close. Of course she deserved a bit of punishment. She had told Damian that she would start packing tonight and that she preferred to do it on her own. She didn't feel good about lying to him, but somehow she couldn't bring herself to tell him the truth. 'Listen, I'm having a nice chat with my gay ex-customer and his new boyfriend. Hope you don't mind. There's even a small chance it might *not* turn into a sweaty sex-orgy.' Sounded just like the thing any man wanted to hear from his girlfriend. For sure, for sure.

Charlie grumbled under her breath. She was too soft. Who had ever heard of a retiring hooker making a courtesy call on her ex-customer? *Gay* ex-customer, if you please. To have tea and cookies with his new honey. This could really only happen to her.

At last. The red and blue underground sign. Charlie's mood lifted a notch.

The entrance to the tube station was cordoned off with police tape. A friendly officer nodded at her. 'This station is closed for the night, miss.'

Her mood plummeted two notches. The most efficient tube system in the world, and you couldn't use it because of some jackass calling the police with nonsense terrorist threats. That's London for you.

She peeked down the dark stairway. At the end of the steps lay a grey blanket that covered ... something. She stared harder. There was a shoe peeping out under the blanket. Her eyes widened in horror.

'Would you please walk on, miss?' The police officer stepped into her field of vision and gave her a gentle nod. 'Please?'

She made a few hesitant steps away from the tube entrance. Ok. A bus. She would take a bus to get to Notting Hill. No problem. Everything under control. She focused her thoughts on something else. On anything but that shoe. Which, of course, made it pop up even more vividly before her inner eye. Damn.

'Hi, honey. There you are,' screamed Blake from two floors up. 'You're late.'

'I had to take the bus. They had closed the tube station.'

'Why?'

'There was a body lying at the end of the stairs.'

Blake stared down at her over the railing, his mouth wide open. He looked like he was about to throw up. Realizing that she was strategically ill-placed for such an incident, Charlie hastened up the steps.

Blake followed her movements, his lips opening and closing without a sound. He blinked twice, then swallowed. 'Forget that I asked. Let's wind the last ten seconds back, ok?'

She arrived on his floor. Out of the trajectory. Good. She gave him a hug. He still looked badly shaken.

Then he said, automatically, 'Hi, honey. There you are. You're late.' It sounded much more toneless than the first time around. A bit like a hoarse croak.

'Hi, Blake. I had to take the bus because they'd closed the tube station. Probably some nonsense terrorist threat.'

'Poor honey. Come in and meet Ned.' Blake's powers of self-delusion worked impeccably. Nothing beats years of hard training.

He took her coat and gently pushed her into his loft. 'Ned, meet Charlie. Charlie, this is Ned.' Two grand waves across the room.

The handsome guy from the internet pic gave Charlie a warm smile. 'Hello, there. Blake has told me so much about you.'

'I bet.' She grinned at him. 'If you believe even a third of it, I swear I will drop dead with shame, right here.'

He laughed. 'Between the two of us, I settled on about a seventh,' he confided in a low voice.

'I heard that,' Blake screamed. 'I am seriously offended, honeys.' Looking rather pleased than offended, he dropped down onto the couch. 'Hava thingy, willya.'

Since his hand motioned towards the liquor cabinet, Charlie took it to mean that she was invited to help herself to some sugar-brew. She ignored the offer, and had a look around his apartment instead. She spotted a new work of art. 'I see you've been creative.'

'Oh yes.' Blake jumped up and dashed to the window. He proudly stood next to a glazed flower-vase drying on the sill. A vase with two round and quite unnecessary appendages on both sides. That's ART, Charlie thought. Annoying Recurrent Testicles.

A slender finger pointed first to the one ball, then to the other. 'Say hello to Boule et Bille, Charlie.'

Charlie squinted at him. Sometimes she wondered whether he lay awake at night to come up with such nonsense. It probably beat counting sheep. 'A flower vase, how homely.'

Charlie's sarcasm was, as always, lost on Blake. 'Yes, I s'pose I'm getting more sedate with age.' He swirled around on one foot, and grabbed the air in front of him. 'Come here, honey,' he commanded.

Ned being in his field of vision, Charlie supposed he didn't mean her, and had another look through the loft. Everything looked clean and orderly. He had put on the heater, too. Probably to make Ned feel comfortable. Or maybe to make his statuettes dry faster.

A sucking sound struck her ear. She turned around and immediately felt touched. How sweet. The true Christmas spirit. Two men smooching. Charlie sighed. She really was too soft.

The little white angel on her right shoulder kept nodding wisely and chanting, 'I told you so.'

The little red devil on her left shoulder just grinned. True winners don't feel the need to hold speeches.

Curled up in Blake's lap, Charlie rubbed her nose against Ned's warm, flat belly. He had such an athletic body. Just the right mixture of muscles, soft skin and a pinch of puppy fat. Gently toned boyish curves, rather than hard manly edges. A lick-your-lips-and-feast-on-it body. No wonder Blake had fallen in love with him.

'What do you work?' asked Ned in a conversational tone. Who would have thought that, only two minutes ago, she had been sucking him, while Blake had made mincemeat out of his ass.

Charlie smiled. 'I'm a student at COBEL.'

Blake jumped up, knocking his pelvis hard into Charlie's jaw. 'What?' he cried, 'you're a student?'

Charlie rubbed her cheek and gave him an accusing look. 'So? I told you that on the first day we met, as far as I remember.'

'Well, yes, but I didn't believe you.'

'And why not, pray tell?'

'Well, because you're a hooker.'

Sensitivity, thy name is definitely not Blake.

'Business school doesn't sound too exciting.' Ned tried to swing the discussion around to less offending ground.

'Oh, but it is. Actually, it's not all that different from being a hooker. In both situations, you learn how to be friendly to assholes, in order to get to their money.'

Ned laughed. 'A very philosophical way of looking at things.'

Blake was sulking.

Charlie reached for her glass. Blake had finally agreed that she could drink orange juice instead of liqueur. But somehow, even his juice tasted sweeter than most. Sigh.

Ned let his hands glide up and down Blake's spine. Charlie noted that he had very beautiful hands. Neatly clipped nails on strong, slender fingers.

Blake arched his back and purred like a kitten. Then he let himself thump onto Charlie's back. She spilled some juice on the linen. 'Blake!'

'Ah, never mind that. Some juice or other on it, doesn't really matter. I'll change the sheets anyway, tomorrow.'

Blake - the perfect housewife. Charlie grinned to herself.

Blake's hands roved down her back and squeezed her butt.

'Ouch!' White-hot pain shot through her legs and spine. Oh damn, she'd forgotten all about that.

She wanted to turn around, but it was already too late. Blake peered curiously at her butt, then recoiled in horror. 'What the hell did you do?' he yelled.

Charlie sighed. 'Don't get all excited. It doesn't look that bad.'

'Not that bad?' Blake pulled her up and dragged her into the bathroom. He made her stand in front of the full-body mirror opposite the toilet seat. He pointed accusingly at the purple bruises on her ass. 'Not that bad?' he asked again, accusingly. 'What's bad for you, then? A holiday in the Iron Maiden?'

Charlie shrugged him off. 'It's a rash, nothing more.'

'Oh, right. And I fell down the stairs, too.' He grabbed her arm and made her look him in the eye. 'Is he beating you up?' he asked, concerned.

'What are you talking about?'

'Your pimp. Is he giving you a hard time? Is that why you want to stop?'

'You're out of your mind.' Charlie turned on her heel and headed back to the bed. 'I'm cold.'

She cuddled up into the blanket and hugged her knees. Ned gave her an encouraging smile. She smiled back, and rolled her eyes in the direction of the bathroom.

Blake stomped back into the room, eyes blazing and blonde locks flying around his face. The Angel of Righteous Wrath.

He snatched up his blackcurrant liqueur and scratched his balls. 'Move over. I'm cold, too.'

Charlie and Ned obliged.

# 16

'I'm sure I put it in the box with my socks and underwear. I distinctly remember thinking it would be nicely padded in there.' Charlie rummaged wildly through a big cardboard box. Pushing panties and bras to the side, she probed and groped. Nothing. At least nothing hard and metallic. She swore.

Damian was watching her stoically. 'Why is it so important where you put it?' he asked. 'You don't need your laptop right now. It'll show up eventually, when we unpack later on.'

Such practical thoughts did not convince Charlie. With a sigh, she collapsed onto a chair full of books. 'Damn, we haven't yet packed those in, either,' she whined. She gave Damian a stern look. 'It *is* important that I find it now. I might not have packed it in at all. What if I forget it here?'

'What, in an empty flat? Hardly.' Damian put the books that Charlie handed him into a box, then covered them with two sheets and a blanket. Charlie started a new attempt at finding her computer. Damian pushed a lock out of his forehead and looked through the apartment. The more they packed, the more crowded the room seemed to become. Strange, somehow. 'I thought you wanted to pack yesterday evening,' he asked tentatively.

'Found it!' Charlie triumphantly held up a cable.

Damian looked blank.

'This cable is attached to my notebook,' she explained.

'Uhuh?'

'My laptop.'

'Oh, I see. So you found it. Great.' Damian opened the fridge door. 'How about we have a break and drink some juice?' He came back to the table with two glasses of orange juice and a bar of chocolate.

Charlie shook her head. 'No, I first want to get this finished.

It's already noon and this place is still a mess. I never knew moving was such a hassle.'

Damian handed her the glass. 'Don't stress yourself so much. We'll finish eventually,' he said with philosophical calm.

There was a knock at the door. They looked at each other.

'You've got a visitor,' Damian pointed out, quite unnecessarily.

'I never get visitors.'

As he was standing next to the door, Damian thought he might as well open it. He found himself face to face with a girl, who beamed at him with candid curiosity.

'Hi, Alice, what are you doing here?' Charlie shot Damian an accusing look, as if it were entirely his fault that the girl had come over.

'Oh, hi, Charlie. I was in the neighbourhood, so I thought I'd drop by. For a chat, you know.'

Charlie gave her a noncommittal smile. 'I really don't have time for a chat, Alice. As you can see, we're a tiny bit crowded in here. But thanks for dropping by, anyway. See ya.'

'Are you redecorating?' asked Alice, unimpressed by her rude reply. She took a step into the apartment.

'No, she's moving in with me,' explained Damian.

'Really?' Alice gave him the twice-over. 'Wow. Are you her boyfriend or something?'

'Why, yeah.' He grinned sheepishly and proceeded to push an imaginary lock out of his forehead.

'Wow.'

Charlie looked from one to the other. 'Are you done socializing? May I point out that we are still sitting on a heap of disorganized mess?'

Alice looked around. 'It does look a bit disorganized. Can I help you? I love to put things in order.'

Before Charlie could object, she had stepped into the room and critically eyed the piles of laundry, books and crockery. 'You might want to start with emptying one corner and piling up the finished boxes there. Like under the window, for instance. So that they're out of the way.'

'Great idea.' Damian pushed a heavy box full of books into the corner, then heaved a lighter one onto the first. Alice added a third box and pushed the empty chair under the table. Much to Charlie's distress, the room looked instantly less crowded.

'Well, of course it *looks* better this way. Doesn't mean it really *is* better.' She knew it sounded lame.

'No, I think this is the way to do it,' Damian backstabbed her. 'Thanks for helping us, uhm, Alice? We appreciate.'

'No problem.' She beamed at him. 'Are you the guy with the black Mercedes?'

'Huh?' Damian was puzzled. 'No, I don't have a car.'

'Oh, because I thought ...'

'Right,' said Charlie, 'if you really want to help, you can do so, but I'd appreciate it if we could delay the small talk till later. Thank you.'

They set to work. After half an hour, three rows of boxes stood neatly piled up in one corner, and Charlie was making a last round of inspections, to make sure that nothing had been forgotten in a cupboard or under the bed. Damian emptied the fridge and divided the remnants of chocolate and juice equally between the three of them. Then he dropped down next to Alice on the bed. 'Finished,' he declared happily.

'I think we did a great job,' said Alice, satisfied.

'Thanks to you,' he agreed.

'Team effort.'

Stepping out from behind the bathroom curtain, Charlie felt an unreal pang of jealousy. Her boyfriend was bonding with her annoying classmate and they seemed to be getting along just great. Someone please tell her this was a nightmare.

'Come over,' called Damian good-natured, and patted the mattress next to him. 'Have a sip of juice.'

'Maybe we should call a taxi, now? I don't want to leave Bobby alone for too long,' she said.

'Oh, right. Yes, we should be going.' Damian turned to Alice. 'Wanna help us unpack, too?'

The moment the door closed behind the girl, Charlie spun around and glared at Damian with angry eyes. 'How *could* you?'

He turned to the dining table and proceeded to bring the dirty cups and plates into the kitchen. Charlie watched him, puzzled. Why wasn't he joining in her quarrel? It was no fun, quarrelling all by yourself.

'I'm talking to you.' She followed him into the kitchen.

He was brushing crumps of cake into the trash bin and stowed the used dishes into the dishwasher. Charlie stood her ground next to him, her hands firmly lodged on her hips. 'Mister Winter?'

'Miss Morgan?' At last he turned around and faced her. She had expected him to look either angry (which would have been really uncalled for, since she was the one who had been wronged here), or rueful (she would have appreciated that, and might even have given up her well-deserved quarrel), or astonished (she wouldn't have been surprised if he had not even noticed how annoyed she had been about him inviting Alice over). Instead, he looked sad and concerned. How very inappropriate. It completely ruined her speech.

'Why did you do that?' she finally managed. It sounded more like a plea than an accusation.

'What *did* I do?' Damian stooped and placed a tablet into the appropriate compartment. He closed the dishwasher, pushed the start button and waited for the machine to come to life. Then he turned around again. 'I invited one of your school friends over. She had offered, quite unselfishly, to help us pack your things. We unpacked some boxes, and then we had five o'clock tea. And throughout this rather pleasant afternoon, you kept pulling faces and being very unfriendly towards our guest. So somehow, I have a mind to ask *you* why you did that.'

Damian's voice had remained levelled and calm throughout, but Charlie felt like he had hit her with his fist in the stomach. She was close to tears. 'She's not my friend. And I didn't want her here.'

'You made that clear. I just wonder, why?'

She didn't answer. Somehow, she had the very unpleasant feeling that her voice would quiver if she attempted to speak.

Damian looked like he was about to cry, too. He took her hand in his and lifted it to his lips. He placed a warm, tender kiss on the palm and the back of her hand, before nuzzling his face into it.

'Why did you invite her over?' Charlie felt it was very important that she understood this.

Damian sighed and pulled her close. 'Because she was nice enough to help us pack. She was funny, friendly, competent and most of ...'

'Alice isn't funny,' she interrupted him. 'She's awkward and has a stupid laugh and ...'

'Can I finish my sentence, please?' When she nodded, Damian continued: '... and most of all, she was very alone and she was happy that we spent some time with her. And,' he added forcefully, 'I still think that she's funny.'

Charlie felt misunderstood. Damian was supposed to see her side of things, not Alice's. Why was he so keen on making a girl happy whom he didn't even know? He was supposed to want to make her, Charlie, happy ...

All these thoughts rambled through her mind and she knew she had to communicate them to him, in order to make him understand. If you don't talk to each other, you cannot expect your partner to know how you feel.

'I don't want you to like her,' she mumbled.

'Uhm, sorry. Can't be helped. I like her.'

Charlie looked up angrily. 'Don't you care at all how I feel about this?'

'Of course I care. You feel angry that I like to talk to someone that you don't like. But you still haven't explained why you don't like her. Has she been mean to you? Has she laughed about you? Has she stolen from you? Has she attempted to kill you?'

Charlie had to laugh against her will at the funny faces he was making. 'Be serious, will you?'

He shook his head, quite determined not to be serious right now. She punched him in the ribs and he went to the floor with a theatrical groan, eyes rolling up in his head. 'I'm so dead.'

She straddled him and started counting. 'One, two, three ...'

Damian opened one eye. 'What are you doing?'

'I'm counting to ten. Four, five. Unless you want to declare defeat right away. Six, seven ...'

He grabbed her with both hands under her shoulders and heaved himself up. Screaming in mock alarm, she was lifted into the air, her legs wrapped tight around his hips, her arms clinging to his neck.

'Help. You're suffocating me.'

Charlie barely released her grip on his neck. 'Sorry.'

'So has she?'

'Has she what?'

'Tried to kill you?'

'Of course not. She's just annoying. Hanging on me like a leech on a wound.'

'Like you right now, you mean?' Damian grinned.

Charlie ignored the remark. 'I just don't have the time to hang around in cafés, drinking coffee and gossiping about school.'

'Why not? Remember when we first met? We had a drink and talked. You didn't seem to be in such a terrible rush. And we would still not have finished packing those boxes, if it hadn't been for Alice.'

'Look, do I *have* to like her? Is it compulsory to like her in order to be your girlfriend?'

'No. But when I watched you this afternoon, the way you snapped at her and rolled your eyes, I had to think of something you told me.'

'And what would that be?' Charlie let herself glide down and hopped onto the kitchen tiles.

'On our first meeting, you told me why you liked your management studies. You told me that it was all about understanding people, finding out about their needs and motivations. I liked that approach a lot. I think that was what made me fall in love with you in the first place.'

Charlie said nothing.

'And you were very emphatic. You had a great way of handling Bobby. And you were so tolerant and understanding, talking about that poor guy who doesn't want to be touched. And you knew how to make me feel good when I was embarrassed because of my dyslexia. I thought you were so wonderful.'

'You thought?' whispered Charlie. 'Meaning you don't think that anymore?'

'I still think you're wonderful, dummy.' Damian lifted her up and placed a big, noisy smack on her cheek. 'Do we have to stand in the kitchen to discuss this? I'd love to cuddle up on the couch.'

'Couch cuddling coming up.'

They settled down in smooching position. Bobby wriggled his tail and joined them.

Tickling the westie's expectantly exposed underside, Damian continued: 'With Alice, you behaved completely differently. It almost seemed like you were another person. And if you tell me that she has done nothing to offend you, I can only think of one explanation.'

'I'm listening, Doctor Watson.'

'That's Dr Freud for you,' he chided her gently. 'You're only compassionate and understanding with men. And you're nasty with her because she's a girl.'

Charlie stared at him. She wanted to laugh and discard this diagnosis as ludicrous nonsense, but she had the unpleasant feeling that he might not be so wrong. 'That's nonsense.'

'I'm not saying that you're doing it on purpose. Maybe you just prefer to hang around with men. I mean, I'm quite sure you do. There's nothing wrong with that. I'm just saying, you don't like her, because she's a girl.'

'I'm not jealous.'

He looked at her, thoughtfully. For quite some time. No one said a word. No one moved. Bobby pushed his belly further up, to remind his bipedal friends of their duties.

'I didn't say you were.'

Charlie blushed. She busied herself with tickling Bobby. 'If I promise to be nicer to her in the future, can we then talk about something else?'

'Deal.' Damian stretched his arms and legs. 'How about we unpack some more of your things?'

Charlie looked fondly at the neatly folded underwear in her night dresser. She knew that her panties and socks would probably never again lie in such delicately arranged rows in this drawer. That was the beauty of moving into a new home: you start out fresh and clean, with the firm intention to keep it that way. And even though you know that it will only take the next laundry to transform your wardrobe into the familiar old jumble of clothes, the purity of a new beginning nevertheless feels good. Very good.

She looked over to the other side of the bed. There stood the same dresser. Damian's. Charlie eyed the wooden piece of furniture curiously. When they had started to unpack her clothes, Damian had suddenly become all agitated. Out of the blue, he had asked her to fetch a jug of orange juice from the kitchen. He had wanted her gone from the room, that much was obvious. Feigning not to notice, she had left the bedroom, and when she had returned, he had been his usual laid-back self. Only when she had wanted to open his dresser (admittedly, to have a peep into it), he had become all embarrassed and had mumbled something about a chaos in there, which he wanted to clear out first.

Charlie grinned to herself. She would give him a few days or weeks. As long as he needed to admit to the pink bear socks, the Hustler mag, the porn DVDs or whatever else it was he was hiding in there. She was curious, but not so curious as not to respect his privacy. She remembered how her brother used to snoop through her things when she was still living at home, and how he had teased her about a Playboy magazine she had once bought out of sheer teenage curiosity. For months on end, he had got on her nerves with sexist innuendos about her being a secret lesbian. She had never felt attracted to girls, but with a brother like Ronnie, it was a wonder she had not become disgusted with the whole male species. In any case, that experience had shown her how important it was to carve out a safe haven for yourself, a place that belonged to you alone. And she had sworn never to intrude on someone else's privacy. If Damian wanted to have his little secrets, that was fine with her.

Charlie threw a last look into her night dresser and pushed the drawer shut. Damian was taking awfully long in the bathroom. Considering that she had not spotted a single magazine in there. A man that could take a poop without the help of a music, football, bike or porn magazine? One of her first make-yourself-at-home moves had been to place a few popular science mags on the laundry bag. Maybe he was checking those out.

Her pocket rang. She flicked the cell-phone open. 'Hello?'

'Hello, honey. I have a question.'

Hm. Blake sounded serious. 'Shoot.'

'You told me that you were supposedly a student ...'

'Not only supposedly. I *am* a student.'

'Alright. So far, so good. Now you may find this silly and I agree that it might just as well be only a coincidence, but you know what they say, it can't be all coincidence, too many ...'

'Blake, what are you talking about?'

'If you didn't keep interrupting me, I'd already have made my point.'

'I'm all ears.'

'So, to put it in a nutshell, my brother called me this morning and he ...' Blake stopped in mid-sentence. Charlie heard him mumble to himself, then swear under his breath.

'Blake?' she ventured.

'If this is what I think it is, I will kill him,' Blake declared grimly.

'What happened?'

'Nothing. Everything's fine. I was just fumbling on my dick and I found this very strange spot ... Honey, I'm sorry, but I fear we will have to postpone our interesting discussion. Important body matters, you understand. Don't forget what you wanted to tell me.'

'But you were the one who ...'

He had already hung up. Charlie stared at her phone, puzzled. He had been fumbling on his dick while talking to her? With Blake, you sometimes felt like in the twilight zone.

'Hey, Princess.' Damian gave her a bear hug from behind. 'Wanna come with Bobby and me? We have to go do number two.'

'Both of you?' Charlie laughed.

'No, just Bobby. I've already done mine. By the way, there are some amazing close-up shots of flowers in that book you put in the bathroom. With morning dew and snowflakes on the petals and stem. Fantastic.' He beamed at her.

'Glad you like it.' She reached for her coat, while Damian fastened the leash on Bobby's collar. Time to go on their evening stroll.

'So which picture was it you liked best?' asked Charlie, leafing through *Nature* magazine.

'The one on the side closest to the window. Somewhere at the beginning of the book.'

Charlie smiled to herself. The side closest to the window. That sounded so much more poetic than a simple 'left-hand side'.

She looked up and watched Damian wash his hands. He had such a sexy body. Young and slender. She still couldn't believe he was really thirty-two. Sometimes he stared at her in wonder and awe, with happy eyes as bright and candid as a child's. Right now he rubbed his hands on a towel and beamed at her through the mirror.

'I forgot to tell you something,' he declared proudly.

'What is it?' She was still looking for that one-of-a-kind flower pic.

'On Christmas Eve, we're having a family dinner at Gerry's. You're invited.'

She looked at him in horror. 'A dinner with your whole family? Do I really have to go? I don't know any of them.'

'You know me. And that way, you'll get to know the others. They're not that bad. I'm sure we'll have a great time.'

She gave him a suspicious squint. 'Was that Gerry's idea?'

Damian neatly folded the towel before hanging it back on the rack. 'He wants to meet you. There's nothing wrong with that,' he added, defensively.

Charlie said nothing. She didn't feel like socializing with Damian's family. She hated holiday get-togethers. In her experience, such family meetings were boring at the best of times. Usually, they made you feel all the nasty little pinpricks of humiliation and anger that remained safely tucked away for the rest of the year. Conventional wisdom had it that during the season, more people than usual committed suicide because they felt lonely and left out. Charlie had her own little idea about this. What if the reason for the suicides lay in the family dinners themselves? Such festivities could have a lethal effect on people's psyche.

'What if I don't feel so good?' she made another attempt at chickening out.

'It'll only be for a couple of hours. But, hey, it's your choice. No need to fake a headache or something. If you don't want to go, I won't force you.'

Charlie was thinking it over. How bad could it be, really? Some food, some wine, some polite chitchat, and soon it would be time to head back home. She remembered Damian mentioning that this Gerry had kids. Maybe she could play with them. It might be fun. Besides, she had nothing to be ashamed of. She was a business school student, nothing more, nothing less. And she couldn't postpone meeting his family forever. She was already grateful that he had not suggested a visit to *her* parents.

'Ok, I'll come with you.'

'Great.' He beamed at her, then motioned to her lap. 'Will it take much longer?'

'No. Actually, I was just sitting around, waiting for you.' She got up and reached for the toilet paper.

'Oh, I see you've found it.' Damian pointed to a full page picture. A close-up shot of a thistle, dark colours standing out sharply on the glossy paper. The winter sun sparkled on a fine coat of snowflakes that covered part of the plant. The subtitle was: *A ray of hope*.

'How beautiful,' she whispered.

'Mhm.' Damian took her in his arms. 'Let's go to bed, Princess, you're getting cold.'

# 17

'Damian!' No answer. Charlie threw a quick look into the living-room, then concentrated back on the task at hand. They were supposed to be at Damian's brother's place around six. It was already after five, and she had still not decided on what to wear. Standing in front of the full-body mirror opposite their bed, she filed through her wardrobe in growing desperation. Woollen pullovers, wide sweaters, old jeans and leggings, socks and hiking boots - all her clothes were comfortable and fun to wear, but none of them qualified for a Christmas dinner in a posh London suburb. Damn.

'Damian, I need your help!' Still no answer. Where the hell was he?

Her phone went off. She threw a look at the display. Blake. Oh no. She let her voicemail take the call. She wasn't in the mood to be honeyed just now.

At last, she heard footsteps in the hall. Strolling leisurely over the parquet. Charlie peered out from behind the open wardrobe door. 'There you are.'

'I am heeding your call, Princess.' Damian placed a kiss on her nose and said: 'How can I be of help?'

'I have nothing to wear.' She thumped down on the bed in desperation. 'Your family will think I'm a pauper.'

Bobby compassionately licked her naked ankles.

Damian stared into the closet. 'What do you mean, you have nothing to wear? The closet's full of clothes!'

Charlie held up her hand. 'Stop! This feels like a scene out of a cheesy old novel. Of course I have things to wear. Comfortable clothes. Clothes that I feel good in. But nothing that I can wear on Christmas Eve.'

'If you feel good in them, you can wear them. Easy as that. We're not going to the Queen's Palace. It's only my brothers, you know. Why don't you wear ...' he rummaged through the closet, '... this.' He held up a soft blue and white pullover. 'That one looks great on you. And it's your favourite colour, too,' he added conspiratorially.

'What do you mean, favourite colour? I don't know. That one's at least four years old. My granny knitted it for me, and she died the year after I passed my GCSEs.'

'Oh, it's that old? Then you cannot wear it, of course. What do you reckon? Can we still give it into the collection of old clothes, or will its age offend the people in the Third World?'

Charlie shot him an I-can-take-the-piss-myself-thank-you look, and pulled the pullover over her head. 'Actually, I love that pullover. I just thought ...'

'... that you needed a long robe to be allowed into the Winter Palace?' Damian finished her sentence.

'So you think I can wear jeans, too?'

'I don't know if *you* can,' he said, 'but you can be damn sure that I will.'

He pointed to the pants she had been wearing that afternoon. 'Put those on. Your ass looks great in them.'

Charlie put her tongue out at him and crammed herself into the jeans. 'How about my hair? Long, ponytail, braided ...'

'Military cut. Definitely.' He nodded gravely.

A hiking boot flew in his direction. He ducked, and the boot landed with a thud inside the wardrobe. Bobby's ears propped up to high alert: maybe she'd also throw something for him to fetch. He was definitely better at this than his master.

'Help, she's gone bonkers.' Damian hid behind the closet door.

'You just hide,' said Charlie unimpressed, 'you can hide, but you can't run.'

'Wasn't that the other way round?' he asked, and peeped out.

The second boot followed the first. Damian ducked back into hiding. 'I'm being mistreated,' he complained, and rubbed a nonexistent bump on his forehead. 'I will seek shelter at the Association of Beaten Boyfriends, first chance I get.'

'What if I make sure you don't get a chance?' asked Charlie with a honey-sweet voice.

'You'll fall asleep eventually.'

'Not before I've tied you to the bed.'

'Oh no!'

'Hands and feet.'

'Help!'

'Gagged, too.'

'Arrggghhh!' Damian fled to the door, but Charlie was quicker. She grabbed him around the waist and held tight. Going down on his knees, he groped helplessly for the doorknob. Too late. She roughly tore his shirt out of his belt. Naked male flesh. Mmmuarghhh!

'Someone help me, pleeeease!'

Bobby circled around them, yapping with glee. Playing rape was so much fun. Almost as much as catch the cookie.

After a quick quickie (Charlie swore she had counted the seconds and it had taken Damian only sixty-three seconds to come. He in turn swore he could have come even faster, but her blowjob just felt so damn good, so he had concentrated very sharply on something else. Charlie demanded to know what he had thought of, and when he proudly announced that he had been thinking of the pan with spaghetti-sauce that still awaited washing in the kitchen sink, she had been speechless. He was thinking of dirty dishes while she rubbed her mouth bloody on his penis? Her fists took a gruesome revenge on his body.) So after said quickie and the ensuing fight, Charlie, Damian and Bobby crammed themselves into a taxi and headed west towards Jekyll's Alter Ego Park.

'I haven't done anything with my hair,' Charlie noted matter-of-factly.

Damian looked at her. 'You could hide it under your scarf,' he proposed.

'I haven't put on any make-up, either.'

'You own make-up?' he asked disbelievingly. 'You never wear make-up.'

'I think I look better without,' she admitted.

'You do,' he agreed.

'You've never seen me with make-up.'

He grinned. 'I'm a psychic.'

The conversation died. The cab was making good speed on the A40, passing along golf courses, quiet residential areas and bustling high streets. Charlie watched the last-minute Christmas shoppers hustling in and out of shops. They didn't seem to have picked up on the spirit of Christmas yet.

*In every shop, in every store*
*They fight and battle as they can*
*With tearful eyes the Gods deplore*
*Man's inhumanity to Man*

Charlie decided that she was definitely getting better at rhyming. That quatrain could easily pass for a famous quote. A genuine Charlie, as Blake would say. Hm, but thinking of Christmas presents ...

Charlie turned to Damian: 'Are you sure it will be alright?'

'Of course.'

'You don't even know what I'm talking about.'

'You are wondering whether my brother will appreciate your ass in these pants.'

'No! I'm thinking of the Christmas presents. They invite me to dinner and I don't even buy them presents.'

'I told you, the presents I bought will be from us both,' explained Damian. 'You only got invited two days ago. And you don't even know them. Don't worry. They don't expect anything. Well, maybe Elsa will, but she's a spoilt bitch anyway, and I'm sure that Gerry ...'

Damian's voice droned on, but Charlie wasn't listening. All she could think of were two names: Elsa and Gerry. No, that couldn't be. Of all the people in London ...

'Who is Elsa?' she finally managed.

'That's Gerry's daughter. Actually he has two girls: Elsa and Nicky. They ...'

Charlie closed her eyes. If she hadn't been absolutely sure that she had never told Damian of Gerald, she would have thought he was playing some sort of mean joke on her. But this could simply not be true. 'I think I'm being sick,' she moaned.

Damian gave her a worried look. 'Motion sickness?' he asked sympathetically.

'Look, I don't think I can go to this family party after all.'

'But we're almost there!'

The cab had left the A40 a while ago and was now cruising north through a quiet residential neighbourhood. Elegant family homes nestled in private parks behind high walls and watchful CCTV cameras. Charlie was feeling claustrophobic. She had to get out of this car. She grabbed the door-handle. Bobby's tail wriggled excitedly. At last, time to go for a walk. Seeing what she had in mind, Damian leant forward and told the driver to stop. With shaking hands, she opened the door and climbed out onto the sidewalk. She took several deep breaths of cool night air. Her thoughts raced. What should she do? What *could* she do? One thing was clear, she couldn't face Gerald. If he was Damian's brother (and by now she was pretty damn sure that he was), she couldn't just intrude on his family. Another thought crossed her mind, and hot blood shot into her face, while ice-cold showers ran down her spine: Gerald was Damian's omnipotent brother! He knew how she earned her money. And he would never allow his little brother to have a girlfriend who was a hooker. Charlie felt tears welling up in her eyes. Shit. What the hell should she do?

Damian put his hand on her shoulder. 'Are you ok, Princess?'

She didn't trust her voice to speak. She shook her head.

'Listen, Katie can give you a glass of water. And you can lie down if you want. That's no problem at all. They're nice people, you'll see.'

Damian took her arm and led her up the gravelled driveway to a house. Enjoying this unexpected bout of freedom, Bobby raced up and down the road, and darted sideways like a rabbit. With a sinking heart, Charlie realized that the cab had come to a halt right in front of Gerald's house. But maybe ... a glimmer of hope shone up. Maybe she was imagining things. After all, he had never called his brother Gerald ...

She grabbed his elbow. 'Your brother ... Gerry ... is that his real name?'

Damian looked at her, puzzled. 'Well, his name's Gerald, but everyone in the family ...'

Charlie almost screamed in frustration. Ok, this was it, she would not take another step. After all, this was Christmas Eve and not Good Friday, and she didn't feel at all like walking up to Calvary, thank you very much.

Feeling extremely foolish, she pleaded: 'I want to go home.'

Before Damian could answer, the front door opened. The blonde girl from Harrods peeped out, shouted: 'It's them alright,' and disappeared into the hallway. A nasal voice from further inside the house said: 'I told you I recognized that stupid dog's yap.'

Charlie stared in horror at the front door. The girl had left it slightly ajar, but not enough to make out any figures in the dark hall. Now a shadow moved behind it, bigger than the girl's. Slowly, the door creaked open.

Damian held her arm and said happily: 'Hey, Gerry. Here we are.'

Charlie felt the blood pump through her ears, like waves thundering against a rough seashore. If Damian hadn't held her, she would have turned and run. Or, more likely, she would have dropped dead and spared them all the shame.

Gerald looked as calm and spotless as ever. He had changed his usual dark business suit against a comfortable brown sweater and beige pants, and Charlie thought, quite irrationally, that the colour didn't suit him at all.

Two seconds ticked by. Gerald's face was a study in self-control. He stared at her, and slowly his expression changed into a welcoming smile. 'So you must be Damian's friend. Please, come in.' He opened the door wide and let them step into the hallway. Charlie stared hard at a quaint glass console, and tried to ignore his look that seemed to singe a hole into her back.

Damian called for Bobby, who didn't feel like giving up his bit of freedom just yet. 'Bobby, heel! Bobby!'

Gerald kept staring at her without saying a word. Charlie clenched her jaws. She was convinced that she would faint any moment now. Maybe if she just gave in to the feeling and let herself drop down on the floor? She might be lucky and die ...

Damian pushed Bobby through the entrance door. 'He's been chasing imaginary cats, the little rascal,' he laughed. Then he noticed her face. 'Oh damn, Princess, you're all pale. Come here, I'll take your coat and you can go into ...'

Turning around to let Damian take her coat, Charlie found herself face to face with the second figure that had emerged from the sitting room.

'There you a... Charlie, honey, what are *you* doing here?' screamed a voice that had probably been cluttering her answering machine during the last hour.

Charlie gagged.

'You know each other?' Damian sounded genuinely puzzled.

'Uh, well, uhm, actually, *yes*! She's your girlfriend, right? Charlie, yes, a wonderful name, so very rare. Uhm, goes to reason. So, yes, we do know each other, she, uhm, admires my art.'

Now both Gerald and Damian stared at her. Like needles and

pins. Quite irrationally, she had that old sixties hit in her head. Needles and pins'uh. She had never understood why there was this 'uh' at the end of the line. But somehow it made the charm of the song. Who knows, *Needles and Pins* might never have become a hit, if it hadn't been for those millions of people wondering why there was this 'uh' after pins ...

'You've seen Blake's sculptures?' asked Damian, dumbfounded.

She tried a weak smile. As it threatened to turn into a lip quivering, she quickly resumed her former close-to-death expression.

Quite unexpectedly, Damian got the don't-ask-stupid-questions hint. 'She doesn't feel well,' he explained, and led her past Blake into the sitting room. Nicky and Elsa lounged on two cream-coloured couches. On the third couch, a young man busied himself with ruffling Bobby's coat. A serene calm came over Charlie. She suddenly realized that Fate could shove and push you down only so far. At one point, you just lie there and laugh into Her face. No matter how much more She dishes out, you can just let Her do Her thing and need not worry. Down is down, and the basement is sure to stop the falling elevator.

Blake pushed past her and made a huge gesture into the room. 'Uhm, Damian, Charlie, this is my new boyfriend, Ned. Ned, meet my brother Damian and Charlie, whom you don't know yet.'

Damian was naive enough to swallow this. 'Hi, Ned,' he chimed merrily. He even added: 'Merry Christmas.'

Charlie felt a nervous laugh bubbling up in her throat. She had to sit down. As neither Elsa nor Nicky seemed inclined to make room for the newcomers, she dropped down next to Ned.

Gerald's wife, whom she recognized from Harrods as well, entered the room, balancing a tray of glasses. She sat them down on the low tea table and gave Charlie and Damian a hearty smile. 'Hello, you two. So, Damian, this is your girlfriend. Welcome to our home.' She eyed Charlie, worried. 'You look a bit pale, girl.'

'She feels sick because of the cab,' Damian hastened to explain.

'Poor love. Do you want a glass of coke, maybe? The sugar will help you get on your feet again.'

Charlie nodded gratefully.

Blake thumped down next to her and patted her knee. 'You'll be alright, honey,' he promised ominously.

Charlie didn't know where to look. Damian was still staring at her with a worried look. Gerald was arguing with his daughters to sit properly on the couch. And Ned had decided to live according to the adage that he who does not say a word, will not say anything wrong.

Bobby jumped onto her lap. Grateful for his unconditional love, she ruffled his coat. Damian smiled at her.

As far as Charlie was concerned, this evening might easily have run under the heading *Nightmare Before Christmas*. Katie was admittedly a very pleasant host. Realizing that Charlie wasn't interested in classical music, she engaged her into a conversation about musicals. Charlie admitted that she had always been dreaming of seeing *The Phantom of the Opera*, but had not yet found the time to do so. Katie recommended the play, as well as *Les Misérables*. Then Charlie mentioned Agatha Christie's *Mousetrap*, which she had also been wanting to see for a while. Katie teased her about the most unexpected ending which she, as everyone else who had read or seen the play, had sworn not to reveal.

Damian didn't say much. He looked lost in thoughts, and from time to time, his hands fretted nervously with his clothes. Charlie was sure that he shot more than one inquisitive look from Blake to her. He was probably wondering what sort of a relationship the two of them had.

Blake, as expected, was performing his usual one-man show. Sipping enormous quantities of blackcurrant liqueur (Charlie secretly wondered how his pancreas managed to produce enough insulin to neutralize these vast amounts of sugar), he told them about his newest art phase. It was, he proudly announced, his anal phase. A time to produce rings and things in the shape of the human rectum. Blissfully oblivious to Elsa and Nicky's childish giggling, he moulded the air in front of him into tiny undulating sphincters, inflating and constricting with every move of his carefully manicured fingers. Gerald was listening politely. He didn't seem to mind that his daughters heard their uncle's thinly veiled sexual fantasies. Maybe he would lie in bed later on, imagining how he spanked them for listening to Blake's perversities. Naughty - little - girl. Charlie took another sip of her coke.

'I especially like *The Music of the Night*,' said Katie. 'It's a very beautiful song, full of feeling and emotions. I have the original cast recording on CD, I can lend it to you, if you would like to listen to it.'

Charlie opened her mouth to reply, when she heard from three sides at once:

'Nicky, will you please sit straight, people can see your underwear.'

'Ned has just come back from Paris. Paris - la ville de l'amour. The Eiffel Tower, such a sensual sex-symbol ...'

'Uhm, feeling any better yet, Princess?'

What a charming evening. A true Winter Tale.

She smiled pleasantly at Katie. 'Thank you, that is very kind of you.'

'... and the Bois de Boulogne, such an interesting place. It has a very cosmopolitan feel to it.'

'Unlike London, you mean?' Ah, Gerald, ever the nationalistic Englishman.

'If you'll excuse me, I shall have a look at our dinner.' Katie shot her husband an intense glance and smiled at her guests. 'I will be right back.'

The dinner, prepared by a cook who had been hired for the occasion, was excellent. First they were offered delicate little bread slices with molten cheese and tomatoes on them. Next came an exquisitely arranged piece of salmon, decorated with minced vegetables, chives and parsley. After that, they ate a delicious soup, a sort of chicken broth with pieces of meat and peas in it. Charlie was wondering how many more dishes this cook had in store, when the maid brought in the main course: a Christmas turkey, generously stuffed and most appetizingly roasted. Charlie had been worrying that she might not be able to eat much more, but when she saw this turkey, her stomach obediently inflated to twice its usual size.

'I'll gain at least five pounds tonight,' she laughed.

Blake gave her a conspiratorial wink.

Damian caught the wink and almost choked on his wine.

Nicky picked her nose, bored.

Elsa gave Charlie the once over, assessing how five additional pounds would look on her.

Gerald eyed his daughter, seemingly assessing much the same thing.

Katie watched her husband.

Ned's eyes went from one member of the Winter family to the other.

Charlie concentrated on her turkey.

After dinner, the family assembled around the Christmas tree, where a colourful heap of presents awaited opening. Gerald insisted that Nicky and Elsa play a duet on the piano, and after much sulking and sighing, the girls finally obliged. Charlie had to admit that their performance sounded very professional, at least to her untrained ear. She had never got any further than a single-finger *Jingle Bells* performance, in which enthusiasm made up for lack of talent and musical training.

Then it was time to open the presents.

'This is for you, Princess.' Damian handed her a tiny package, wrapped in baby-blue silk. Charlie took it gingerly and undid the wrapping. Beneath it appeared a delicate little box, of the kind that jewellers use.

Charlie looked up at him.

Damian beamed like a leaking reactor. 'Come on, open up.'

With a beating heart, she clicked the lid open. Inside lay a pair of finely wrought silver earrings, each with a tiny blue sapphire. Charlie's heart melted. He was such a darling.

Damian put his hand over hers. 'They're your favourite colour. Sky blue. Almost as beautiful as your eyes. Merry Christmas, Princess.'

He took her in his arms and gave her a long, warm kiss on the mouth. Charlie closed her eyes. She wanted to relish this moment, savour every second of it. If tomorrow Gerald persuaded his little brother that she was no good for him, that he should throw her out, cast her aside like an untouchable, she would still have these memories. Damian's warm breath in her ear, his soft cheek against her mouth, his curls playing in her eyes. A magic moment.

Behind their back, Nicky played air-fiddle and rolled her eyes theatrically. Elsa grinned and mouthed: 'Pathetic.'

Bobby was beyond himself with joy when Charlie opened his Christmas present. He insisted on tasting the biscuits on the spot, and gave his approval with several happy barks. Damian was so touched when he unpacked his mug, that his active vocabulary reduced itself on the spot to the phoneme /m/ and its many allophones. Sweet.

Then the rest of the presents were distributed. Blake generously bestowed his collection of fine arts on his family members. Vases and book-holders for the adults, and two finely chiselled rings for the girls. Much to Charlie's surprise, he had the decency not to mention their anal connotation again. Instead, he ceremoniously handed them their presents and declared, 'Bagues d'amour, in love toujours.'

Elsa eyed her ring sceptically. It displayed an unmistakable similarity to Frodo's ring in Tolkien's novel, but the beauty of the incisions were lost on her. 'I don't do French,' she said aloof, and added quickly: 'in school.'

Freud would have had a field day with this family.

'Oh, but I'm sure you do, honey,' moaned Blake, his voice as sticky-sweet as cotton candy. Gerald shot him a warning glance. Blake grinned.

'I never liked French, either,' Damian hurried to her rescue.

Elsa gave him a contemptuous look. 'Of course you didn't,' she sneered. 'It's hard enough to try and get your mother tongue right, huh?'

Damian's face turned crimson red. Charlie calmly wished for the arrogant little bitch to transform into a frog, on the spot. She would gladly have overcome her aversion against frog legs this once. Mmmh, yummy little legs, stewed in garlic and pepper. Apparently frogs were still alive when they had their legs pulled out. No, that would be too cruel. In Elsa's case, the little bugger would simply be roasted alive in the pan. A slow, painful death.

Blake was watching his niece thoughtfully. When she finally averted her eyes, he leaned forward and frowned. 'Is that a zit on your nose, honey?' he cried. 'Oh my, what a canker. Ah, but don't worry, it doesn't really disfigure you too much.'

Elsa shot him a look of such hatred, that he couldn't help grinning. She snorted like an enraged bull and dashed out of the room.

Blake watched her exit with candid astonishment. 'Oops. Did I say something wrong?'

Nicky hissed: 'Asshole,' and hurried after her sister.

Blake shook his head, bemused. 'Ah, such nasty language, tststs. You should teach your girls some manners, Gerry.'

Gerald nursed his brandy. 'Maybe I should,' he murmured into the glass.

Charlie had a surreptitious glance at her watch and sighed. Not even eleven. Bobby licked her boot in sympathy.

# 18

'Brr, it's cold.'

Funny, how we always resort to talking about the weather when situations become too awkward. Your brother has brought down five people while running amok at work? - Mention the sun that burns your eyes. Your husband announces that he will trade you in for a cute twenty-year-old piece of ass? - Whine about the continuous rain or that terrible draught (whichever fits best). Your boyfriend has just found out that his gay brother has probably paid you for sex? - Talk about the cold December air.

'Yep. I wonder when we will get the first snow.'

How reassuring, Damian was adhering to the same principle. Your girlfriend has witnessed your entire family making complete fools of themselves? - Talk about the snow. Note: this works especially well when your family name correlates with the season.

'I'm glad when we're home.'

Damian hesitantly reached for her hand. Outside, the city lights sped by. London by night. How serene the city looked, when you drove through it in a cab.

He put his head on her shoulder and placed a kiss into the soft wool of her pullover. His hair smelled of fruit shampoo. Mango and kiwi. 'I love you,' he whispered.

Charlie squeezed his hand. 'I love you, too.'

Ten minutes later, Damian locked the door of their apartment behind them. Bobby ran circles around them. Charlie correctly interpreted this as his cookiemaker dance and provided the goodies. Soon after, a happy pup retired to his night basket behind the yucca.

Looking out at the deserted street, she felt Damian stepping up behind her. He slung his arms around her and hugged her tight. 'Wanna go to bed, Princess?' he murmured into her neck.

She nodded. It was so much easier to talk with the lights out.

After they had brushed their teeth, rid themselves of the better part of the Christmas dinner, and undressed, Charlie and Damian snuggled up in bed. Damian shamelessly rubbed his icy toes against her legs. Charlie didn't mind. Her body was so numb with cold that she couldn't even feel it. Besides, she couldn't really complain, as she had her cold fingers firmly tucked under his warm back. Talk about mutual abuse in a partnership.

'You're cold,' Damian pointed out.

'So are you,' she countered.

'I want a warm girlfriend.'

'Then go out and find yourself one.'

'No.'

'Why?'

'It's too cold.'

They both laughed and huddled closer.

'How about we have sex,' proposed Charlie.

'Great idea.'

They started kissing, bestowing soft, tentative caresses on each other's skin. Charlie closed her eyes and concentrated on the tiny waves of electric current tingling through each stimulated nerve ending.

Vibrations release energy. Energy creates heat. Thus sex keeps you warm. Basic physics. Also works with your fingers, by the way.

Damian wedged his leg between her knees and moaned. Charlie's hips started to work up a steady rhythm against his thigh. Her teeth grazed his earlobe, kneading the soft flesh into little balls of pleasure. With a gasp, Damian pressed closer. She slung her legs around his hips and rolled on top of him. Her lips moaned into his neck, her breasts rubbed against his chest, her hips beat their rhythmic tattoo against his belly. She grabbed his hair with both hands and moved up and down on his body. Mmmh. Now *that* felt really good ...

Damian growled happily. 'I love our sex.'

'Me too.'

'I could fuck you ten times a day.'

'Me too.'

'Oh damn.'

Charlie laughed. 'Don't promise what you can't keep,' she teased him, 'because I won't say no.'

'Help, my girlfriend is a nymaphoniac!'

'A nymphomaniac.'

'That too. She's sex crazy.'

'I am? Shit.' Charlie sounded concerned. 'Do you think there's something we can do about it?'

'I don't know. I hope not.'

Charlie giggled and nuzzled into his neck. 'I'm afraid your brother doesn't like me too much.'

'Gerry? Of course he likes you.'

'What if he doesn't?'

'What makes you think he doesn't?'

'I asked first!'

'He likes you. And if he doesn't, he can go and suck what you just sucked.'

'Your earlobe?'

'Yeah, that too.'

They both laughed and Damian rolled over, presenting her his backside. She huddled closer into their preferred feel-good position.

'So, do you like his art?' he asked his night dresser.

'Whose?' she asked his back. 'Blake's?'

'Mhm.'

'It's ... special,' she answered his left shoulder, 'but yes, I like it. It's funny, somehow.'

'Yeah, it is, huh?' Damian still stared at the dresser. 'Practical, too. He made me a glowing dick for Easter. Said I could use it as a bedside light.'

'And you've never used it?'

'Yeah, I have.'

Charlie was quiet. The forbidden drawer. 'But you don't like it anymore?' she finally asked.

'I didn't want you to see it,' he admitted to his dresser.

'Because you thought I would be shocked?'

'No, I didn't really think you would be shocked. I thought you would think I was ...' He hesitated. '... you know,' he finally concluded.

'... into dicks?' she helped him along.

'Mhm.'

'Why would I think that? It's just a present from your brother. It doesn't say anything about you.'

'Yeah, but I thought you might be disgusted if you thought that I was ...'

'... into dicks?'

'Mhm.'

'Damian: we have great sex. You're a wonderful lover. I know you're not gay.'

'Because I'm not.'

'I know.'

For a while, they lay together in silence. Charlie nibbled on Damian's shoulder.

'He's got such an engaging laugh, huh?' he started anew.

'Blake? Mhm.'

'Makes you feel good.'

'Yes.'

'And such roving hands.'

'Look, Damian, I'm sorry. I didn't know he was your brother. I ...' Charlie stopped short. She suddenly had the feeling that Damian was not really trying to find out if she had had sex with

Blake. He was trying to tell her something. She bit her lip and took a deep breath. 'Yes, he's got lovely hands.'

'They're very tender, even when they push you down.'

Charlie closed her eyes. Damn, she was supposed to be shocked now. Or disgusted. Instead, she felt herself getting wet. 'Yes, they are. Very gentle.'

They were both quiet. Damian seemed to fight an inner conflict.

Charlie decided to make it easy on him. 'And his cum tastes kinda sweet, what with all that blackcurrant liqueur he's washing down.' When Damian didn't reply, she added softly: 'Don't you think?'

She could feel him hold his breath. Five seconds ticked by.

'Yes,' he finally said, and slowly exhaled.

Charlie gently brushed a lock behind his ear. The skin behind his earlobe felt so soft. 'Wanna sleep?' she asked.

'No.'

'Wanna tell me your story?'

'Yes.'

For a long time, no one said a word. Charlie thought he had fallen asleep, when Damian finally began to speak.

'It was two days after my parents' death. It was September, and I had just got back to Lambert's Oak, settling down for a new school year. One afternoon, I remember it was after a particularly terrible English class ... our teacher, Mr Williams, had handed us our essays back. When he got to my desk, he stopped and just looked at me. His look was so full of scorn that I cringed. And then he started reading my essay aloud, pronouncing every single spelling mistake I had made. It sounded like some foreigner trying to speak English. Utterly silly. The others howled with laughter. He read through the whole text - three entire pages. When he had finished, some of the boys were rolling on the floor, laughing.'

Charlie's heart hammered in her chest. She wished that sadistic asshole a very slow and painful death. She suddenly realized that she was grabbing the sheet so tight that her knuckles stood out white. She relaxed her grip and nuzzled closer against Damian's back. 'That man is an asshole,' she declared matter-of-factly, 'a stupid, mean asshole, and so are your schoolmates. But you don't have to be around them anymore. Hm?'

Damian nodded. 'Anyway,' he continued, 'after class, I found Gerry standing in the hallway. He looked awful. Tired and grey in the face. Back then he was twenty-five, he and Katie had just married and they were expecting their first baby. He wouldn't say why he was there, just insisted that we go to my room. And there he told me that our parents had died that morning. He said: 'There was a car accident. A truck ran into father's car. They're both dead.' Just like that. Then he went on saying that I would of course stay at Lambert's Oak, that he would take care of everything, that I need not worry. Not worry! He'd just told me that our parents were both dead! That my mum was dead! And then he said I should not worry. I hated him so much for that, for saying that I should not worry ...'

Damian's voice had become ever more unsteady and incomprehensible. Finally, it trailed off, and Charlie felt his shoulders tremble with quiet sobs. She gently stroked his back. She felt so sorry for him. She didn't understand what all this had to do with Blake, but she knew better than to ask. Whatever he had to tell her, she would listen.

'Back then, I didn't understand how difficult it all was for Gerry. He had only been working in the company for a very short time, and now he had to make all the important decisions. If it hadn't been for him, the company lawyers probably would have grabbed the biggest part of the cake, and Winter Towers would have been sold off to the highest bidder. Without me or Blake ever seeing any money for it, I guess. But back then, I didn't understand this. All I knew was that Gerry behaved cold and business-like, and that I hated him for it. I felt so alone. I simply turned my back on him and waited for him to leave. Then I cried for two whole days. I refused to leave my room, I didn't go down for classes or meals. I just stayed in bed and cried, and I guess I just waited for him to come.'

'Blake?'

'Mhm. I was sure he would come. He had never had a good relationship with my father. Dad disapproved of everything he was doing - the fact that he refused to go to university, that he flaunted his relationships with men, that he wanted to be an artist and wasn't interested in working in the company. In the end, Blake simply stopped coming home. But we still saw each other. He had always been my best friend.'

'That's wonderful, to have such a close relationship with your brother. So after two days, he came to your school?'

'Mhm. When he knocked at my door, I let him in and got back to bed. All the others had tried to get me out of bed. The prefect, the nurse, some classmates, the head of house teacher, the rector. They'd all stood before my bed and tried to reason with me.'

'And Blake didn't?'

'No. He simply climbed into the bed and hugged me.'

They were both quiet. After a while, Charlie asked: 'And then you made love?'

'You know, I'd never made love before.'

'Well, you were only sixteen. So it just happened?'

Damian nodded. 'Mhm. We hugged and cuddled, and then he started stroking me. Very softly, very gently. I wasn't at all afraid. I knew he wouldn't hurt me.'

Charlie thought back at her own sexual encounters with Blake. He hadn't struck her as particularly sensitive to other people's needs.

Damian must have guessed what she was thinking, because he added: 'I know Blake often comes across as selfish and focused on his own pleasure. But he can also be sensitive and caring. And he was, that day.'

'I believe you.'

Damian was quiet. After a while, he asked: 'How old were you when you first had sex?'

Charlie thought back at a certain embarrassing scene behind the Swallop Youth Centre's football field. But this situation called for honesty and she decided not to lie about it. 'I was fifteen.'

'Wow, that's pretty young, huh?'

'Mhm. It wasn't that great, though,' she admitted. 'I didn't really know what to do, and he didn't, either. So it was more a series of painful embarrassments, rather than real sex.' She laughed self-consciously.

Damian nodded thoughtfully. 'I can imagine. I was thirteen,' he added.

Charlie was puzzled. 'Thirteen? I thought Blake had been the first?'

'Well yes, as far as making love goes, he was.'

Charlie felt that Damian was trying to tell her something important. Something that he might not ever have told anyone before. She put her hand on his arm and held him fast. His skin felt very cold. She pulled the blanket higher. 'But there was someone else?' she helped him on.

'Mhm. You know, there's a kind of ritual at Lambert's Oak.'

Charlie drew in a sharp breath. She knew what was coming now.

'Every boy had to go through it. It was just the usual initiation humiliation. You know, dunking your head into cold water until you turn blue in the face, making you wear girl's clothes, taking turns fucking you ...'

Again, his voice trailed off. Charlie hugged him very tight. She wished all public schools and their cruel rituals to Hell.

'Do you still love me?' he murmured.

Charlie wasn't sure if she had heard correctly. 'Whether I still love you? Baby, I've never loved you more. I just wish I could kill those bastards that did that to you.'

'The ritual wasn't that bad, you know. It didn't even really come as a shock, as Blake had been hinting at it for years. But Dad always made him shut up. I remember he once beat the shit out of him for saying that Lambert's Oak was a meeting place for gay fuckers.'

Charlie grinned. That was Blake alright. His sexual predilections might be fairly bent, but as far as speaking his mind went, he was straight as an arrow. Another thought crossed her mind: if all new students had to go through that ritual, Gerald had suffered the abuse as well. She couldn't imagine strong, proud Gerald to harbour such shameful memories.

'So you think your brothers had the same experience?'

'The ritual, you mean? Oh yeah. Every new boy had to go through it.'

Charlie knew that she would never again be able to look a surgeon, lawyer, company director or other member of the High Snobiety in the eye without imagining them on their knees, cheeks blazing with shame and humiliation.

'Couldn't they have helped you?'

'No, they were already out of school when I got there. Besides, there was nothing they could have done.'

Charlie was quiet.

'But the ritual wasn't really that bad.'

So he had said before. Charlie waited quietly for him to tell her what *was* that bad.

'It was more the things they did later on,' he murmured into the linen.

'What did they do, baby?' Charlie softly kissed his neck. She felt so much tenderness for him, she could have cried.

'There was this sort of tradition that some of the elder boys had pages,' explained Damian to his pillow. 'First-years, that were supposed to do stuff for them. Especially sexual stuff.'

Charlie could feel his neck burn with shame. 'I'm so sorry, baby,' she said quietly.

'Me too.'

'I love you.'

'I'm so happy about that.'

Charlie gave him a kiss on his earlobe. 'What do you think? Should we put Blake's bedside light to use again?'

She felt Damian smile. He nodded and reached into his drawer. The shape of the thing he took out would have made any porn star proud. Damian plugged it into the socket and turned the light on. The penis gave off a soft, rosy glow.

Charlie nodded approvingly. 'Rose-coloured. Very cute.'

'It's made of saltstone. That's a material that keeps the air around you clean.'

'Like an air freshener? How practical.'

Damian lay back down. Charlie turned her back to him and reached over her shoulder to grab his arm and pull him closer. Feel-good position.

'Wasn't the evening too horrible for you?' Damian asked into her neck.

No, apart from realizing that two of my customers are your brothers, Charlie thought. 'Your niece is a bitch, but the others seem to be alright,' she said.

'They liked you, too,' declared Damian, with unshaken faith in the good taste of his family. 'The coffee mug you gave me is so sweet. I'll use it every day, I swear. And it'll get a place of honour on the sideboard.'

'Under the kitchen window?'

'Mhm.'

'Right next to the phalaenopsis?' Charlie was proud of the new word she'd learnt yesterday. Damian had informed her that what she had so derogatively dismissed as a 'nice flower' was in fact a phalaenopsis, which had its place on the sideboard because it stood under a north window. And orchids liked north windows. For a guy who had problems keeping left and right apart and who refused to read words that had more than two syllables, that speech was quite amazing. Charlie had been very proud of her plantophile boyfriend.

'Right there,' he agreed. He nuzzled against her neck and asked sheepishly: 'So how do like your earrings?'

'I love them. They're the most beautiful present I ever got.'

'And the stones are your favourite colour, too,' he said.

'Yes, they're my favourite colour. Sky blue.'

Smiling happily, Damian was soon fast asleep.

# 19

'There's way too much information on this paper.' Damian stared defeated at the electricity bill in front of him.

'No, not really. There's plenty of things on it that you don't need to read. Let's tackle this logically: what do you think is the most important thing on this paper?'

Damian chewed on his lip while he thought that question through. 'The sum total at the bottom,' he finally spurted out.

'Correct, that's pretty important. And as you rightly pointed out, it's the number at the bottom. Here,' she tapped on a figure, 'that's the amount you have to pay to the company.'

'What company?' asked Damian.

'I see you're asking the right questions. Ok, so how do we find the name of the company who sent you the bill?'

'We ask Charlie.' Damian smiled boyishly at her. 'Look, Princess, I'm no good at this. I'm ...'

'I'm waiting. Hint: bigger letters might carry important messages.'

Damian sighed and turned his attention back to the bill. His finger traced the fat black letters in the centre of the page: 'E - le - tir - city.' He beamed up at her: 'It's the electricity bill.'

Charlie hugged him. 'Right, it's the electricity bill. For what month?'

'What month?' Damian was puzzled. 'For December, I guess.'

'Don't guess, read.'

His finger wandered over the page, tracing ever larger and more playful circles. 'It doesn't say,' he finally declared. 'Can we have a break now?'

'Damian, you're not trying!' Charlie grabbed the bill and pointed to a line. 'What does it say here?'

Damian gave the paper a quick glance. 'It says, Charlie is a tyrant.'

Charlie's hand sank down. 'I thought you wanted to do the mail yourself,' she said unhappily.

'I did. I just didn't expect it to be so ... difficult.'

'It's not difficult. You're just not used to it. I got news for you: the next electricity bill will look exactly the same, except maybe for the sum total at the bottom. And the one after that, too. So it's just a matter of familiarizing yourself with it.' She handed him a yellow marker. 'Tell you what: we'll highlight the relevant words on the bill, that way you'll find your way around more easily next time.'

Damian sighed and bent over the paper. He highlighted the sum at the bottom and the word *Electricity*. After a further careful analysis of the bill, he tapped on a date. 'Is that the month?' he asked hopefully.

Charlie felt so sorry for him. 'No, baby, that's the date on which the bill was issued. The month for which we have to pay is here.'

She pointed to a note on the left.

'No - env - der,' spelled Damian. He looked up. 'It's the bill for November.'

'Right. You can highlight that as well. And what do we have to do now?'

'Have tea?' he suggested.

'No! We have to pay the bill.' Charlie motioned to the pile of transfer forms that lay in front of them. 'Your brother gave you those so that you can pay the bills yourself. But you have to pay them, otherwise you'll get a reminder. And that means, yet more things to read,' she threatened, and gave him a wink.

Damian took a form and seized his pen. His jaw was set, his stare determined. He was ready to tackle the task.

'First we fill in the sum. Here.' Charlie waited until he had copied the sum in large, careful figures into the correct box. 'Very good. Now we look for the company name.'

When Damian had filled in each case, he looked sceptically at the form. 'I'll never remember that. How about I copy everything onto a second form and keep that one as a reference?'

'That's a great idea, baby.' Charlie hugged him.

When the copy was safely tucked onto the bill and the transfer form stowed away in an envelope, Damian leant back on his chair and yawned. 'This is so much work. I didn't expect it to take so long. We've been sitting here for half an hour, and we've only done one single bill.'

'Yes, but that was the most difficult one. The others will be easier, you'll see. Let's see what else we've received.'

Damian looked at the three remaining items that had been in the mail on Wednesday and Thursday. Two more envelopes and a leaflet. He reached for the nearest envelope. It turned out to contain a bank account statement.

'What's this?' he asked Charlie.

'That,' she announced, 'is a bank account statement.'

'Uhuh.'

'It tells you what transactions you have made, respectively your brother has made for you. The next statement you get will show that you have paid your electricity bill. So let's see what your brother has paid over the last month.'

They read the statement together. The phone bill had been paid, Damian's visa card had been debited and Gerald had wired 2000 £ onto the account. When Charlie saw the figure at the bottom of the statement, she swallowed hard. 'Why on earth do you have that much money in a normal bank account? Your brother should have put some of that into a savings account.'

Damian looked puzzled. 'That's for my everyday expenses,' he explained. 'Gerry puts money in it, so that I always have enough when I want to buy something.'

'What a life you have.' Charlie sighed enviously. 'Anyway, we'll put that statement away into a separate folder. One folder for the bills, and one for your bank account statements. Next item.'

Damian reached for the leaflet.

'Ah, that one's easy,' said Charlie encouragingly. 'That's junk.'

'Junk?' Puzzled, Damian looked towards the kitchen door.

'No, not that sort of junk. It's junk mail. Here's something useful for you to remember: colourful leaflets that come without an envelope are most probably advertisements and can be discarded right away.'

'Oh really?' He stared at the paper in front of him. It was a leaflet announcing a children's Christmas fair in Bloomsbury Hall. But more importantly, it was very colourful. 'That's junk,' he declared.

Charlie nodded.

He hesitated. 'Can I simply throw it away?' he asked.

'Of course. That's what you do with junk, right? But maybe you want to know what it's about?'

'No,' said Damian, and the paper wandered onto the floor, much to Bobby's delight. Rather than just slouching around under the table, he decided to make himself useful as a canine shredder.

'Last item,' announced Damian enthusiastically, and reached for the remaining envelope. It contained a folded card. A colourful folded card.

'Stop!' cried Charlie, as he joyfully set about to rip it in two. 'What are you doing?'

'It's junk,' he defended himself. 'See: it's yellow with a cartoon on it.'

'Yes, but it came in an envelope,' countered Charlie.

'Damn, you're right.' Damian bit his lip and eyed the card wearily. 'It's probably not junk then, huh?'

'Maybe you should read what it says?' she offered.

He opened the card. It contained a short message, written in large, easy-to-read letters. 'Have fun,' spelled Damian, 'with your mail. Gerry.'

'It's a message from Gerry!' He beamed at her.

Charlie smiled. She would never have thought that Mr Mercedes could be so sensitive. 'You've just read your first private letter. Congratulations. And you've finished your mail for today. Congrats again.' She hugged him.

'Great. And now we can ...'

The first notes to *I was made for loving you, baby* interrupted him. Just an hour ago, Charlie had downloaded the Kiss song as new ringtone for her cell-phone.

'Paul Stanley's calling,' remarked Damian.

Charlie grabbed her phone. A look at the display: Caller unknown. Hm. 'Hello?'

'I need to see you.'

Fuck. 'Look, I'm just sorting through my bills with Damian,' she said and mouthed: 'Brother.'

Damian nodded and retired to the kitchen to make coffee.

'We'll meet in an hour in front of your library, ok?'

'No! I cannot ...'

'Yes, you can. See you there.' Gerald hung up.

Charlie stared at the phone, speechless. Who the fuck did he think he was? Her father? Arrogant asshole. As if she would come running, as soon as he snapped his fingers. Power hungry perv.

Damian came out of the kitchen, carrying two mugs and a box of biscuits. 'Tea-time.'

She smiled at him. 'I thought I smelled coffee.'

'Yes. We're having tea with coffee.'

'That makes sense.' She jumped on his neck and kissed him. 'I love you.'

'I love you too, Princess. So, your brother is in town?'

'Yes, he wants to see me in an hour. I don't feel at all like meeting him.'

'Have you invited him over?'

'No!' Charlie smiled nervously. 'No, he doesn't have much time, anyway. We'll meet downtown, for a quick chat. I won't be long, I promise.'

Damian gave her a peck on the cheek. 'You take all the time you want. In the meantime, I'll go walkies with Bobby.'

'Great idea.'

A faint beeping announced that coffee was ready. 'I'll fetch the coffee, so that we can have tea,' she declared, and sauntered off into the kitchen.

The black Mercedes stopped at the kerb. Charlie took a deep breath and opened the door. 'Hi.'

'Get in.'

Charlie obeyed, and the car set into motion. For the first half minute, no one spoke. Then Gerald said irritably: 'Put your seat belt on, will you?'

'Most victims of car accidents have their seat belt on, you know,' Charlie snapped back.

Gerald's face went rigid. He didn't reply. Feeling sorry for her outburst, Charlie fastened her seat belt.

After a ten-minute drive, Gerald parked the car in a quiet residential area. He turned the engine off and faced her. Oops. He looked very angry.

'Why did you want to see me?' asked Charlie. It didn't come out as self-assured as she would have liked. In fact, it sounded almost frightened. Not good. 'I didn't know he was your brother,' she added, more forcefully.

'I don't want you to see him again,' said Gerald quietly.

'What? Who do you think you are? I'm not taking orders from you. This isn't one of your little games, Gerald. And while we're at it, I think you've bossed Damian around long enough, too.'

Gerald grabbed her coat collar. His eyes were blazing angrily. Charlie suddenly realized that the street was deserted. No one around who would hear her scream. She reached for the doorhandle.

'Don't be silly, I won't hurt you,' said Gerald, and released his grip. 'I simply want us to discuss the situation.'

'What situation?' Charlie gave him a challenging look. 'The fact that you have been keeping Damian in total dependence for the last sixteen years? The fact that you have completely destroyed his self-confidence? Alright, let's discuss that.'

'You don't know what you're talking about.' Gerald sounded tired and weary. 'Do you think I was happy when I had to take over the family business? Do you think I rejoice putting in sixty hours a week most of the year? Certainly not. But someone has to do it. Blake isn't any help, and, let's be frank, Damian isn't, either.' The names seemed to trigger a new train of thought. 'You've fucked Blake as well, haven't you?'

'Watch your language, Gerald,' she warned him.

'Why should I? Because of some little cunt who has fucked herself through my whole family and probably the rest of London, as well? I don't think so.'

Charlie's cheeks were burning. 'You arrogant asshole.'

He slapped her on the cheek, hard. Charlie took a deep breath and successfully resisted the urge to cry out in pain. Her heart beat fast and painful against her ribs, but she managed to keep a cool outward appearance. 'You're just a sad old wanker, who gets off on beating little girls,' she said very calmly. 'I will leave your car now.'

'No!' Gerald grabbed her arm, but he was careful not to hurt her this time. 'I'm sorry I hit you. I apologize, ok? I shouldn't have done that. I have an offer for you.'

She was surprised. 'An offer?'

'I will wire ten thousand pounds into an account of your choice, if you leave my brother alone.'

Charlie didn't believe her ears. 'Are you crazy?' she finally managed.

'No, I'm not crazy. And there is no need to try and bargain. Ten thousand is my last offer.'

'You're a real scumbag, aren't you, *Gerry*?'

'In fact, I think I'm being very generous.'

'In fact, I think you're straight out bonkers. Do you really believe I can be bought?'

'Seeing that I have bought you on several occasions before, yes.' He put in the door security lock. 'You're not getting out before you have promised to leave Damian.'

She was beyond herself with rage. 'What?' Glaring angrily at him, she took a deep breath and settled back in the seat, arms folded on her chest. 'Ok. Fine. Let's sit it out. In a few hours at the latest, Damian will call and ask where I am. And I will tell him that his nutter of a brother is keeping me prisoner in his car.'

'Don't be silly. You don't want Damian to find out, either.'

'Find out what? That I had sex with you? No, not really. And do you know why? Because he loves you and admires you. I don't want him to find out what a crazy perv you are.'

'Now hold it, Charlie, I'm not that bad. You liked our games as well.' He moved closer, until his face was only an inch from hers, and stared at her with those intense hazel eyes of his. Damian's eyes. She could have kicked herself for not seeing the resemblance. Gerald was more broadly built and overall more imposing than his brother, but their faces bore many similar traits. His eyes still boring into hers, Gerald said softly: 'I made you come, didn't I?' His deep, velvety voice ran down her spine and flowed into her jeans, throbbing warm and steady against the fabric of her panties. Damn, she hated it that his voice had such an effect on her.

Satisfied with her reaction, he leant back and said coldly: 'I will not allow Damian to fall in love with a hooker.'

'I'm not a hooker,' she said. 'I've quit the job.'

He laughed mockingly. 'You don't seriously expect me to believe that, do you?'

'Of course I do. Because it's true. I've promised Damian.'

His eyes widened. 'You have *told* him that you have been working the streets?'

'Actually, he found out by himself. And he doesn't mind, because a) I'm not doing it anymore and b) we love each other and c) he isn't as narrow-minded and conceited as a certain brother of his. Can I now please leave your car?'

He ignored the request. 'I don't believe that you will stop doing what you do. It's too easy to make money that way.'

'Oh but you can believe it. I didn't want to spoil our last meeting for you, so I decided to tell you only after your skiing holiday. Speaking of which, shouldn't you be on your way to Switzerland?'

'Our plane is leaving tomorrow at eight,' he replied, thoughtfully. He gave her an inquiring look. 'So you didn't want to see me again?'

'Correct. Of course, now that I know you're Damian's brother, we will have to see each other from time to time. On family get-togethers,' she added sweetly.

Gerald was quiet. He seemed to have a hard time digesting the fact that he now had to look for someone else to play games with. It wouldn't be easy to find one as good as her. Charlie grinned inwardly. Too bad for him.

'If I find out that you're just after Damian's money ...' he started.

'Don't be silly. If I was after the Winter fortune, I could make a lot more money blackmailing you, then by moving in with Damian. Don't worry. I know you can turn off his money tap whenever you wish. I love Damian. Not because, but in spite of your money.'

He shook his head, as if she had just uttered a particularly silly sentence. 'We won't have any more of our games,' he declared.

'Ok, daddy.'

He gave her a stern look. 'I mean it.'

Charlie rolled her eyes, exasperated. 'I mean it, too. It's not as if it had been my idea in the first place.'

Gerald ignored this. 'I don't want Damian to be hurt.'

'Me neither. What Damian needs is a friend and partner, not a mother. He has had a father figure looming over him for far too long.'

'If you ever reveal the smallest thing about our ... games, I will make sure that you will never find a job in this city, nor in any other town in Great Britain.'

'No need to threaten me, I can keep a dirty little secret. Can I now please get out of the car?'

Gerald unlocked the security lock. 'Suit yourself.'

Downstairs, the elevator door opened and closed. They heard the low whir of the machinery as the cabin set slowly into motion.

Damian rubbed Bobby's coat. 'What do you think, old boy, will she tell us whom she has been with?'

Bobby looked at his master with attentive, intelligent eyes and wriggled his stiff little tail. *If you don't want to be lied to, then don't ask her. I never ask any questions. I'm just grateful for whatever attention I get.*

Damian sighed. 'You think I'm worrying too much, right?'

Bobby yapped in agreement and licked his master's nose.

The elevator door opened and Charlie stepped out, her face glowing red from the cold. 'Pewh, it's icy outside. Hi, baby. I'm sorry it got so late.' She threw her coat over the couch and crouched down next to Damian. 'Hello, Bobby.' Kiss on the nose. 'Hello, Damian.' Kiss on the nose. 'Brr, your nose is wet.'

'So's Bobby's and you didn't complain about that. He just gave me a kiss.'

'I see. My two men are smooching when I'm not around. Do I have reason to be jealous?'

'No. Bobby's part of the family, and you cannot be jealous of family members. Do I?'

Charlie unlaced her boots. 'Do you what? Have reason to be jealous?' She looked up into his eyes and said earnestly: 'No.'

Five minutes later, all three of them lay comfortably intertwined on the couch and were listening to Katie's *Phantom of the Opera* CD.

Christine pleaded softly *If you ever find a moment, spare a thought for me.*

'Blake called,' said Damian.

'Oh really?' Charlie propped her head up. 'What did he say?'

'He congratulated me on my courage. I don't know. The conversation was kinda surrealistic. He asked me whether I'd bought you off your pimp or whether I was hiding you from him. I wonder where he got that idea?'

Charlie stared at him open-mouthed. 'He told you I had a *pimp*? Wow, how very sensitive of our artist. Trust Blake to tell the world how I've been earning my money.'

'Actually, he didn't just spurt it out. He was very secretive about it all, almost like he was conducting a criminal investigation. Watson-style.' Damian massaged her toes and blew a kiss on each one of them. 'Asked me if I knew about your past. Whether you'd told me anything about "it". Made it sound like you were Mata Hari or something.'

They both laughed. Damian reached for her other foot.

'So, you told him?'

'I figured he knew anyway. I didn't have the heart to let him stew in his curiosity, so I told him that, actually, I'd been one of your punters.'

Charlie's head jerked up, making her foot kick out at the same time to keep her balance. '*What?*'

'Ow.' Damian rubbed his face. 'You jabbed your big toe into my nose, Princess.'

'I'm sorry, baby. But how could you say that to Blake? How did he react?'

'He thought it was fantastic. Sort of made his day, I guess. He rambled on about it being our social duty to use such services from time to time. I didn't really get what he meant by that. Anyway, he offered his help, in case your pimp was making problems.'

'How sweet of him. And so heroic. I didn't think he had it in him.'

'He hasn't. In fact, he stressed that his help could only involve non-violent acts, thank you very much. He also explicitly excluded gang-fights and stunts in the East End, him being an artist and all.'

Charlie nodded understandingly. 'Blake has a very low pain-threshold.'

'I see you know my brother.'

They both laughed. On the CD, the Phantom sang *And though you turn from me to glance behind, the Phantom of the Opera is there - inside your mind.*

Charlie shuddered with pleasure, and moved closer to Damian. She sang along with Christine: *'Those who have seen your face, draw back in fear ...'*

Damian pouted. 'I don't look that horrible, do I?'

She grinned and sang: *'I am the mask you wear, it's me they hear ...'*

'You cannot sing both Christine's and the Phantom's part,' he objected.

'Then sing along.' She nudged him in the ribs. *'Your spirit and my voice ...'*

*'My spirit and your voice ...'* he chimed in, half a second too late.

Charlie snuggled up in his arm, and together they brought the title song to a thunderous finale. Bobby retreated to his cot behind the yucca. As much as he loved his two masters, their mating howls couldn't be qualified as anything else than ear-shattering.

'He's invited us over for New Year's Eve,' Damian started anew, while the Phantom launched into his *Music of the Night.*

'That's nice of him. Did you accept?'

'I told him I would ask you first. Ned will be there, too. He is only driving back to Manchester on New Year's Day.'

'I think Ned is good for Blake,' said Charlie thoughtfully.

'Mhm. He deserves a boyfriend who is not only after his money.'

'Well, you know, somehow it's his own fault, though,' she said energetically and sat up. 'He's looking for love in all the wrong places. Pick-up bars, boys from the streets ... that's a sure recipe for heartache, if you ask me.'

As soon as the words were out, Charlie realized her error. Damian grinned good-naturedly at her. She bit her lip. 'I'm not after your money,' she mumbled.

'I know that, Princess.'

'How can you know?'

'Because I don't have any. I couldn't just go out and buy you a fancy sports car or a big apartment or some expensive piece of jewellery. Gerry's got his thumb on the family money, and he's making sure I don't spend too much of it. Not that I've ever tried,' he added hastily.

'You're lucky to have a brother like Gerald.'

'I know. I might have problems spelling my own name correctly, but I do know that without Gerry, Winter Towers would have gone downhill a long time ago. I'd probably be a bum on the streets by now. Without him.'

Charlie was quiet. She knew Damian was right. Her thoughts went back to her conversation with Gerald. Now she wished that they had parted on better terms. She shouldn't have called him a perv. It had surely hurt him, even though he had not let it show. And after all, there was nothing wrong with enacting a fantasy ...

She shook off these gloomy thoughts. 'Winter Towers. That's a very poetic name for a company. What is it trading in?'

'They're a consulting company, whatever that means. I never really understood what they are doing. Damian shrugged his shoulders.

'Hm. Sounds interesting.'

'You think so? Well, maybe for you, seeing that you study management.'

Suddenly he seemed to have an idea. 'Why don't you do your practical training at Winter Towers?' he asked excitedly.

Charlie laughed. 'It's not as easy as that. There are a lot more students waiting to do practical trainings than companies that are willing to train them. You need top connections to the business world to grab such an internship. Any internship. And unlike me, many students have families with connections. Talk about democracy here. I will be happy if some third-rate company agrees to take me on. Some sleazy businessman looking for one more worker to exploit. But a big company like Winter Towers? Forget it.'

'But you have connections, Princess.' Damian beamed at her. 'You have me.'

Charlie thought about it. Gerald would have a heart attack if Damian suggested this.

'I don't think ...' she began, but Damian interrupted her. 'No, seriously, Princess, I can talk to Gerry. In fact, I will do it, as soon as he gets back from Saas-Fee.'

There was no use trying to dissuade him. Gerald would come up with far better arguments than she ever could. She let the subject drop, and instead wriggled her toes as a polite reminder of his duties.

'Can I nibble at your toe?' asked Damian.

'Please do.' Charlie gracefully placed her foot into his outstretched hand and purred with pleasure when he gently grazed her skin with his teeth.

On the CD, the Phantom urged Christine to *Let the dream begin, let your darker side give in to the power of the music that I write - the power of the music of the night.*

Katie was right. This song was really very emotional. And the Phantom had such a sexy voice. Charlie sighed happily. 'I wish I could see that musical live.'

# 20

'I received a postcard,' Damian called out, when he opened his mailbox.

It was two days later, and they were setting out to bring Bobby to Blake. Charlie stood at the entrance door, keeping a lookout for their taxi. It should be arriving any moment now.

'Who is it from?' she asked, and tried to keep Bobby from dashing down the hallway.

'Uhm.' Damian squinted at the card, trying to decipher the handwriting. 'It says: Hello lil-tle Pi-rate ...'

'Pirate? Are you sure this card is for you?' Charlie picked Bobby up and walked over to him. Standing on tiptoe, she glanced curiously over his shoulder. Her eyes scrolled down to the signature. 'Damian! This card is addressed to me! It's from Paul.' She snatched the postcard from him.

Damian looked blank. 'Who is Paul?'

'Remember I told you about the guy whom I met after throwing a salad bowl at my employer? The one who's now living in Seattle?'

'Oh, right.' Damian's face lit up. 'I remember: your first punter.'

Charlie ignored this. 'He's wishing us both a Merry Christmas and a Happy New Year,' she declared. 'And he thinks he will be back in London by February.' As Bobby was struggling to be set free, she put him down on the floor. He happily skittered along the tiles, chasing imaginary cats and rabbits through the entrance hall.

'Great.' Damian smiled at her. 'Why is he calling you Pirate?'

'Oh, we went to see that movie, *Pirates of the Caribbean* ...'

'... with Keira Knightley.' Damian nodded knowingly.

'... with Johnny Depp and Orlando Bloom,' Charlie finished her sentence. 'I guess I got a bit excited about Orlando, so Paul started calling me his little Pirate ...'

'Hm. How come he has your new address?'

'I wrote him an e-mail, telling him that I'd be moving in with you. He's very happy for me. He's really a great guy.'

'Cool. Can't wait to meet this extraordinary bloke.' He peered over her head into the street. 'I think our taxi has arrived, Princess.'

Blake opened the front door in his pyjamas. He looked extremely tired.

'Did we wake you up?' asked Damian, astonished.

Blake uttered a non-committal 'uh' and rubbed the sleep out of his eyes. He motioned for them to come in and slouched back to the bed.

Charlie felt strange, standing beside Damian in Blake's apartment. When she had been here the last time, she hadn't known that Blake was Damian's brother.

'Where is Ned?' asked Damian, and looked searchingly around the room.

Blake waved his hand towards the bathroom. Ned emerged, dressed in one of Blake's bathrobes, white foam playing before his mouth. He has rabies, Charlie thought. If he bites us, we will all die a painful death. Bobby sniffed suspiciously at a container with sticky yellow liquid. She pulled him away and turned to Ned: 'We will be back around eleven. Can you please make sure that he won't lick or chew on any of this stuff?' She made a gesture encompassing the whole studio.

Ned nodded reassuringly and went back to the bathroom to finish brushing his teeth. Blake moaned from the bed.

Damian eyed him worriedly. 'Are you ok?'

Blake shook his head and motioned to a small box of pills lying on the bedside table.

Damian sighed. 'Oh, it's that time of the month, huh?' When Charlie shot him a questioning look, he explained: 'Blake has migraines. They come at regular intervals. He thinks it has something to do with the moon phases.' He looked at Bobby, unsure whether he could burden his brother with the care of a pup right now. 'Is it still ok that we leave Bobby here?' he asked hesitantly.

Blake waved his consent and buried his face in the pillow.

Charlie crouched down and hugged Bobby. 'You be nice, ok? We'll be back in a few hours.' She placed a hearty smack on the dog's nose and turned to leave.

Bobby eyed them with big, fearful eyes. When Damian closed the door behind them, he let out a sad little howl and scratched his paws against the wood.

Charlie bit her lip. Damn, this was so hard. Damian hugged her. 'Don't worry, Princess, he'll be ok.' She sighed. Maybe the musical hadn't been such a great idea after all.

Charlie and Damian walked up the staircase to the balcony of Her Majesty's. Holding on to Damian's arm, Charlie slowly took each step backwards, so that she could admire the huge painting of a lady that hung on the wall above the stairs. The red carpet and the quaint little lamps gave the place a delightfully fin de siècleish look. When they finally entered the balcony and she saw the long rows of red plush seats high above the stage, Charlie let out a little scream. 'Oh Damian, this is so exciting.' In order to vent her enthusiasm, she boxed his belly. 'I'm happy.'

'I'm happy too, Princess.' Smiling at his excited little girlfriend, Damian followed her to their seats in the third row.

Charlie discovered that every seat had opera glasses attached to it. She produced a fifty-pence coin to release them from their hold, and held the binoculars to her face. 'You look very strange,' she said, eyeing Damian through them.

'You too,' he retorted, and turned her head towards the stage. 'That's where the music's playing.'

'Not yet.' She turned back to him. He stuck his tongue out at her. She recoiled in mock horror. 'Eek, a monster!'

'Wrong,' he said and grabbed for her with claw-like fingers, 'The Phantom, huaaahhh!'

An elderly lady in an evening gown had been watching them disapprovingly. Her purple perm stood out like a halo around her head. Much to Charlie's delight, she even sported a jewelled headdress that would have made any accomplished young lady in a Jane Austen novel proud. On her, it looked admittedly a bit silly. When Damian let out his phantom-cry, she raised a thinly pencilled eyebrow.

'Don't worry,' said Damian good-naturedly in her direction, 'I'm just kidding to scare my girlfriend.' He hugged Charlie tightly and placed a noisy smack on her cheek.

The lady turned away, disgusted.

Damian grinned. 'She's a bit stiff, huh?' he whispered into Charlie's neck.

'As in: dead since the middle of the century, yes,' she whispered back.

Damian chuckled and tickled her waist.

'Hey, what do you think you're doing, Mr Winter?'

'I'm being a naughty phantom,' he grinned. 'I'll frighten you from time to time during the show.'

'I can't wait for it.'

'Oh, but you'll have to.'

Charlie leaned forward and scrutinized the stage. Three big veiled objects stood in front of the heavy grey curtains, each with an inscription on it. 'Le cygne,' she read, 'chandelier ... and the last one I cannot make out.' She turned to Damian. 'That's French, right? What does *le cygne* mean?'

He shrugged his shoulders. 'No idea. You'll have to ask Blake for this.'

'Can he really speak French?' asked Charlie sceptically. 'Sometimes I wonder whether he's just making the words up.'

'Oh no, he can speak it alright. Spanish and German, too. And Latin and Old Greek. And he started learning Russian once, when he fell in love with a Russian dancer. Dimitri was his name, I think.'

'Wow.'

'Yeah, I know, pretty amazing, huh?' Damian shook his head. 'So you thought he was bullshitting you when he was using French words? I can assure you he's not. But the problem is, Blake is so smart that most people think he's really dumb. I guess that's why he's monkeying around all the time. What's the use of showing how bright you are, when no one understands your puns?'

Charlie was thinking this through. 'I'm glad I'm not that smart,' she finally said.

Damian smiled. 'Yeah, me too.'

The lights in the room dimmed, and they directed their attention to the stage. The curtains parted. An auctioneer loudly banged his gavel on the desk. 'Sold!'

Charlie squeezed Damian's arm. The musical had begun.

'This was soooo erotic,' sighed Charlie, when the lights went on during the break. 'I want that Phantom.'

Damian recoiled in mock horror. 'Help! My girlfriend is in love with a ghost.'

Charlie laughed. 'That sounds like the subtitle to a talk show.'

'Hm. Right.' Damian thought for a while. 'I thought you would prefer Raoul,' he finally said.

Charlie considered this. 'In fact I do,' she admitted. 'But the Phantom is so torn, such a sad and bitter and lonely character. Don't you think that's sexy?'

'No.'

'Oh.' She snuggled closer. 'I loved Raoul and Christine's duet,' she mumbled into his shirt.

*'Say you'll share with me one love, one lifetime ...'* began Damian.

She giggled. 'You better stop. I don't want it to rain when we get out of the theatre.'

Damian was unimpressed by her teasing. '... *Anywhere you go let me go, too* ...' He looked into her eyes and added softly: '*Love me - that's all I ask of you.*'

Charlie purred happily and buried her face in his chest. 'You're a terrible singer, but a perfect boyfriend.' She stretched and stood up. 'Now if you'll excuse me, I have to pee.'

Hopping up the stairs to the toilet, her glance fell on an ice-cream vendor passing through the rows. She stowed this information away for further reference.

After queuing for a ridiculously long time in front of the ladies' toilets (why was it that there never seemed to be a queue in front of the gents?), she returned to their seats, where she found Damian in animated discussion with a Japanese couple.

'Hey, Princess!' He made room for her to move in. 'This is Yuki and his girlfriend Tsukiko. They're on their honeymoon through Europe.'

Tsukiko nodded eagerly. 'We have visited Naples, Rome, Florence, Nizza, Paris and Berlin already. Next stop is Helsinki.'

Charlie was impressed. 'You have seen a lot more of Europe than I ever have. How long have you been in London?'

'We arrived this afternoon,' replied Yuki, 'and we stay till the day after tomorrow. We have been to Buckingham Palace and Westminster Abbey already. Tomorrow, we will make a boat ride on the Thames to Greenwich and drive to Oxford and Blenheim Palace. England is very beautiful.' His girlfriend nodded.

Charlie looked from them to Damian. 'I want to visit my country, too,' she said.

'You've already been to the Tower, Princess,' Damian tried to comfort her.

Charlie pouted.

Meanwhile, Tsukiko had taken out her camera. 'Souvenir photo,' she declared and eyed them through the lens. Charlie and Damian snuggled closer and grinned into the camera. Tsukiko was about to click on the button, when a woman hurried down the steps and gave her a stern look. 'If you take a picture inside our theatre, I will have to take the camera away from you,' she declared.

Tsukiko stared at her and turned a crimson red. 'I'm so sorry,' she peeped.

'Try this again, and I will take the camera away,' the woman repeated, and headed back up the stairs, in search for other offenders.

Damian stared after her. 'What an unpleasant lady,' he mumbled, and hurried to reassure Tsukiko: 'Usually people in England are much nicer.' She smiled gratefully at him.

Charlie jumped up. 'I want an ice-cream,' she declared and looked into the round. 'Anyone else wants one, too?'

Yuki looked sceptically at the ice-cream vendor. 'I think we will rather have a glass of champagne,' he said, and they headed off to the bar.

'How about we have some champagne, too?' proposed Damian, and stood up.

'I wanted some ice-cream,' said Charlie, unhappy.

Damian looked down at her. She looked up at him.

'I'm waiting,' he said.

'For what?'

'For you to tell me.'

'Tell you what?'

'Chocolate, vanilla or strawberry?' asked Damian.

# 21

Damian was watching Charlie hack away on her laptop. It was amazing how fast her fingers flew over the keyboard without hitting a single wrong key. Her eyes were focused on the screen, and she only looked down from time to time to assess whether her fingers were still in the right place. Her lips were slightly parted in concentration, and Damian had the impression that her breath was synchronizing with the parts of sentences she wrote: tap-a-dee-tap - breathing pause - tap-a-dee-tap-tap - breathing pause. Funny.

'I don't like being watched when I answer my mail,' said Charlie.

Damian, head propped up in his left hand, looked sternly at Bobby, who slouched under the table, completely exhausted from their walk in the park. 'Bobby, stop watching Charlie, she doesn't like that.' Bobby gave him the equivalent of a canine rolleyes.

Charlie looked up. 'Don't blame the pup for what you do.'

'What, you meant me? But I love watching you. Can't I, please?'

'No.'

'Pleeeease?'

Charlie sighed. 'Don't you have anything to do? How about you take a shower and get dressed? We're supposed to be at Blake's place in two hours.'

'Who are you writing to?' Damian asked, ignoring her suggestion. 'Paul?'

'No, I'm sending an e-card to my friend Babsy in Munich.'

'Babsy?'

'A German exchange student at my school in Swallop,' explained Charlie. 'We still write to each other occasionally, these days it's mostly cards from holidays, though.'

'What's an eek-art?' asked Damian, intrigued. 'Sounds like something Blake could come up with.'

'An e-card is an electronic card. Like e-mail being electronic mail. Wanna see the card I'm sending her?'

Damian got up and walked around the table. He bowed down and kissed her neck. 'Mmh, what a delicious little eek-art we have here,' he mumbled.

Charlie fought him off. 'The card's on the computer, silly, not in my neck. There.' She pointed at the screen and pushed a button. A card unfolded: A bulky Father Christmas gliding through a tight chimney, while his reindeer stood on the roof and looked down in amazement. When Santa landed in the hearth with a thud, a writing appeared at the top: *Fröhliche Weihnachten, Babsy!*

Damian laughed. 'That's a funny cartoon.' Then he squinted at the screen. 'For-chel-lice ... damn, why don't these letters stop moving?' He turned to Charlie and asked defeated: 'What does it say?'

'It's German, baby. It means: Merry Christmas, Babsy. I know I'm a bit late with my wishes. But she's on holiday anyway and won't get the card until she gets back. So it doesn't really matter.'

'You could have wished her a happy New Year,' Damian proposed. 'Would have been more suitable on December 31st.'

'Maybe. But I can't remember how to say that in German. So it's gotta be Christmas wishes.'

'Mhm.' Damian hugged her around the neck. 'I'd like to write an eek-art, too,' he declared.

'Ok. Do you have an e-mail account?'

Damian looked blank. 'I don't know,' he admitted. 'I would have to ask Gerry. He's running all my accounts, you know.'

Charlie shot him a look. 'How about we sent a card from my account?' she offered. 'We can sign with both our names. Whom do you want to write to?'

Damian thought for a moment. 'How about Bobby?' he proposed. 'We could give him the card and let him tear it to pieces. He'd love that.'

'Well, an e-card is kinda virtual. It's a bit hard to tear to pieces.'

'Bobby has good teeth,' countered Damian, undaunted.

Charlie thought for a while. Damian didn't seem to have any friends, which was strange, because he had a very easy-going manner with people. But during the two weeks she had been living in his apartment, he had not once invited someone over, or gone out with people. He seemed to be leading a completely isolated life, right here in the heart of one of the most bustling cities of Europe. It was sad, somehow, that you could nowhere be more truly alone than in a big city ...

'How about we write a New Year's greeting to Alice?' she proposed.

'That's a fantastic idea!' Damian pulled his chair close and stared eagerly at the screen. 'How do we proceed?'

'Well, first we have to decide on a card.' Charlie clicked on a link, and several rows of thumbnails popped up, all displaying motives of the season. She scrolled down the page. 'Anything here you like?'

Damian pointed to a naively painted winter landscape. 'That one looks nice.'

Charlie clicked on it, and an empty card appeared on the screen. Then a virtual brush dipped into a bucket, and painted a snowy meadow. The brush dipped in again and splashed a tree upon the page, followed by a cottage, a moon and stars. Finally, snowflakes danced down through the dark night, and an invisible hand wrote *Merry Christmas!* into the sky.

Damian was impressed. 'Terrific.'

'Yes, but it should rather say *Happy New Year*.' Charlie scrolled down and found the box which allowed you to edit the message. She deleted the original text and replaced it with *Hap-*

*py New Year, Alice.* She thought for a while, then added: *from Charlie, Damian and Bobby. See you next week.*

Damian's lips moved, while he read the message. 'That's a very nice message,' he finally said. 'What do we do now?'

'We'll sent it to her.' Charlie typed Alice's address into the appropriate box and clicked on the send button. 'Next time she's checking her mail, she'll see our card.'

Damian smiled. 'She'll surely be happy about it.'

'Surely.' Charlie hugged him. 'How about we take a shower together? I can soap your back.'

'Only my back?'

'Among other things ...'

'Sounds great ...'

The taxi came to a halt at a red traffic light. Everywhere on the sidewalk, groups of people were on their way to bars and restaurants, ready to welcome the New Year, each according to their preference. Charlie noticed a tall man with a prominent red 2005 painted on his forehead. He waved a British flag and held hands with a pale young girl sporting rasta locks and a Bob Marley T-shirt. Behind them, a family with three small children seemed to be on their way home. One of the kids, a boy of around eight, blew his toy trumpet right behind the girl's back and made her jump. She turned around and laughed, and her companion waved his flag at the boy. The kid beamed proudly.

The lights changed, and the taxi sped on through the brightly lit streets of London.

Charlie took Damian's hand. 'I'm so excited. In four hours, we'll be in a new year.'

He smiled at her. 'Blake told me on the phone that he has a New Year's gift for us.'

'Really? Help!'

'Maybe it's another lamp? Or an anal ring, like he gave them to Nicky and Elsa.'

'I'm prepared for the worst. From salad bowls in the form of a uterus to Fabergé testis, I refuse to be shocked by Blake art.'

Damian laughed. 'Have you ever been to one of his happenings? I wanted to take you last time, but you already had an appointment ...'

Charlie stared at him. 'Of course! That private view at the Galeria Mundo! So *that's* were you wanted to take me? Blake had invited me too, but when I ...' She stopped short. Damn. She couldn't tell him that she had left because she had recognized Gerald. '... I got held up,' she finished lamely.

'It was really funny. We had a little stage, with sand dunes and snakes. And Blake was dressed in nomad clothes, with long linen robes, it looked really cool.'

'A pity I couldn't see it. But I'm sure there will be other happenings. Blake also wanted to introduce me to some of his friends ...'

'Like the Contessa?' asked Damian.

'You know her?'

'Her ... er ... yes,' Damian replied. 'She's ... nice.'

Charlie looked sceptically at him. 'You sound ominous. Blake told me she's one of his best friends. The only woman he's ever had.'

'He said that, huh?' Damian laughed. 'Well ...'

'Well, what?' Charlie eyed him curiously.

'Well ... I thought he had you too?'

'That's not what you really wanted to say,' she said accusingly.

'Yes, it is!'

'No, it's not.'

'Yes, it is. Don't try to change the subject.'

'What? Me? I'm not.' Charlie leaned back in her seat. 'What was the subject, anyway?'

'I said I thought Blake had you too,' Damian reminded her.

'Well, that depends on the definition ...'

'It does?'

'Kinda.'

'I see.' Damian eyed her thoughtfully.

'Look, whatever I did with him, it was before I met y... - before I decided to stop working,' she corrected herself.

'I'm not angry, Princess.' Damian snuggled up to her, much to Bobby's annoyance, who saw his rightful place in Charlie's lap challenged. He shortly lifted his head and shot his master a most determined that's-my-lap look. Damian obediently limited his snuggling to Charlie's upper body.

'There you are, honeys.' Blake opened his arms wide and gave each of them a bear hug. 'Say hello to Ned.'

'Hey, Ned.' Damian freed himself from his brother's embrace and stepped into the studio. 'How's it lying?'

Ned, propped up on Blake's couch in truest Oscar Wilde fashion, waved at them. 'Thanks, Damian. Everything's just fine. Blake and I have been visiting the London Dungeon today. A trip into the bowels of Mankind's sadistic inventive mind.'

Charlie shot a concerned look at Blake. 'Didn't you get sick in there?'

'No, honey, I was just about able to hold it in,' said Blake, with a sorrowful face.

Ned grinned. 'In some rooms he simply refused to open his eyes.'

Damian nodded thoughtfully. 'I remember him doing that on the ghost train, when we were kids. I always had to promise not to tell Dad.'

Charlie was amazed. 'You're seven years younger than him,' she pointed out.

'Yes, I must have been five and he was about twelve,' said Damian. 'I had to hold his hand and tell him when the end of the ride was in sight.'

'Hello?' Blake waved his hands about theatrically. 'I'm still here, you know. I don't like being gossiped about when I can hear it.'

They looked at him.

'Sorry, Blake,' said Ned.

'Was fun while it lasted, though,' added Damian.

Charlie grinned.

Blake pouted. 'I want a red thingy,' he whined.

Ned got up and poured him a blackcurrant liqueur. 'Anything I can offer you two?' he asked Charlie and Damian.

'Juice for me.'

'For me too, thanks,' said Damian.

'No!' In two quick strides, Blake was at the kitchen door and held his arms in front of it. 'No juice on New Year's Eve.'

'Huh?' Damian stared at him, puzzled. 'You're refusing to serve your guests?'

'No, I'm just refusing to serve non-alcoholic drinks on New Year's Eve. Hava coloured one.' He motioned to the liquor cabinet.

Charlie sighed and eyed the bottles wearily. 'Make it a Baileys then.'

Ned poured her a drink and looked quizzically at Damian.

'Amaretto,' he mumbled. 'Can Bobby at least get some water?'

'Alright, I'll make an exception for the pup,' conceded Blake. He dropped onto the couch that Ned had vacated, and motioned to his guests to sit down as well. Looking around the room, he suddenly realized that there were not enough seats available to accommodate four people. He got up again. 'How about we move over to the bed, honeys?' he asked.

Charlie felt light-headed. Too much sweet liqueur on an empty stomach. She reached for another canapé. Blake had finally condescended to feed his guests, and Charlie had to admit that the little slices of bread topped with salmon, egg-paste, ham and various herbs were delicious. A compliment to the deli that had delivered them. She decided on a ham-and-gherkin topped one.

Blake moved into the billiard room and announced: 'I take Reverend Green, in the billiard room, with a candlestick.'

Damian muttered: 'You wish,' and moved his piece next to Blake's. Then he flashed a card at him and grinned. 'So wrong, hehe.'

Blake shook his head. 'Strategics, honey, it's all strategics,' he mumbled, and tickled his brother's neck.

Charlie sighed and tried to move out of his legs' trajectory. Blake was lying on his belly across the huge bed, his feet rowing annoyingly through the air, and his hands just seemed to be everywhere. It was bad enough that he almost knocked the board over each time he propped himself up to give Ned a kiss, but Charlie really resented him fondling *her* boyfriend.

Damian didn't seem to mind, though. He bore his brother's caresses as stoically as a bull bears a fly walking leisurely over its back. He even smiled good-humouredly at Charlie. 'It's your turn, Princess.'

'It's your turn, honey,' Blake chimed in, and rubbed her belly.

Charlie got up. 'I have to pee.'

'Suit yourself, honey.' Blake held her glass for her.

'Me too.' Damian thrust his glass into Blake's other hand and followed her to the bathroom.

'Don't cheat!' Blake yelled after them.

Damian closed the door behind them and scanned Charlie's face. 'Are you ok, Princess?'

Not trusting her legs to carry her, Charlie collapsed onto the toilet seat. 'No, I'm not ok. This situation is highly embarrassing.'

Damian crouched in front of her and gently stroked her hands. 'Do you prefer to leave, maybe?'

She slouched down, confused and miserable. 'I don't know. I don't know what I want, or what I should think.'

Damian was still caressing her hands. 'Look, I love Blake. He's my brother and he means well. And Ned seems to be ok, too. But if you're not comfortable with this, we can leave. Anytime.'

Charlie looked up at him. 'He wants to have sex,' she stated the obvious.

'No, he doesn't.'

'Yes, he does, and you know it. Besides, I don't want him to rub my belly like that.'

'Then tell him.'

'I wonder why *you* don't tell him?'

'Me?' Damian was astonished. 'Why would I tell him to stop rubbing your belly?'

'Because you're my boyfriend ...'

'Is that what you want me to do?' Damian eyed her questioningly. 'You want me to tell him that you don't like it?'

'No.' Charlie was close to tears. 'I'm just saying: you're my boyfriend. You're supposed to be jealous and to defend me ...'

Damian blew a kiss into her palm and sighed. 'Look, Princess, if you want me to help you keep Blake at bay, I will do that, of course. You just have to tell me. But if you're just sitting there with an unhappy face, without saying what it is that you don't like, you cannot expect me to read your thoughts.' He added, sheepishly: 'You know I'm not that good at reading.'

Charlie smiled sadly. 'So you're not jealous?'

Damian gave her an earnest look. 'No.' Charlie opened her mouth to reply, but he put his hand on her lips and continued: 'Let me finish, Princess. What I mean is: if Blake does something you don't like and you protest and he goes on doing it, and you ask me to help you, you can be sure I'll fry his balls sunny side up. But if Blake rubs your belly and you just let it happen, then I suppose it's ok for you. And as long as it's ok for you, it's also ok for me. Do you understand what I mean?'

Charlie eyed him unhappily. 'Don't you want me to be faithful?'

Damian gave her tender smile. 'I want you to be happy. And I want you to enjoy your life. And I want you to feel free and strong and loved. *That's* what I want you to do. As for being faithful ...' His eyes smiled boyishly up from under his unruly mop of hair. He took a deep breath and sang softly, with lots of feeling and very little talent: *'Love me - that's all I ask of you.'*

Charlie felt tears coming to her eyes. He was so sweet, and she was so tipsy. She nuzzled her face into his neck. 'I love you, Damian.'

'I love you too, Princess.'

When they returned to the bed, Charlie eyed Blake suspiciously. 'You didn't look at the cards, did you, Blake?'

Ned grinned. 'He tried to, but I wouldn't let him.'

Blake pouted.

Damian let himself drop on the bed. 'It's your turn, Princess,' he said.

Charlie rolled the dice and entered the lounge. 'I accuse Miss Scarlet, in the lounge, with a lead pipe,' she intoned.

Blake pulled a face. 'A lead pipe, how gruesome. I wouldn't like to be hit with such a thingy. Besides, you cannot accuse yourself.'

'Why not?' Charlie reached for the file.

Blake's hand shot forward. 'Uh-uh. Not so fast. How come you're so sure it was you?'

Charlie grinned. 'Most murderers can remember their kill, don't you think?' She gently took Blake's hand from her breast. 'Blake, can you please stop touching me like that? I'm with Damian, and it's kind of tiring to fend off your hands all the time.'

Blake stared at her, open-mouthed. 'I'm just trying to show my affection for you,' he protested. To Charlie's relief, he wasn't monkeying around, but sounded worried that she might have misinterpreted his intentions.

Charlie gave him a fond peck on the cheek. 'How about you show your affection by letting me check those cards?'

Subdued, Blake handed her the file. Charlie opened it and grinned triumphantly. She held up the three cards, for the others to see. 'I was right: I was the killer,' she declared proudly.

Ned laughed. 'Congrats, Charlie.'

Damian kissed her knee. 'Well done, Princess.'

Blake proceeded to redo his ponytail. He put the blue rubber band between his lips and brushed his fingers through his hair. 'I never really liked Cluedo that much,' he mumbled.

Ned nudged him in the ribs. 'Come on, be a good loser, Blake.'

Blake sighed and placed a kiss on Charlie's forehead. 'Well done, Miss Scarlet. I'm just glad you didn't knock that lead pipe over my head.'

'You know I love you too much for that, Blake.' Charlie smiled fondly at him, and snuggled closer to Damian. 'It sounds like they're setting about to rip Notting Hill apart,' she remarked dryly, as someone down in the street let loose a particularly wild yowl.

Blake got up and walked to the window. The streets of Notting Hill were crowded with people, as thousands of merrymakers congregated to welcome the New Year the British way, that is to say, with lots of beer and good humour.

'I have a New Year present for you two,' said Blake.

'I was so hoping he had forgotten about it,' whispered Damian to Charlie, making her almost choke on her drink.

'Thanks, now I have Baileys in my nose,' she complained.

Blake returned to the bed with an eight-inch long ship, made of burnt clay. It featured, quite out of all proportion, a huge cannon with a ball on each side.

Damian eyed the object without saying a word. At last he commented: 'A warship? Sweet.'

'It's the ship that shall guide you safely into the haven of a happy permanent relationship,' cried Blake, offended that his present was not duly appreciated. 'And the cannon represents, well, a happy sex-life, I suppose. Yes, that's it. Some good sheet ruffling. Besides, it fits the spirit of New Year.'

As on cue, the first fireworks exploded into the night sky.

Ned eyed the clock over the bed. 'They're early. It's still five minutes to midnight.'

'Quick, we have to be prepared!' Blake handed the ship to Damian and ran towards the CD player. He rummaged through his man-high CD tower and swore under his breath when he didn't immediately find what he was looking for. At last he jumped up, proudly waving a CD case in his hand. He put the disk into the player, and pushed the button for song number two. A heavy guitar sound emanated from the loudspeakers, followed by an occasional drumbeat.

'What song is this?' asked Charlie, and tapped her feet to its catchy rhythm.

*Two Minutes To Midnight,*' declared Blake. 'The perfect song to welcome a new year.'

Bobby hid behind the couch, yelping.

'He doesn't like your music,' remarked Ned.

'No, he's afraid of the fireworks,' explained Damian, and crouched next to Bobby. 'Right, old boy? No need to be afraid, that's just some silly people out there, having fun.' He ruffled the dog's coat reassuringly.

Blake kneeled next to him. 'Poor pup,' he said compassionately, and tickled him behind the ears.

Meanwhile, Charlie and Ned had gone to the kitchen, and were wrestling with the champagne bottle. A loud pop announced the successful outcome of their efforts. Charlie stepped up to Damian and Blake, and handed them two glasses of Dom Perignon. Then all four of them stared spellbound at Blake's big clock on the wall. Two more minutes ... On the streets, a many-throated jeer rose up to them. 'Happy New Year!'

Charlie looked accusingly at Blake. 'Your clock is two minutes slow.'

'It's not,' he defended his furniture. 'They're two minutes early.'

On the CD, Bruce Dickinson sang *Two minutes to midnight, to kill the unborn in the woo-oomb!*

Damian hugged Charlie. 'Happy New Year, Princess. May all your dreams come true, and may a lot of them involve me.'

Charlie laughed. 'The same to you, baby, the same to you.'

They all hugged each other and clinked their glasses.

Blake looked out the window and motioned for them to come nearer. 'They're shooting up numbers into the sky,' he said, and pointed to the colourful lights that flashed up high above the London skyline. Charlie followed his gaze. A huge yellow *2005* illuminated the night over their heads. Eruptions of red and blue stars followed. It was so beautiful.

Bobby cowered deeper into Damian's lap, who tried to soothe him by mumbling reassuring words into his coat. It didn't seem to help much.

'Any New Year's resolutions?' Charlie asked Blake.

'To try and walk through life without hurting anybody,' he replied, without taking his gaze from the spectacle outside. 'Least of all me, of course. And to create art that makes people happy.'

'That's very sweet of you.' Charlie patted his hand and turned to Ned. 'How about you?'

Ned sipped his champagne. 'I don't make New Year's resolutions. I prefer to do things right away, instead of storing them away until the first of January.'

Charlie nodded. 'Clever. Also, that way, you don't have to break any.'

'Correct.'

Charlie kneeled on the couch and looked down on her two men. 'How about you, baby?'

Damian gazed up at her. 'I told you before, remember? I want to make my Princess happy.'

They smiled at each other, their faces illuminated by the afterglow of the fireworks outside. Just when the situation threatened to become too cheesy, Bobby gave a sad, little whimper. Charlie looked at their frightened pup, worried. 'Is he ok?'

'Mhm, I think he'll soon come out of it. Give him a few more minutes.' He continued to stroke the dog's coat. Charlie's phone went off. She hopped onto the bed and reached into her coat pocket for the cell-phone. A look at the display: Caller unknown. Hm. 'Hello?'

'Hey, little girl.'

Charlie smiled.

- to be continued -